TERRIBLE BEAUTY

TERRIBLE BEAUTY

A Novel

PETER T. KING

ROBERTS RINEHART PUBLISHERS

Published by Roberts Rinehart Publishers
A Member of the Rowman & Littlefield Publishing Group
4720 Boston Way
Lanham, MD 20706

Distributed by National Book Network

ISBN 1-56833-225-4 (paperback : alk. paper)
Library of Congress Control Number 2001087295

⊖™ The paper used in this publication meets the minimum requirements of
American National Standard for Information Sciences—Permanence of
Paper for Printed Library Materials, ANSI/NISO Z39.48–1992.
Manufactured in the United States of America.

*For the republican
women of Ireland*

Foreword

Terrible Beauty is a work of fiction. The injustice and the oppression it describes in the Belfast of the early 1980s, however, are all too true. Much has changed since then. President Bill Clinton granted Gerry Adams a visa and made Ireland an international issue. Tony Blair became the first British prime minister in this century to address the Irish issue honestly. Irish Prime Minister Bertie Ahern committed the Irish government to speaking for nationalists in the north of Ireland. And Mary McAleese, a Northern Irish national- ist, was elected president of Ireland. The result was the historic Good Friday Agreement of 1998. Time will tell whether the Good Friday Agreement will succeed. This book recounts the suffering of Catholic nationalists that made this agreement necessary.

In writing this book, I am indebted to many courageous people throughout the six counties, who never realized how much they inspired me by their unyielding courage and tenacity.

I also owe particular thanks to Oistin MacBride for painstakingly assisting me in capturing the Northern Irish dialect and idiom.

Many thanks also to my publisher, Roberts Rinehart, for taking a chance on me, and to my wife, Rosemary, and my children, Sean and Erin, for putting up with me.

I write it out in a verse—
MacDonagh and MacBride
And Connolly and Pearse
Now and in time to be,
Wherever green is worn,
Are changed, changed utterly:
A terrible beauty is born.

—"EASTER, 1916"
WILLIAM BUTLER YEATS

Glossary

Gerry Adams—President of Sinn Fein, a member of Parliament from West Belfast and the acknowledged political leader of the republican movement.

Craic (pronounced "crack")—A Gaelic word for a good time; humorous moment; commotion. It is used often and randomly.

Diplock Courts—Special courts in Northern Ireland in which defendants charged with terrorist offenses are tried by a judge with no jury. They were created in the early 1970s following a report issued by Lord Diplock, a British judge.

Falls Road—Nationalist stronghold in West Belfast.

Garda Síochána (Gardai)—Police force in the Republic of Ireland.

Irish Republican Army (IRA)—Outlawed guerrilla force waging armed struggle to end British rule in the north of Ireland. Also referred to as "Provos" and "the Ra." It is comprised of Active Service Units (ASU).

Long Kesh—British prison near Belfast for men convicted of terrorist offenses. The official British designation for the prison is "The Maze."

Loyalists—Supporters of continued British rule in Northern Ireland. They are predominantly Protestant and support paramilitary forces.

Nationalists—Opponents of British rule in the north of Ireland. They are predominantly Catholic.

Northern Ireland—The six northeastern counties of Ireland, which remain under British rule. They were partitioned from the rest of the country in 1921 following the Irish war of independence. Because republicans do not recognize the legitimacy of the Northern Ireland state, they refer to it as "the north of Ireland," "the six counties," and "occupied Ireland."

Orange Order—Large Protestant organization in Northern Ireland committed to preserving British rule. Republicans often refer to loyalists as "orangies."

Ian Paisley—Free Presbyterian minister who heads the Democratic Unionist Party (DUP) and is a member of the British Parliament.

Republic of Ireland—The nation comprised of the twenty-six counties on the island of Ireland that are not part of Northern Ireland. It received autonomy as a "Free State" in 1921 following the Irish war of independence and declared itself a Republic in

1949. Northern Irish republicans disparagingly refer to the Irish government as the "Free State" because of what they perceive to be its pro-British sympathies.

Republicans—Nationalists who support Sinn Fein and the IRA.

Royal Ulster Constabulary (RUC)—The Northern Ireland police force. Its members are disparagingly referred to by republicans as "peelers."

Shankill Road—Loyalist stronghold in Belfast.

Sinn Fein ("Ourselves Alone")—The political arm of the republican movement. It supports the IRA's armed struggle against British rule.

Social Democratic And Labour Party (SDLP)—A predominantly Catholic and middle-class political party in Northern Ireland. It favors the reunification of Ireland by nonviolent means. It is opposed to the IRA and Sinn Fein.

Ulster Defense Regiment (UDR)—A 10,000-member unit of the British Army that is recruited entirely from Northern Ireland and serves only in Northern Ireland.

Ulster Volunteer Force (UVF)—Outlawed loyalist paramilitary organization.

Unionists—Supporters of continued British rule in Northern Ireland. They are predominantly Protestant.

Prologue

The Irish Tri-Colour had been removed and the coffin lowered into the ground. The piper had played his final dirge.

Ignoring the driving rain that swirled about the Belfast graveyard, Bernadette Hanlon stared at the coffin that bore the remains of a man she loved. As the hundreds of mourners stood silent, all she could hear were clumps of mud hitting the wooden coffin below.

After a long moment, she turned from the grave and began to walk slowly toward the cemetery gate. Pressing her hands deep into the pockets of her soaking-wet raincoat, she cursed the spiral of death that encircled her being.

She had no way of knowing when it would end. But she could think back to when it had begun.

It was more than a year ago.

On Holy Thursday.

After another funeral.

PART ONE

ONLY OUR RIVERS
RUN FREE

I wander her hills and her valleys
And still through my sorrow I see
A land that has never known freedom
And only her rivers run free.

—NORTHERN IRISH FOLK SONG

CHAPTER ONE

Holy Thursday, one year earlier.

Brendan and Siobhan had just finished their breakfast and rushed out the door, eager to finish their last day of school before the Easter holiday. Maura, the baby, swallowed the last bit of her oatmeal, and Bernadette carried her into the living room, where she caught a glimpse of the sun struggling to break through the somber Belfast sky.

"Is there much on the funeral?" she asked her husband.

"Aye, front page," Dermot answered, handing her the newspaper on his way into the kitchen. While Maura played on the floor with her dolls, Bernadette sat down on the couch and looked at the picture of Eamon Riley's funeral in the *Irish News*. It was a three-column photo and showed Eamon's wife, Rita, and their six children following the coffin shrouded in the Tri-Colour. Mourners crushed in around them. Eamon had been a good friend of Bernadette and Dermot. He had also belonged to Dermot's IRA unit.

Poor Eamon, Bernadette thought, he never knew what hit him. When he had opened his front door last Sunday evening, two UVF men shot him dead, three bullets through the face.

Bernadette had sat with Rita at her house for both nights of the wake. And, of course, she'd been at the funeral yesterday, including the long procession to Milltown Cemetery. But now Bernadette wondered whether she'd done too much. She was three months pregnant and had been bleeding slightly when she was at the clinic two weeks ago. They had told her to rest and stay off her feet as much as possible. And how was she supposed to do that with a fourteen-month-old baby to take care of? My God, Maura weighed more than two stone now and was into everything.

Bernadette had been feeling weak for the past few days. Yesterday, when she came home after the funeral, she saw how heavy the bleeding was. She rang the clinic, who told her she should go to the Royal Victoria Hospital today. Her first thought had been to put it off. But the bleeding was even worse this morning. She would have to go to the Royal. She had told none of this to Dermot, who was coming back from the kitchen with a cup of tea. His face was grim. He has so much on his mind already, she thought.

"Eamon was a good man," she said as he sat down.

"None better," he answered.

The telephone rang and Dermot answered it. The call lasted less than twenty seconds. All Dermot said was "aye" and "dead on" before putting down the receiver.

"I have to be away now," he said, and got to his feet.

"Do you know when you'll be back?"

"I don't."

When Dermot received these calls, Bernadette would never ask him where he was going or what he was to do. It was safer for both of them that way.

She followed him into the kitchen. As he opened the back

door, he threw her a glance over his shoulder, forced a laugh, and said, "Cheer up woman: There's no law against your smiling!"

Bernadette smiled weakly and went back to her chair. She lit a cigarette and picked up the newspaper. Maura was still playing with her dolls. Quietly, thank God. After she finished the paper, Bernadette went to the phone and rang her mother, who was always willing to mind the children.

"Mommy, do you think you could keep Maura while I run down to the Royal? I'll be leaving in about an hour."

"Of course, luv. Are you still having the problem with the bleeding?"

"I am and it's getting worse. I better do something about it."

"I'm sure you'll be fine. But it can't do you any harm to get an examination. I'll be by in half an hour, so I will."

"Thanks, Mommy."

"Cheerio."

Bernadette looked at Maura, who was still occupied with her wee dolls. She had not expected to become pregnant again so soon. But she did and that was that. Besides, a baby would be so good for Maura. Siobhan was ten years old and Brendan thirteen. A new baby would give Maura someone her own age to play with. My God, she thought, I hope Mommy was right. I hope everything will be fine.

Later, as her taxi headed out of Andersonstown toward the Royal, Bernadette stared out the window and thought about Rita and the looks on the faces of the six Riley children as they followed their daddy's coffin.

And then she found herself thinking back to when her brother Rory had been killed, more than nine years ago. Like so many boys who grew up in Ballymurphy, Rory had joined the IRA soon after the Troubles began in 1969. Bernadette had never asked Rory which operations he was involved in, but she did know he was considered good at what he did. And just as important, Rory had always been lucky. Some of his mates had been shot. Many more were interned. But Rory had never even been arrested. Christ, he thought he was Superman, Bernadette said to herself, smiling grimly.

It ended all of a sudden outside Springfield Road Barracks one night when Rory's own bomb blew him apart. Tiny pieces of bone and flesh were scraped up from the street and sidewalk.

Rory's death had devastated Bernadette. Three years older, he had been her shield against the terrible reality of Belfast life. He would walk her home from school and look after her at the dances. He revealed the magic of poetry to her and spoke lyrically of an Ireland free of British rule. Later, he helped her look after Siobhan and Brendan while Dermot was interned.

Bernadette knew that Rory killed—and killed often. She never discussed it with him but she knew it and she accepted it. After all, she thought, there's a fucking war going on in Belfast and people get killed in war. Still, Bernadette could never bring herself to visualize Rory killing anyone.

Bernadette had never thought she knew all the answers to the war that raged outside her window. But she did know that she hated the Brits. She hated their guns and their armored cars, their sneering accents and their leering looks. And she knew they didn't belong in Ireland.

The taxi stopped in front of the Royal Victoria Hospital, bringing Bernadette back to her own problem. She paid the driver, then walked across the Falls Road and entered the hospital. She went to the main desk, gave her name and explained her situation to the clerk, a sober-looking young woman with brown hair.

"I'm three months pregnant, and have three children at home. There was some slight bleeding when I was at the clinic two weeks ago, and now it's got worse. I have some pain and discomfort. The clinic told me to come here today . . ."

The clerk took the information and asked Bernadette to take a seat. "It will be at least fifteen minutes before Dr. Watkins can see you," she said.

Bernadette smiled politely, walked over to a window and sat down in a blue plastic chair against the wall. No matter how they try, she thought, a hospital always smells like one. She lit a cigarette, dragged on it heavily and stared out the window. She could feel light perspiration on her forehead.

She wondered if her baby was a boy or a girl. She and Dermot had agreed that if the baby was a boy, they would name him Rory, after her brother. Bernadette wondered whether naming a son after Rory would upset her mother. Bernadette vividly remembered how devastated her mother and father had been at Rory's funeral. She also recalled how they had fiercely maintained their dignity through the long agony of the wake, the Mass and pious incantations from the church pulpit, followed by the walk, holding her sister Eilish's hand, to Milltown Cemetery.

The streets of Andersonstown had been filled with mourners by the thousands along with masked IRA men. Through it all, up to the final volley over Rory's coffin, Bernadette had stared blankly and stifled suffocating sobs. Later, they told her that she never lowered her head, not even once, during the ordeal. When it was over, she realized how much Rory had shielded her from the pain of life in Belfast. Even though death had been all around her for so long, she was unprepared when it intruded so savagely into her life.

Bernadette had never joined the IRA, but when Rory was alive, she had helped them when they had asked, passing along information on army foot patrols, stashing weapons in her home and protecting volunteers on the run. But after seeing the sorrow etched in her parents' faces the day Rory was buried, and then when her father died of a heart attack just a month after Rory's funeral, she vowed she would never do any of that for the IRA again. And for several years she stopped her work for Sinn Fein.

A nurse called her. The doctor was ready to see her.

After the initial examination, around four-thirty, Bernadette lay in a hospital bed waiting to see Dr. Watkins again. For the past several hours she'd been answering questions and undergoing tests and examinations. She didn't know what to expect, but the bleeding had been going on for too long. The faces of the nurses and the doctors betrayed their concern. Bernadette feared there was something wrong, but she would do whatever she could to save the baby.

At last Dr. Watkins came into the room and stood at the side of the bed while he spoke quietly.

"Mrs. Hanlon, I'm afraid there's no easy way to tell you this." Bernadette stiffened, preparing herself for bad news, yet still hopeful.

"The tests show no sign of life in the fetus," Dr. Watkins went on. "We will have to take it from you. I've scheduled you for tomorrow morning."

"Are you telling me the baby is dead?" asked Bernadette.

"None of the tests showed any sign of life."

"But that can't be." Bernadette's voice rose higher. "I know I've felt the baby move. I know I have."

"Mrs. Hanlon, you may think there's movement, but I can assure you there is no sign of life. The fetus must be taken and it must be done as soon as possible so that you don't develop complications."

Bernadette said nothing more, and when Dr. Watkins left the room, her eyes filled with tears. She stared at the ceiling trying to sort out what was happening. What had she done to cause this? How would she explain it to Brendan and Siobhan? And where might Dermot be?

Some time later a nurse came by with tea and toast. "It's better that you not have too much," the nurse said. "But you should eat something."

Bernadette sipped the tea and nibbled at the toast. When the nurse returned to take her tray, Bernadette asked, "Would it be all right if I went out into the corridor and rang home?"

"Just get back into bed as soon as you can. You shouldn't be on your feet any more than you have to be."

Bernadette put on her robe and walked to the pay phone. She placed the call. Siobhan answered. "Hello, luv, is your granny there?" asked Bernadette.

"Aye, Mommy, she is. Where are you?"

"I'm in hospital. But I'll be fine. Let me talk to your granny."

"But when will you be home?"

"I should be home in a few days, luv. Granny'll explain to you."

Bernadette could hear Siobhan handing the phone to her grandmother.

"Bernadette, are you all right?"

"They say the baby's to come away, that it's dead." She spoke quickly, trying to keep from crying.

"How could they tell you that?" demanded her mother.

"Mommy, it's true. I don't know why it happened but it's true."

Her mother said nothing more, so Bernadette asked, "Have you heard from Dermot?"

"No, luv, I haven't. I'm sure he's fine, so he is."

"If he rings or if you see him, tell him where I am. I have to stay here overnight."

"I will, of course. But will you be all right tonight? Should I ring Eilish?" she asked.

"No, there's no need to be bothering her."

"I'll be there to see you in the morning."

"Thank you, Mommy. Is Maura asleep?"

"Aye, we just got her up in the cot."

"And is Brendan home?"

"Aye, he's watching the TV, so he is."

"Thank you, Mommy. I'll see you tomorrow."

"Good night, luv. God bless."

Bernadette went back to bed. A few moments later, another nurse came by and handed her two tablets and a cup of water. "You might want to take these," the nurse said. "It's important that you get a good night's sleep."

Bernadette put the tablets in her mouth and swallowed them with the water. She put her head back on the pillow and closed her eyes.

As she lay there in the darkened room, her thoughts turned again to Dermot. Like so many other Catholic wives in Belfast, she didn't know her husband well. She knew she liked him and, yes, she was sure she loved him. But she didn't know him—certainly not as well as she should. They married when she was nineteen and he was barely twenty-one. She liked his sandy hair and his being tall—almost six feet. During their fourteen years of marriage, with three children to show for it, they almost never had what anyone would call a serious row—except once, over her involvement with Sinn Fein. He enjoyed being with the children, particularly reading to them at night. He was protective of Bernadette but never smothered her. He knew she was smart. He knew she was strong. And she knew he was proud of her.

Yet there was so much he never spoke about. He was a skilled bricklayer but had been out of work for thirteen years. Jobs didn't come easily for Catholics in Belfast. She knew how much it tore at Dermot's insides to be living on the dole, but never once in those long, lean years did he ever say a word to her about it. Dermot was one man who would never drop his guard. Then, of course, there was the IRA. Dermot was an IRA man, although Bernadette never knew exactly when he had joined. She wasn't even certain if he was in it before they were married. So many Ballymurphy men were in the IRA at that time that it would have been unusual if he weren't. But she didn't know for sure because he didn't talk about it.

They'd been married less than a year and had just moved to Andersonstown when he was interned for the first time. She was six months pregnant with Brendan. Just before dawn, the Brits crashed through the front door and dragged Dermot from their bed. Bernadette remembered the wild panic that came over her. She had no idea what was happening. The screaming, the cursing, Dermot being pulled down the stairs and out the door, the room being ripped apart and she sitting on the side of the bed, crying hysterically. The neighbors rang her mother, who rushed down to the flat. Rory came with her.

Bernadette smiled as she recalled her mother putting her back into bed that night, as if she were still a wee child. Bernadette also recalled how Rory had held her that night and told her not to cry.

How he had reminded her that he always protected her and then assured her that everything would be fine this time also. And how, two weeks after the break-in, an armored car was rocket-bombed down the corner from Bernadette's flat. Two British soldiers were incinerated.

Dermot was interned for ten months that first time. In those days the Brits didn't even have to formally charge them. Just arrest them, lock them away, and only God knew when they would get out. They put him on the *Maidstone*, a prison ship in the harbor. Whenever she would visit him, he was always happy and cheery, especially after Brendan was born and she would bring him pictures. Dermot never complained and kept telling her that the conditions were "not too bad." It was only later that she found out from others about the brutal beatings, relentless interrogations, burning cigarettes crushed into skin. When Dermot was released, he was a different man. He had not changed much outwardly, but there was a part of him that she could no longer enter. A dark corner hidden away, a corner she knew was lethal. Bernadette had long ago lost count of the times Dermot was arrested or the times their home was raided. She did know that at one time or another he'd been in every jail in the north of Ireland. Fortunately, he was never sentenced to more than eighteen months. All told, he served close to five years. She realized it did no good to ask him what he was doing or planning. She knew how brutal and sadistic the treatment could be at Castlereagh Interrogation Centre. The less you knew about anyone else's business in Belfast, even your husband's, the better off everyone was. But she also knew that the secrecy and all the furtive comings and goings were widening a chasm between them. Marriage can be difficult enough under the best of circumstances,

Bernadette thought. How the hell can it survive in this madness of guerrilla warfare?

But Jesus, she'd never felt more alone. She needed him now. He was so damned strong and had fucking ice water in his veins. He'd reassure her and keep her together. If Dermot didn't come home or ring the house tonight, he wouldn't even know she was in hospital.

Bernadette turned onto her back again. The sedative was beginning to work. She needed sleep. Not that it would be the sleep of peace. Her baby was dead.

It was Good Friday morning. Bernadette looked at the clock beside her bed: ten minutes before noon. The last thing she could remember was being taken to the operating room earlier that morning and Dr. Watkins telling her she was about to be given anesthesia.

Her mother came in and stood at the foot of the bed. "Has Dermot been by yet, Mommy?" Bernadette asked. The anesthetic had almost worn off, and she felt only a bit groggy.

"The doctor says you have to get some sleep, luv," her mother said softly. Bernadette tensed. Her mother was pretending to be calm as she spoke. "You've been through so much. Eilish is minding Maura, and Brendan and Siohban are fixing up the house for when you get out tomorrow. And Dermot is just great, so he is."

Don't do this to me, Mommy, Bernadette wanted to scream. "What's happened to Dermot? Tell me."

"Dermot is in Castlereagh. He and Mick McAllister got lifted last night at a checkpoint in the Markets."

"Oh, Jesus."

"From what we can find out, it might not be too bad," her mother said. "There was nothing found and they've nothing on him."

Bernadette felt the last grips of the anesthesia vanish as her anger rose. "But Christ, Mommy, you know that it doesn't matter what evidence they have. They'll find some supergrass, give him a thousand pounds, and he'll say whatever they want him to say."

Her mother moved over to a chair next to the bed and sat down. "We've already got in touch with Paddy Ferguson and he'll go to Castlereagh and talk with Dermot as soon as the forty-eight hours are up," her mother said. Bernadette knew she was trying to evince more assurance than either of them felt. "I know one thing about Dermot," her mother added, "he'll never sign a statement. No matter what they do to him."

Bernadette watched as her mother put her hand to her mouth, as if to force her words back into her mouth. The last thing her mother had wanted to do was remind Bernadette of what the peelers could be doing to Dermot in Castlereagh. But it was too late.

"Poor Dermot," said Bernadette, as her eyes welled up with tears. At least they'd been fortunate enough to get hold of Paddy Ferguson, she thought. Paddy was a brilliant solicitor and he was tough. His two brothers were in the IRA and serving life sentences in Long Kesh. He knew what the Brits were all about and he fought them at every turn with a spirit as fiery as his red hair. There were no juries, of course, and most of the judges did what the Brits told them to do but, by Jesus, Paddy made it rough for them. Whenever Paddy got involved in the case, the Brits had to decide whether or not it was worth the effort. Not only would he do whatever he could to tie them up in procedural knots, he had developed solid media contacts that he never hesitated to use. As far as Paddy was concerned, the law in Northern Ireland was not an institution to be venerated or respected. Not after what the Brits had done to it. Torture, police perjury, and now the latest, "supergrass" informers.

"If anything can be done for Dermot," Bernadette said, "Paddy Ferguson will be the one to do it. Right, Mommy?"

Her mother brushed back Bernadette's auburn hair from her sweating brow. "It's time for you to rest," she said.

"You're right about that," said a nurse as she walked into the room. "Everything went well during the operation, and Dr. Watkins will come round later to see you. It seems fairly definite that you will be home tomorrow in time for Easter."

"Cheerio, luv," her mother said. She kissed Bernadette's cheek and pressed her hand.

"Thanks, Mommy. Would you ask Paddy to come up and see me if he gets the chance?" Bernadette clutched her mother's hand. Then she let go.

"Sure, luv, I'll ring him as soon as I get home."

"Say hello to the children for me. Tell them their mommy will be home tomorrow."

After her mother and the nurse had gone, Bernadette looked again at the ceiling. In only twenty-four hours her world had become a merciless maelstrom. Her baby was gone from her forever. Dermot was in Castlereagh.

"Oh, Jesus," she murmured as she closed her eyes, and after a few fitful moments, fell into a deep sleep.

CHAPTER TWO

On the way home in the taxi on Holy Saturday afternoon, Bernadette mulled over what Paddy Ferguson had told her when he came by to see her in the hospital. She was eager to talk to her mother about what he'd said and glad she had arranged to stay with the family for a few days. Her mother could help take care of Maura and do the cooking—especially the Easter dinner. The doctor had told Bernadette she needed at least a week's bedrest. No sooner was she out of the cab than Brendan and Siobhan rushed up to kiss her and help her into the house. Then, as soon as she went through the door, her mother took her coat, and led her upstairs to the bedroom, with the children following.

"I saw Paddy," Bernadette whispered.

Her mother nodded. "Good. Tell me later. All that you have to do now is lie in bed and relax. I'll get you a cup of tea. Maura's sleeping, and I'll bring her to you as soon as she wakes."

She went downstairs, and Bernadette lay down on the double bed fully dressed. The children looked at her, concerned. She smiled at them and they seemed to relax, but stayed standing at the foot of the bed. She wondered how they were going to manage. Thank the Good Lord for her mother, always there when she was needed.

She had also been truly blessed with Brendan and Siobhan. Even with Dermot getting arrested so often, and the house raided regularly and there never being any money, the children never complained. They did well in school and had common sense besides. She never had to worry about them when they were on their own. They knew which streets to stay away from and developed the uncanny knack that Belfast children seemed to have of sensing trouble seconds before it happened. Somewhere in the back of her mind she knew that in a few years they would be old enough to join the IRA, but she wouldn't allow herself to think about that.

Poor children, she thought. The miscarriage would have been enough for them to get used to. They were looking forward so much to another baby. Paddy had warned her it was likely Dermot would spend at least the next two years in jail. That will break their hearts. God, he's so gentle with them. He never even raises his voice. And, Jesus, all the shouting I do! But I'll have to tell them the truth. They would know straightaway if I didn't.

"How are you, Mommy?" Siobhan asked finally.

"A wee bit tired, luv, but it's great to be home and be with you," Bernadette replied. "I want the two of you to be helping your granny. Do you hear me now?"

"Aye, we do, Mommy," answered Brendan.

"How is our daddy?" asked Siobhan. "Will he be home in time for dinner tomorrow? Granny says she will cook us a roast."

Bernadette was thrown off her stride for a moment. Struggling to recover and hoping that the children wouldn't notice her distress, she answered in as calm a voice as possible.

"Daddy won't be home for a while, I'm afraid. The Brits are cracking down, and your daddy's lawyer thinks they may keep him inside for quite a few months."

"Can they keep our daddy in jail forever, Mommy?" asked Brendan.

Bernadette forced a smile she hoped would be reassuring. "They won't hold him forever. We just have to make sure we're as strong as Daddy is. And until he does get out, we'll visit him at the Crum as often as they let us."

"Oh, Mommy," said Siobhan, "I hate the Crum. Those screws are so mean, the way they yell at us and make us wait so long."

Bernadette hadn't realized that Siobhan even remembered the Crumlin Road prison. It had been more than four years since Dermot had been in Crumlin Road, and Siobhan had been only five when they visited him. She had never mentioned it since. Until today.

"No one likes the Crum, luv, except the screws," said Bernadette, "but it will make your daddy very happy indeed if he can see you. So we'll visit the Crum and we'll do no complaining. If your daddy's not complaining, then there is no need for us to be fussing about."

"Aye, Mommy. I'm sorry," said Siobhan. "I'm just going to miss Daddy so much, especially on Easter."

"I know, luv, and I am sure that he's missing us as well. But we can never be weak and let him down."

"Aye, I'll be good, Mommy." Siobhan smiled.

"Mommy, Granny told us about the baby," said Brendan, scuffing his foot on the rug. "Will you be okay?"

"Aye, Brendan, I'll be fine. I know how disappointed you both are. But God, well, He has His reason for doing things. And sometimes we just aren't able to understand those reasons."

"Aye, Mommy," said Brendan with a tone of resignation, indicating that he was unable to understand a number of God's decisions lately.

"Maura wants to see her mommy," said Bernadette's mother, as she came into the room carrying the baby. Bernadette sat up, took Maura and held her tight. Still half asleep, Maura put her arms around her mother's neck and nestled her head on her shoulder.

"Come on," Bernadette's mother said to Brendan and Siobhan. "Your mommy needs her rest."

"Wait, luv," Bernadette said to Siobhan. "What will you be wearing to church tomorrow for Easter?"

"Now don't be worrying yourself about that," her mother said. "We'll find something for her to wear."

Brendan and Siobhan kissed their mother lightly on the cheek and went downstairs.

"Did you talk to them about Dermot?" her mother asked.

"Yes, I did. I think they understand," she said. "Sometimes I think they understand too much."

"I'm afraid you're right," her mother sighed.

"Mommy," said Bernadette, "I remember when Brendan and Siobhan were Maura's age. Jesus, for the life of me, I never thought the war would still be going on after all these years."

"At least you know that Dermot is alive. God, poor Rita Riley. What that poor woman must be going through. And what she has ahead of her."

"Yes, I suppose we're lucky," said Bernadette, feeling guilty as she thought of Rita Riley.

Her mother pulled a chair up to the bed and sat down. "What did Paddy say to you?"

"He told me the peelers wouldn't let him see Dermot until the forty-eight hours are up. He also told me to prepare myself for some tough times ahead. He said Dermot knew what to expect and was ready for it."

"What about the evidence against him?"

"He said there wasn't any evidence, but that Frank McGrath was brought to Castlereagh last night."

"Jesus, Mary and Joseph," Bernadette's mother sighed. "That rotten informer."

"The word is that Frank will finger Dermot for murdering a UDR man in Downpatrick three years ago," Bernadette said. "Not that it matters very much, but I don't think Dermot's ever even been in Downpatrick. But it doesn't matter one bit. Paddy says that once McGrath identifies Dermot, that'll be enough to charge him, and you know Dermot'll never get bail. So he could be on remand for the next two years before he even gets a trial."

"Frank McGrath, that tout. Him, always knocking about on the Falls saying what a republican he was and now he's doing all this," said Bernadette's mother.

"Paddy thinks the only real hope we have is that this whole supergrass system will collapse before Dermot's case is finished."

"What are the chances?"

"The Brits are hoping if they can get enough supergrasses to tout for them and if they move quickly enough, they can throw half the republican movement in jail. Frank McGrath's not the only informer, Paddy told me. Bill White from Ardoyne and Mickey Cahill from Turf Lodge are talking as well."

"Ach, Mickey Cahill. How could the Brits expect anyone to believe anything he says? Wasn't he the one caught stealing from his own mother?" Bernadette's mother asked.

"Paddy thinks almost two hundred of our people will be charged by the end of the month. But there'll be at least three trials before Dermot's. McGrath'll be the supergrass in one of them, the one where the thirty lads from Ballymurphy are charged."

Bernadette's mother listened intently, saying nothing.

"Paddy also told me pressure is building on the Brits. Already there's been some talk in England and America about the supergrasses."

"Don't ever sell the Brits short," Bernadette's mother said bitterly.

"That I won't. Paddy told me that when they held the hearing in the Cahill trial last week, they brought Mickey in to identify the eight Turf Lodge lads in open court. Well, by Jesus, you wouldn't have recognized him, Paddy said." Bernadette lowered her voice an octave. "There he was dressed in a new suit, his hair neatly cut and his voice sounding like he was a university professor. The Brits have remade the wee trout." She leaned back against the pillow, Maura still nestled in her arms, thumb in mouth.

"Let me take Maura so you can get some sleep, her mother said, smiling. "The one thing these children don't need is a sick mother." She leaned down and picked up the baby.

"I'll try to sleep, but Paddy will be seeing Dermot tonight at Castlereagh. If he rings, ask him if he could stop by to see me after he's with Dermot. It doesn't matter what time it is."

"I will, luv. Now you try to get some sleep. I'll have dinner for you when you wake up." Her mother pulled a blanket up around Bernadette and closed the curtains to keep out whatever sunlight had made its way through the dark afternoon clouds.

Bernadette looked about the darkened room, which seemed even smaller than it was. As she felt her eyes closing, she sensed the ceiling inching its way toward her and the heavily papered wall closing in on her. She turned her head to the right and gazed at her wedding picture on the dresser. She and Dermot were smiling then. She fell asleep moments later.

"Ah, Bernadette, that was a great sleep you had," her mother said as she turned on the low lamp light.

Bernadette opened her eyes. She could smell bacon. Her mother had brought up a tray. "Jesus, Mommy, I didn't know where I was. I slept so sound. What time is it anyway?"

"It's half eight, luv. Paddy rang up awhile ago. He'll be stopping by at half nine."

"Did he see Dermot?"

"He was on his way to Castlereagh when he rang."

"Did he say anything else?"

"No, not a thing. He just asked how you were keeping and whether you were well enough for him to come by."

"Ach, I'm feeling fine."

"I'm not so sure about that, luv. But here, I've fixed you some tea, a little bacon and some spuds. Eat what you can. You need your strength."

"Aye, thanks, Mommy," Bernadette said, sipping the tea and picking at the bacon and potatoes. "How are the children?"

"They're just grand. Siobhan was a big help to me with dinner, and Brendan reminds me so much of his father. There he is picking up around the house, cleaning the windows and looking out for the Brits. And, Jesus, whenever the other kids would be shouting in the street, he was after them to be quiet because his mommy was sick."

Bernadette smiled. "And Maura?"

"Maura's been no bother at all."

Bernadette drank two cups of tea and ended up finishing almost all of the bacon and potatoes. This brought joy to her mother who she knew was convinced that a healthy appetite was the cure for almost everything.

"Mum, would you get me the brush, please. I'd like to fix my hair before Paddy arrives. With the way I look, he'll be thinking it's Halloween rather than Holy Saturday."

"Now, luv, don't be saying that. You look beautiful. But here it is."

As she brushed her long auburn hair, Bernadette remembered the hours she had spent as a young girl brushing her hair and looking at herself in the mirror, imagining how wonderful it must be to be married and have children and have all the clothes and jewelry and money that you could ever want. Ah, sure, she thought, it's truly a wonderland that I'm living in, all right!

She heard a knock at the door below.

"Ah, Paddy, come on in. It's starting to rain," she heard her mother say. "Let me take your coat and I'll bring you up to Bernadette. She's waiting for you."

"Bernadette, the man himself is here," her mother called as she and Paddy climbed the stairs to her room.

"Ah, Paddy, God love you. Doing all this on a Saturday night—and Holy Saturday no less, when you would sooner be home with your family, I know," said Bernadette.

"I'll be downstairs with the children," said her mother. "Will you be wanting a cup of tea, Paddy?"

"No, thank you, Missus, I'll be fine," Paddy answered. He pulled up a chair beside the bed.

"Well, how is Dermot?" asked Bernadette.

"Dermot is great. He's asking for you and the children and, from what I can see, the Brits are not being very tough on him at all. Of course, there is the questioning, slapping him about, but nothing he can't handle."

"Paddy, be honest with me. How badly do the Brits want Dermot?"

"I'm afraid they want him pretty badly. Christ, I don't know what Dermot has been doing and I'm sure you don't know either. But we both know that the Ra has stepped up its campaign lately—especially in Andytown. The Brits can't have that. How can they say the IRA is defeated when foot patrols are being ambushed right on Andersonstown Road? They have to get the likes of Dermot off the street," Paddy said.

"Jesus, will it ever end?" said Bernadette.

"There's more. Just this afternoon, they brought McGrath to Dermot's cell, and Frank said, 'Aye, he's your man!' "

"Jesus, what did Dermot say?"

"You know well enough what Dermot said: 'Fuck off, tout.'"

Bernadette smiled. "That's what Dermot would say, all right. When will I be able to see him?"

"The RUC will get the seven-day order, so I don't think you should plan on seeing him for at least another five or six days. Besides, it will be at least until then before you're in any condition to put up with their harassment."

"I suppose you're right, and I don't want to keep you any longer. But what's happening to Mick McAllister?"

"Same as Dermot. Tommy Mullen is his solicitor, and Tommy told me that McGrath said Mick planted the bomb in that card shop in the Markets last year."

"Mother of God. The Ra had nothing to do with that one at all. That was a UVF bomb. Poor Mick. That bastard McGrath is really following the script, isn't he, though?"

"That he is, Bernadette. But Mick is strong like Dermot. Thank God we have men like them." Paddy paused, then went on. "You better be careful with your Sinn Fein work. The Brits love democracy, you know, so long as it's on their terms. What I'm saying is that I know the supergrasses are going to start naming political people and involve them in bombings and shootings and God knows what else. So keep your eyes open and don't make it any easier for them."

"Christ, Paddy, when I asked you to tell me the truth, you really took me at my word," said Bernadette, forcing a smile.

"Well, I must be off now. I'll ring you as soon as I have anything more."

"Thanks, Paddy. Thanks a million for everything. Good night and happy Easter to you."

"All the best, Bernadette."

Bernadette lay back against the pillow. She couldn't help but smile, though, when she thought about Paddy's warning that she might be stopped by the peelers because of her Sinn Fein work.

She remembered when she and Dermot had had a heated argument about Sinn Fein two years ago, the only time in their marriage she had heard him shout.

Several years after Rory died, Bernadette had joined Sinn Fein. She proved herself to be one of Sinn Fein's most effective workers and demonstrated a natural zeal for political organizing. With local elections coming up, the Sinn Fein leadership had seen those contests as the opportunity to show how extensive their grassroots support really was. About two months before the elections, Bernadette had been asked to come to a meeting at the Sinn Fein press centre at 51 Falls Road, the party's main headquarters.

The centre was a three-story brick building with boulders along the footpath to protect it from car bombs. The walls were festooned with colorful republican murals depicting IRA soldiers and downtrodden masses. Bernadette walked up to the cagelike enclosure that surrounded the entrance on Sevastapol Street around the corner from the Falls and pressed the buzzer. She was buzzed in and opened the cage door, then the inside door, and walked into the building. It was dark and damp as ever and the walls were replete with gaping holes in the plaster. Walking up the creaking staircase, she could feel the dust on the splintered banister. She smiled as she passed the minder who had buzzed her in, and he took his eyes off the video camera just long enough to nod polite-ly. Wending her way up the stairs, she saw Susan McGowan filing papers in the cabinet outside Gerry Adams's office. Susan was in her early twenties and spent almost every day at the press centre doing typing and research work.

"Ah, Bernadette, you're looking well, as usual. Why don't you go right in. Gerry's on the phone, but he is waiting for you."

"Aye, thanks very much, Susan. You're a luv."

Seated behind his desk, the phone to his ear, Gerry Adams pointed his pipe and motioned for Bernadette to sit down. Tall and lean, with long black hair, a dark beard and wire-rimmed glasses, Adams appeared almost ascetic in his wool cardigan. He spoke in deep measured tones and was a commanding presence. Though he was only in his mid-thirties, he was clearly the preeminent force in the republican movement.

Bernadette had no idea whether he was in the IRA. And she didn't really care, even though British intelligence and segments of the media described Adams as the IRA's chief of staff or at least a member of its Army Council.

What mattered to Bernadette was that, primarily through Adams, Sinn Fein had become a political force. And she knew how difficult it had been for him to achieve that. Republican hard-lin-ers opposed him, the Brits and RUC harassed him, and the loyalist paramilitaries had him on their death list. So far, he had survived. She was glad about that. There was a lot of work to be done.

Adams finished his call, put the phone down and looked toward Bernadette. "How are you keeping? How's Dermot?"

"Not so bad, Gerry. How's yourself?"

"Just great. Would you like a mug of tea?" He stood up.

"Aye, I would. It's very damp today and this place certainly doesn't help matters at all." She smiled.

"No, I must admit that it's not quite 10 Downing Street," he rejoined as he poured the tea and offered Bernadette some biscuits.

He opened the door to the adjoining office and said, "We might as well get started. Why don't you come in?"

In a few moments, Danny Morrison and Joe Austin walked in. Bernadette had known the two of them for years. Morrison was Sinn Fein's publicity director and Austin was the head of Sinn Fein in Belfast.

Morrison, sandy-haired with a white-flecked beard, had on a tweed jacket over a crewneck sweater. Austin, blond, clean-shaven and wiry, was wearing a maroon cardigan. They exchanged greetings with Bernadette and sat down.

"Bernadette, I don't have to tell you how important these elections can be for us," Adams began. "It will give our workers the experience in the streets that they need and it gives us the chance to show that we have support."

"Aye, I know that," Bernadette said.

"We need someone in the streets to organize and coordinate the grassroots work. Someone who knows what she's doing," said Adams.

"We've given this quite a bit of thought," Morrison added, "and we think you're the one to head up the campaigns in West Belfast, which is where we have our best chance to make a strong showing. You know the communities, you know the workers and you've good political sense. And we trust you."

"Jesus," Bernadette exhaled. "I'd no idea you'd anything like this in mind for me. I just can't say. I still have my children to look after, you know."

"Believe me, Bernadette," said Austin, "no one thinks this is going to be easy. The peelers will be harassing our workers. It will take a lot of your time, but at the end of the day it will be a great leap forward."

"Could I have a day or two to think it over?" Bernadette asked.

"That's all we can ask, Bernadette," said Adams. "Just let us know by Thursday."

"I will indeed, Gerry. And thank you."

Back home a few hours later, Bernadette had made up her mind to accede to the Sinn Fein request. It was only for two months, and her mother could help with Brendan and Siobhan. That night she mentioned the work to Dermot.

She was startled when he reacted so vehemently. She knew he had never favored the political route, but never before had she realized the intensity of his opposition.

"You'll just be wasting your time!" he shouted at her. "These campaigns, these elections, they're wasting money that should be spent on weapons. That's the only thing, the only fucking thing, the Brits have ever respected."

Nonetheless, in spite of Dermot's opposition, Bernadette did coordinate the West Belfast campaigns, and Sinn Fein did better than expected. The party won a number of seats and got a strong vote everywhere. More important, Sinn Fein established itself as a permanent political force.

As the ballots were being tallied, Bernadette received many of the plaudits. Still, it was not an evening she could enjoy.

She knew that she had done the job they had asked her to do, and she was satisfied with the results, but Dermot's hostility toward Sinn Fein and her role in it pained her.

When the elections were over, Bernadette made no effort to reap any benefits from what she had done. She didn't attempt to work her way into the party's ruling circle, nor did she try to get a commitment for a future candidacy for herself.

She went back to work at the advice centre in Andytown and also got involved in the campaign against strip-searching of women prisoners. She never discussed any of this with Dermot, although he was aware of what she was doing. Then, during the later stages of her pregnancy with Maura and for the first six months after she was born, Bernadette limited her party work to addressing envelopes at home. Only in the past few months had she begun to attend party meetings again. It was ironic, but Sinn Fein's growing political influence might now benefit Dermot. She could imagine what Dermot was going through right now at Castlereagh. Some of the strongest men and women had been broken in Castlereagh. Bernadette knew that Dermot would never break, but her entire body trembled at the thought of his torment.

It was a brilliant Easter morning as the blazing sun shone brightly in the heavens. Bernadette awoke at half eight and was immediately set upon by Brendan and Siobhan who had been anxiously awaiting her first stirring.

"Happy Easter, Mommy," they exclaimed as they clambered onto the bed to kiss her. Siobhan handed her a picture of the Blessed Mother that she had drawn in school. "This is for you, Mommy, for Easter."

"Thank you, luv. I don't know what your mommy would do without you. And Brendan, my God, you've even combed your hair. You must really think your mommy is very sick," she joked.

"Mommy, this is for Daddy for Easter. I've been painting it for the past week. I hope he'll like it," said Brendan.

Bernadette felt a rush of tears as she looked at Brendan's painting.

"What's wrong, Mommy, don't you like it?"

"No, Brendan, it's not that at all," she said hurriedly. "It's just so beautiful."

Actually, Bernadette was trying to conceal her trembling as she studied Brendan's work. The drawing was so precise and measured, the colors so carefully chosen. It had almost the mosaic effect of stained glass. At the center was a magnificent Easter lily enveloped in a blazing flame. On both sides of the burning lily were IRA men in full uniform—black beret, sunglasses, army field jackets and trousers, black boots—aiming their M-16 armalites upward and toward the center. Emerging from the flame at its highest point was a crucifix fashioned from chains. Across the bottom of the painting in beautiful, gothic lettering was the inscription "From the ashes, a Nation is born."

"Oh, Brendan, I know your daddy will be so proud of you."

"I hope so, Mommy. I hope so," said Brendan, suddenly looking distinctly older than his thirteen years.

"Look who wants to kiss her mommy for Easter," said the children's grandmother, holding Maura's hand as she waddled across the room toward Bernadette with a new bright yellow ribbon in her hair.

Taking Maura into the bed with her and kissing her mother on the forehead, Bernadette wished them all a happy Easter and thanked them for being so helpful and thoughtful. Her mother said she would be going to the ten o'clock Mass with Siobhan, and

Bernadette knew Brendan intended to go to the annual ceremony commemorating the 1916 Easter Uprising.

"And what Mass are you going to, Brendan?" asked Bernadette.

"Ah, Mommy, I'll be looking after Maura while Granny and Siobhan are at church and then I'm going to the Commemoration. Besides, I'm not much for going to church anyway."

"Jesus, Brendan, that's enough of that type of talk. Well, be sure to at least say a prayer today. You owe God that much," said Bernadette, who was not particularly anxious to pursue the point since she herself had not been to Mass in more than five years.

"Well, Mommy, I'm not so sure who owes what to anyone, but I'll say a prayer for you and Daddy," answered Brendan.

"That's grand, Brendan, and don't be messing about at the parade. Do you hear me now?"

"Aye, Mommy," smiled Brendan.

Brendan came back from the Commemoration just in time for dinner at three o'clock.

Bernadette had decided to get dressed and eat with the rest of the family. She felt a bit weak coming down the stairs but was happy to be out of bed and sitting at the table.

"And how was the parade, Brendan?" Bernadette asked.

"Ah, Mommy, it was brilliant. All the bands and thousands of people marching along the Falls. And then at the cemetery, Gerry Adams gave a brilliant speech. He said the whole world knew that the Brits were murderers, and that the Easter Rebellion wouldn't be completed until every Brit left Ireland. And the Brits just stood there, raging. But they couldn't do a thing about it."

Bernadette could feel Brendan's animation, but she knew that the Brits *could* do a lot about it. Didn't they kill fourteen of ours on Bloody Sunday in a civil rights march in Derry in 1972? And even today, she knew they would be arresting the odd stragglers coming home from the parade and beating the hell out of them. It worried her that Brendan was so defiant of the Brits, so oblivious to their ruthlessness. She would have to keep her eye on him.

CHAPTER THREE

Bernadette found herself getting stronger each day, and by the Thursday after Easter she was able to take care of herself and her home. It was good to be on her own again, alone so she could think. Alone so she could sort out how she would help Dermot and how she would manage without him. And alone to confront her demons.

During the next several weeks, her days took on a deadening sameness. A quick shower, then putting on jeans, a blouse and a cardigan. Fixing breakfast, getting Brendan and Siobhan off to school and finding something that would keep Maura reasonably amused for a while at least.

And then, except while she attended to Maura, Bernadette would sit alone in the living room for hours at a time, with the blinds closed and the curtains drawn shut, smoking cigarette after cigarette. Occasionally, she'd summon the strength to do some of the wash or tidy the house a bit. But for the most part, Siobhan had assumed responsibility for those tasks.

Bernadette's mother would either ring her daily or come by to see her. "Why don't you see a doctor?" she would ask.

"No. A doctor would do me no good," Bernadette would answer. "I don't want to spend the rest of my life filled with Valium."

"Well, what is it that you do want?"

"I don't know. I'm sorry, Mommy, but I just don't know."

Her only respite from the depression would come when she visited Dermot for one hour, three days a week. And even then her relief would only be partial.

On those days she'd comb her hair, put on some makeup and make sure she'd something to bring him. He always wanted newspapers, of course. And books on Irish history. He also wanted to study the Irish language. The last time he'd been inside, he had learned enough Irish to talk with the other prisoners, who used it to confound the screws. This time he told her he'd learn to read Irish and speak it fluently. Paddy was a great help to her in finding many of the books Dermot requested.

On a visiting day a taxi would come by her house and leave her off on Crumlin Road outside the jail. She'd then take her place at the end of the long queue of visitors, which slowly inched along the sidewalk toward the prison entrance. Sometimes the wait would be as long as an hour. Often rain would fall while she was waiting and she'd put the newspapers and books under her raincoat to protect them. Just as often, she and the others in the queue would have to endure the slurs and taunts of the Brit foot patrols walking by.

And all the while as she waited, she could see directly across the street on her right the courthouse where Dermot would finally, one day, go on trial.

Once inside the prison, there were the further ordeals of being searched and questioned by the screws and then waiting still longer until Dermot was brought down to the visitor area. There, they would sit at a wood table while a warder eyed them just several feet away. While they spoke, Bernadette would feel her spirits lifting, but the depression was still there. Dermot told her not to worry, reassuring her that she would soon be fine and her old self once again.

And, indeed, perhaps she might be.

This morning, as she sat in the darkened living room and stared at the heavy wallpaper that covered the wall to stave off Belfast's corrosive dampness, Bernadette felt for the first time since the depression had come upon her that she was able to start sorting out the perplexing array of dark feelings that had made her a prisoner of her own mind.

Tomorrow was Ascension Thursday, but, far more important to Bernadette, it was the anniversary of Rory's death. And as she thought of Rory, she remembered that it was during the days after he died that she had first encountered these dreaded demons. No, they were not as intense then, but they were horrific nonetheless. That same sense of despair, of emptiness, of loss of control over her life and destiny.

She also thought about when she had experienced her truest joy, and it was when each of the three babies had been born.

Rory's death had torn apart Bernadette's spirit every bit as much as the bomb had torn apart his body. To resurrect her spirit so she could go on with her life, Bernadette had severed herself from the republican movement. She would have nothing more to do with it. If Rory had not been in the IRA, she had concluded, he would still be alive. No cause could justify his death. Aye, the Brits are bastards. But Rory is dead—as dead as any man could ever be—and the Brits are still here.

But after several years, Bernadette had realized that she could no long continue to deny the reality of what was going on around her. The Brits were trying to destroy the very soul of her people. That was when Bernadette rejoined Sinn Fein, and created a contradiction within herself that she had never been able to resolve.

She still identified Rory's death with the IRA. Yet, Sinn Fein was the IRA's political wing, Sinn Fein supported the IRA's armed struggle, and many of Sinn Fein's members and leaders belonged to the IRA as well.

To those who'd ask and to herself, she'd say there was no contradiction. Or at least not so much of a contradiction as might seem apparent. As far as she was concerned, Sinn Fein was separate from the IRA. Besides, the IRA was not an end in itself, she would say. It was the means to put military pressure on the Brits to increase Sinn Fein's bargaining position.

Now, as Bernadette looked about the living room, she thought not just of the life of her unborn child that had been lost, but of the lives that faced Brendan and Siobhan and Maura. She also thought of a wall mural in Ballymurphy: "Is There Life After Birth?"

If her children were to have a life—or any hope of a life— Bernadette could not allow herself to be defeated. Yes, she did need Dermot more than ever. But Brendan, Siobhan and Maura needed *her* more than ever.

She got up from the couch and walked toward the window. She drew back the curtains and, after a moment's hesitation, opened the blinds the slightest bit, just enough for rays of sunlight to pierce the darkness that had enshrouded the room for too long. Rory was dead. But Dermot, her children, her mother, her younger sister Eilish were alive. It was time Bernadette rejoined the living.

Eilish had been after her to see the house she had moved into in Twinbrook a fortnight ago. Thursday would be a grand day to visit Eilish, Bernadette thought. Her mother could stay with Brendan and Siobhan, who would be off from school for the holy day, and

Bernadette and Maura could go to Elish's right after she saw Dermot at the Crum.

As the taxi turned left into the Twinbrook estate off Stewartstown Road, Bernadette listened to the news on the car radio about the five Brits killed the previous night in Crossmaglen and saw the inscriptions on the walls honoring Bobby Sands's memory.

On the very edge of West Belfast, Twinbrook was built in the early seventies and was a bastion of republican support. Bobby Sands had lived in Twinbrook. His mother and father still lived there. The taxi drove around the green and dropped her at Eilish's home.

"Bernadette, you look so beautiful, so you do," said Eilish as she greeted her at the door. "And I'm delighted you brought Maura."

"Oh, Eilish, the house is lovely. And my God, Veronica has got so big."

"She was two last week," Eilish said, beaming with pride at the cheerful child.

"Mother of God, the poor child's birthday was last week and I forgot all about it. I'm so sorry!"

"Ach, will you stop your slobbering! After what you've been through, I'm thrilled that you're here at all."

"Well, I just thought it was time for me to get out. After sitting around like a baby all these weeks. Tell me, how is Alex keeping?"

"Ah, he's great, so he is," Eilish answered as she and Bernadette watched Veronica and Maura playfully chase one another from room to room. "He gets lifted now and again but they never hold him more than overnight. Jesus, Bernadette, it's almost three years now he's been out of the Kesh. I pray for you and Dermot. I don't think I could ever face that again."

"Ah, you're as strong as they come. You know that."

"Well, I do know we've had a bit of luck lately," Eilish whispered. "Alex has been doing the double—getting the dole and doing some odd carpentry jobs as well."

"Thanks be to God for that," Bernadette smiled.

"Alex just went to the shop. He should be home any minute. Why don't I show you the house and then we can all have tea together?"

"Aye, that would be gr—"

Suddenly they heard screeching tire and popping noises outside, followed by children screaming. Bernadette looked at Eilish apprehensively.

"Mother of God, Bernadette, this place is filled with those dammed joyriders," said Eilish. She jerked open the front door and Bernadette looked out.

British jeeps and saracens, small, tanklike armored vehicles, were positioned all over the street and children were screaming hysterically: "They shot Mairead Brady. They shot Mairead. They shot her with plastics."

A grocery bag and a carton of milk were off to the side of the footpath. Then Bernadette saw Alex kneeling over a girl about twelve years old. Bernadette ran out to help as Alex screamed to Eilish to get a towel. Blood was pouring from the girl's head and coming up her throat. Eilish raced out of the house clutching a wad of towels.

"Get back, you fucking bastards, or you'll all be fucking dead," a soldier shouted and shoved Bernadette back toward the house. Eilish eluded the soldiers and ran over to Alex. Over the din of screams and sobs, Bernadette heard a woman shout "Michael, call an ambulance. Call an ambulance."

Bernadette leaned around the soldier, trying to see Alex and the girl. He grabbed her arms and told her to hold still. The crowd was shouting, "Murderers, murderers."

One of the other soldiers yelled, "This is for our five mates, you fuckers!"

Bernadette could see that Alex was pressing the towels against the back of Mairead's head. A sobbing woman thrust herself through the Brits and fell to her knees, squeezing the girl's hands and crying, "My baby, my baby."

"Where the hell is the ambulance?" people shouted.

Bernadette twisted out of the soldier's grasp and ran back toward the house where Maura and Veronica were standing at the door. She picked Maura up and held Veronica's hand tightly as she edged forward to the periphery of the crowd.

She saw a priest rushing across the road toward the girl. As the priest prayed over her, an ambulance wound its way around the green. Within minutes the girl was on a stretcher and in the ambulance. The girl's mother and what looked like an older sister followed the ambulance in a taxi.

Eilish ran over and picked up Veronica. Each holding their baby daughters in their arms, the sisters stood on the small pathway to the front door as Alex walked toward them, his hands and clothes covered with Mairead Brady's blood.

"There's no hope for the wee girl at all. It's not just the blood, but brains as well, that spilled out of her head," said Alex.

They were about to go into the house when Martha McEntee came rushing up the path. Bernadette remembered meeting Martha at Eilish's wedding. She thought she had been living in England.

"Eilish, the soldiers murdered Mairead," she shouted. "I saw it with my own eyes. They murdered her."

"Come inside, luv, and I'll give you some tea," said Eilish.

Bernadette, with Maura on her lap, Eilish and Alex sat at the kitchen table as Martha told them what she had seen. Alex had washed his hands in the kitchen sink but his clothes were still blood-soaked.

"I had gone to the front door to call in my wee Erin," said Martha. "I saw there were two jeeps and two saracens racing up the hill and there were still two jeeps at the bottom of the hill. Mairead had just walked along the footpath in front of my home. Alanna Duggan and Colette Sweeney were with her."

Martha paused for a moment to light a cigarette. Bernadette waited anxiously for her to continue.

"Mairead had a grocery bag in her hand. She must have been coming from the shop."

"Aye, she had been there when I came in," said Alex.

"Anyway, the jeeps and saracens went speeding past her. When they reached the corner, they stopped and reversed. I could hear the soldiers shouting and laughing. And just as they drew even with the girl, they fired two plastic bullets from the saracens. I saw the flashes. Then they fired another two and Mairead fell to the ground. And the soldiers kept shouting and laughing, with the poor wee girl lying in a pool of her own blood all the while."

Bernadette sipped her tea. She lit a cigarette.

"I was at the bottom of the hill," Alex said, "when I heard the jeeps and the saracens speeding. And I ran up the hill when I heard the shots. But the first thing I saw was Mairead on the ground."

"It was such a beautiful day. And a holy day as well," said Martha. "Who ever thought this would happen? My God, it could just as easily been any one of our wee children."

As she listened to Martha recount what happened, Bernadette could feel fear and terror growing within herself. Yet, she could also sense that her mind was focusing more clearly than it had since she lost the baby.

Brenda Molloy, who lived across the green, came to the front door with her son, Tommy, who was about fourteen. He was clutching his right side, and his left eye was swollen and discolored.

After quickly introducing Brenda to Bernadette, Eilish asked, "Brenda, luv, what happened to Tommy?"

"It was the Brits, Eilish," said Brenda, standing in the middle of the kitchen. "He'll be okay. But poor Mairead, the wee girl! Those bastards wouldn't let the ambulance into the estate."

"What?" Alex shouted.

"Hold this to your eye," said Eilish, handing Tommy an ice cube.

"When Tommy saw that Mairead had been shot, he and his two mates ran up to Stewartstown Road to make sure the ambulance went the right way when it came into the estate," Brenda continued. "But just when the ambulance began to turn into the estate, two Brits who were there shouted to the driver that it was a fake alarm and that he should turn back. Tommy, tell what happened then."

Sitting at the table holding the ice against his eye, Tommy said, "I shouted, 'No, no! There's been a wee girl shot! She's across the green.' And the next thing I know, one of the Brits clouts me across the face with his hand and batons me in the stomach."

"Jesus Christ!" said Eilish.

Bernadette dragged heavily on her cigarette and clutched Maura.

"Finally, after a lot of shouting from my mates," Tommy said, "the driver went through." He pulled up his shirt. His rib cage was covered with bruises.

"Brenda," Alex said, "you should take him above to the clinic right away. Those ribs could be broken."

"Aye, Alex, I will indeed. Let's go, Tommy."

Knowing how quickly the news would spread, Bernadette and Eilish telephoned their mother to assure her that they were fine. Bernadette then took Maura home with her in a taxi.

Mairead's shooting was the first story that evening on the six o'clock news. "A twelve-year-old girl from West Belfast is in critical condition after being shot in the head with a plastic bullet during a riot this afternoon. Mairead Brady was shot as the Army attempted to quell a demonstration in the Twinbrook estate."

"What lies!" snapped Bernadette as her mother shook her head sadly.

The news reader continued: "The injured girl's brother, Conor Brady, is presently serving a life sentence in the Maze Prison for the murder of an RUC man five years ago. Mairead Brady is at the Royal Victoria Hospital on a life-support system. Doctors say her condition is giving cause for concern."

Bernadette was at the shop early Friday morning to buy the *Irish News*. The headline read "TWINBROOK GIRL NEAR DEATH. Shot in the Head with Plastic Bullet; Accounts of Incident Vary."

The story quoted RUC Deputy Chief Constable George Williamson: "This incident is tragic and regrettable and the direct result of a riot situation." It also quoted Martha McEntee as stating, "There was no riot at all."

When Bernadette finished reading the paper, she rang Eilish. "Eilish, is there any news on Mairead?"

"Aye, there is. But it's not very good. Alex was talking to Mairead's older sister, Elizabeth, this morning. She said the wee girl is on life support at the Royal. They don't expect her to live very long. It could be just days or even hours."

"My God."

"She also said that after they left the estate yesterday and were on their way to the Royal with Mairead, the ambulance and the taxi were stopped for questions."

"Was it the Brits?"

"No, it was peelers. But they knew just what they were doing, so they did."

"Indeed, they did," said Bernadette, her voice trailing off.

"There will be a meeting at Jerry O'Donnell's house tonight. We must do something about this. The Brits might as well have a license to kill. Would you want to stop by?"

"I feel so sorry for Mrs. Brady. That's the least I can do."

"The meeting will start at half seven. I will see you then. Cheerio."

"Cheerio, Eilish."

After hanging up the phone, Bernadette went to the living room window and opened the blinds so that the room filled with daylight. She had to be ready for this evening's meeting.

When Bernadette arrived at Jerry O'Donnell's Twinbrook home that evening at five past eight, he was just calling the meeting to order. There were about twenty people crammed into the living room and overflowing into the kitchen. Bernadette saw Eilish and Alex standing off to the side against the living room wall, and she worked her way across the room until she was alongside them.

Jerry O'Donnell was in his early fifties. Bernadette knew he'd been an accountant who'd been out of work for the past ten years. He had never been affiliated with any political party but had been active in the civil rights movement and in various causes such as the campaign against strip-searching, which was how Bernadette had first met him. His most recent effort had been the establishment of a preschool Irish language program. He opened the meeting by handing out fact sheets he had prepared.

As the papers were passed hand to hand, O'Donnell said, "All of us are here tonight because of what happened to poor Mairead yesterday afternoon. The time has come for us to stand together as a community on this issue. Tonight we are forming the 'Committee Against Plastic Bullets.' All of you who wish to join are welcome. We need your support. I'd like to read the statement that we'll be releasing to the press tomorrow:

"The tragic and intentional shooting of Mairead Brady with a plastic bullet constitutes yet another black page in the book of suffering which the Northern Irish nationalist community has had to endure at the hands of British security forces.

"The plastic bullet is a lethal weapon. It is a five-ounce cylinder, one-and-a-half inches in diameter and four inches long. It has a velocity of more than 160 miles per hour.

"Plastic bullets fired by British security forces kill and injure nationalist civilians. These injuries include severe head wounds, blindness and damage to the lungs, spleen, intestines, liver, legs and arms.

"The use of the plastic bullet by security forces in Northern Ireland has been condemned by an International Tribunal of Inquiry in Belfast in 1981 and the European Parliament in 1982. Yet, British forces continue to fire plastic bullets and nationalist civilians continue to die.

"The Committee Against Plastic Bullets demands the outlawing of the use of these lethal projectiles and calls upon all political and church leaders to assert their solidarity with us in this cause."

When O'Donnell finished reading the press statement, Hugh Courtney, who had organized a number of youth programs in Twinbrook, asked to be recognized. "Jerry, I think it's grand that you've arranged this meeting and formed the committee. But no matter what we say to the press, we must be honest with ourselves. You know—and we all know—that a group of Catholics from Twinbrook isn't going to be able to stop the Brits from shooting plastic bullets. If the European Parliament couldn't do it, then we certainly won't. Still, I think we might make some progress." The crowd murmured, and Bernadette thought about what a plastic bullet might do to one of her children.

"Yes, I believe we can hurt the Brits this time," O'Donnell said. "They shot down a wee girl in the middle of the day, with no riot or demonstration going on." Bernadette wished she could get the picture of Mairead lying in her own blood out of her mind.

"Williamson was on the TV tonight," Courtney said. "I'm sure most of you saw him, saying that plastic bullets are used only against rioters and that—I wrote it down just as he said it—'there are proper procedures for complaints about plastic bullets which assure a thorough and impartial investigation.'"

Courtney paused for a moment as the room filled with ironic and bitter laughter. "Williamson may have given us the opening we need. If people who saw what happened come forward, the peelers will be forced to conduct an investigation. And while I've no doubt the Brits will be cleared, the peelers will have to go through some contortions to do it."

"Hugh," said O'Donnell, "I agree with everything you've said, but I believe we'd be asking too much if we asked a witness to officially challenge the Brits on this. God knows what might happen."

"Excuse me," said a woman getting up from her chair in the corner of the living room. "My name is Martha McEntee and I am a witness. I heard what you just said about what might happen if I challenge the official version. But I may have already gone too far by being quoted in today's *Irish News*."

"Mrs. McEntee," O'Donnell answered, "I'm certain the Brits are quite disturbed by what you said in the *Irish News*, but I'm also fairly certain that they will do nothing at this point so long as you go no further."

"Well," Martha continued, "as most of you probably know, I've never been politically involved. My husband and I are living in Twinbrook because we're Catholics, but my husband was born in Liverpool and we lived in England for five years after we were married. I have no animosity against the British people. But what I saw yesterday was outright murder. So I do intend to file a complaint with the RUC. I don't expect the RUC or the Army to be pleased with what I'm doing, but this is just something that I must do."

The people in the house applauded Martha McEntee as she sat down.

O'Donnell commended Martha for her decision and assured her the committee would support her. He also said that he would ask Brenda Molloy, who was not at the meeting, if she would be willing to have her son submit a statement to the RUC about the Brits' attempt to turn the ambulance away.

As the meeting broke up, Bernadette walked over to Martha, lightly touched her arm and told her, "My God, I'm so proud of you."

"Ah, Bernadette, I'll be fine," Martha replied with a hint of a smile.

Several days later, on Wednesday evening, Eilish and Bernadette sat and talked in Bernadette's living room, attempting to sort out recent events. They had just come from another meeting, which Jerry O'Donnell had called at the Lake Glen Hotel on Andersonstown Road.

Mairead Brady had died Sunday afternoon. On Monday, British foot patrols questioned and harassed mourners attempting to enter Twinbrook to attend the wake at the Brady home. Late Tuesday night, the front windows on both floors of Brenda Molloy's home were shot out with plastic bullets. Mairead's brother, Conor, who was in Long Kesh, was denied compassionate bail to attend the funeral. And the already tragic funeral was further marred when Army helicopters hovered low over the mourners during the procession to Milltown Cemetery.

"Jesus, Bernadette, that crowd was angry tonight, so they were."

"After what's gone on this week, who could blame them? I'm still trembling from the funeral. I've been to so many—I thought I'd almost got used to them."

"I know what you're saying."

"But Mairead's funeral wrecked me. Maybe it's because the wee girl was shot on Rory's anniversary. Or maybe I've just been to too many funerals."

"Ah, Bernadette, I'm sure it's a combination of everything. But Jesus, I think you're doing fine, so you are. After losing the baby and Dermot being lifted, it's a wonder you're doing so well."

"Eilish, do you think Mrs. Molloy will file a complaint?"

"No, I don't. Alex saw the poor woman today. She told Alex they were all in the house when the peelers shot out the windows. She says Tommy is afraid even to come out of the bedroom."

"And Martha?"

"Aye, she was to go to the barracks today after the funeral."

"God love her. But what do you think will come from all this?"

"I suppose I have to agree with what Hugh Courtney said at Jerry O'Donnell's the other night. Nothing we do is going to stop the Brits from firing plastics at us. But this is such a clear case of murder that maybe we can use it to damage the Brits, not just on the plastics but the courts, the supergrasses—everything."

"Jesus, they keep killing ours and we keep trying to make our points."

"Aye, Bernadette, but we kill some of theirs as well and thank God for that."

For the next two days, Bernadette worried about Martha. Early Thursday morning, the peelers had broken into Martha's house and taken her to Castlereagh. That was the last Bernadette heard until about an hour ago, when Eilish rang to say Martha had been released. Bernadette rushed over to Twinbrook after a frantic call to her mother to watch the children.

Bernadette knew that forty-eight hours in Castlereagh could be a lifetime—a brutal lifetime—and as she followed Alex through the door, she was filled with apprehension.

Martha was sitting on the couch, wearing a heavy wool sweater even though it was a hot, humid day. Her body quivered as if it were midwinter. Stooped over, her left arm wrapped across her waist, she dragged heavily on the cigarette gripped between the fingers of her right hand. Her hair, usually permed and styled off to the side, looked thick and matted and was combed straight back. Her face had no makeup and was a ghostly white. Her eyes looked hollow and sunken, the lids swollen and red.

"Bernadette," said Martha anxiously, "it's so good of you to come."

"Ah, Martha, I'm just so happy that you're out." Bernadette glanced at Eilish, hoping for some direction as to what she should say.

"Martha has had a rough time," said Eilish. "And when she was released this morning, the peelers arrested her husband. Her solicitor just rang, though, and said Gerard will be released in a few hours. The fucking peelers couldn't resist the last bit of harassment."

"Oh, Bernadette," Martha said, "I'm so sorry for what I've done. I was telling Eilish that I will never be able to forgive myself. Never."

"Ach, Martha, anyone who's been in Castlereagh for two days doesn't have anything to be forgiven for."

"No, you don't understand. I signed a statement this morning. It said I never saw the soldiers shoot Mairead, that I'd filed the complaint because I was afraid the IRA would murder me if I didn't."

"Martha," said Alex, in an understanding but firm tone, "each of us in this room knows enough about Castlereagh to know what those bastards will do to get you to sign their statements."

"I can't believe all of this has happened," said Martha, giving no indication she'd even heard Alex.

Bernadette could see that Martha wanted to tell all. The best thing they could do for her was listen.

"I went to the barracks on Wednesday afternoon after the funeral," Martha went on, "and insisted on signing a complaint against the soldiers who shot Mairead. Two RUC men and a woman officer took me in a room and I told them what I had seen. They told me I was making a big mistake. But I signed the complaint anyway. As I was walking to the door, the woman came up behind me and said, 'You will be sorry, you bitch.'

"The next morning I was fixing breakfast for Padraic and Margaret and getting them off to school. Gerard was in the living room. The front door was kicked in and six RUC came racing through the house with rifles, shouting as loud as they could that I was under arrest. Mother of God, I didn't know what was happening. Padraic and Margaret were both crying. Gerard was put up against the wall and two female officers took me up to the bedroom and told me to get dressed. After I put on a skirt and blouse, one of the woman officers snapped the handcuffs on me and turned them so tight, I thought my wrists were broken. Then, one of them grabbed my arm and the other my hair and they dragged me down the stairs, pulled me out the door and threw me into the back of a Land Rover.

"The two policewomen and the male officer were in the back with me and the man kept saying over and over, 'When you get to fucking Castlereagh, you'll be fucking sorry you ever signed that fucking complaint.' And every time he said it the two women laughed and laughed."

"Those bastards, they never change," said Alex.

"When I got to Castlereagh," Martha continued, "they took me straightaway to a cell, where they took off the handcuffs and let me sit there alone for about an hour or so. Then a man came into the cell. He said he was there for fingerprints and I was brought down to a room to have them taken. When they took me back to the cell, I could hardly breathe because the fans were blowing hot air and making a terrible noise as well.

"Jesus, I was petrified, so I was. I was alone, I was suffocating, and I'd no idea what was to happen to me. After about another hour and a half went by, a Special Branch man and a police-woman came to the cell and took me to an interrogation room.

"God, it was a terrible room. There was one wooden chair near the wall and a long table in the middle of the room. No windows. They told me to sit in the chair. The woman was standing behind me, the man in front. He started off calmly, telling me he knew the IRA made me sign the complaint and that the RUC would file no charges against me if I withdrew the complaint and signed a statement blaming the IRA. He also told me he didn't believe the allegations against me.

"I told him I knew nothing about the IRA and that I had signed the complaint on my own. And I asked him, 'What allegations?'

"For several seconds there was complete silence, and then the woman grabbed my hair and pulled my hair so hard over the back of the chair that I thought my neck would snap."

Martha crushed her cigarette into the ashtray and lit a new one. Bernadette dug in her pockets and found her own pack. She lit a cigarette and Martha went on talking about the policewoman.

"Jesus, she shouted at me louder than I ever heard anyone shout. 'You fucking liar. You cunt. You IRA whore. You were in the women's IRA—you were in Cumann na Bman—even when you were in England, you fucking bitch.'

"I was crying my eyes out and screaming 'No, no' and the more I cried, the harder she pulled on my hair and shouted that I was a whore. I thought all the hair would come out by the roots, it hurt so much.

"Finally, she let go of my hair and the man put his face next to mine and screamed, 'When we're finished with you, you'll wish you were fucking dead. And there won't be a mark on you.' Then he spit in my face.

"The two of them dragged me out of the room and down a long corridor where they threw me into a cell. Again, no window, and the air was so stale and hot. I couldn't see anyone but I could hear other women screaming and crying. Then the light started to dim and go off and on. This continued for hours and after a while, I didn't know whether it was morning or night or even what day it was—or, Jesus, what month or year it was.

"A matron brought in a tray with a piece of meat and a potato on it. I touched them with my finger and they were cold and greasy. And I could see insects on the meat.

"When I didn't eat, the matron threw the tray down on the floor and slapped me across the face, calling me a 'fucking whore.' I didn't know how much later it was, but two Special Branch men and a policewoman came for me and pulled me down the corridor again to another interrogation room. The men were twisting my arms and the woman was dragging me by the hair."

Martha stopped for a moment to sip some tea. Bernadette realized that the whole time she had been talking, Martha had just stared straight ahead, never blinking her eyes.

"This room seemed smaller than the first," Martha went on, "but there were three chairs and a table. The room was so dark. I could barely make anything out. I felt so sick and so dizzy and I was so damned scared. They sat me in a chair and the two men sat right in front of me. The policewoman stood behind me. She grabbed onto my hair but wasn't pulling it. One of the men was shining a bright light into my eyes, and I couldn't see anything.

"The woman pulled my head back. The other man said that I was a fool for not cooperating with them, that my husband had already signed a statement that we kept weapons for the IRA in our home. I could hear the Branch man turning a lot of papers, and then he said that they had statements and other evidence that Gerard and I were involved in bombings in Birmingham when we were living in England.

"All the time he was telling me this, the woman kept pulling my hair a wee bit harder and harder.

"The man who was holding the light said that if I didn't give them the information they wanted, Padraic and Margaret would be just as dead as Mairead Brady.

"The policewoman started to pull my hair very hard now and my head was almost completely back over the top of the chair. She asked me to tell them the names of the IRA men in Twinbrook. Now, Mother of God, you know that I've nothing to do with the IRA. I don't have a clue who's in it. When I started to tell her that, I found that I could barely talk because my mouth was so dry.

"One of the men then punched me so hard in the stomach, I couldn't breathe. I started to pass out from the pain. Then the woman put a hood over my head and the men tied my feet to the chair legs."

Bernadette glanced fleetingly at Martha's feet and saw the raw, bruised skin around her ankles.

"I was terrified, just terrified," said Martha, "and I went hysterical. I tried to break loose but two of them—I think it was the Branch men—twisted my arms until I sat still.

"Jesus, I heard the most terrible noise. It sounded like dust-bin lids crashing together, pipes cracking against radiator pipes, and God knows what else. It also seemed as if more men had come into the room, but I didn't know for sure.

"I was so scared that I couldn't even scream anymore. Then for what must have been five minutes, there was dead silence. I did-n't know why, but I found that more terrifying than all the noises they had been making. Maybe it was because I couldn't see anything with the hood being on me.

"And then—" Martha started to sob hysterically. Eilish put her arms around her and let her cry. Alex brought her a glass of Powers whiskey. After a few moments, she stopped crying almost as suddenly as she had begun. She drank the whiskey and lit another cigarette. Inhaling deeply, she continued.

"I heard the woman whisper something and the men gripped my wrists much more tightly than they had been. Then, suddenly, the woman—I know it was her—pulled my skirt all the way up. And I just went mad. No matter how hard they were twisting my arms, I could barely feel that pain. I just wanted to cover myself. This went on until I almost collapsed from exhaustion.

"The men were making crude remarks about my legs. The woman said, 'I don't know why this should bother you so much. After all, we know that you fuck every IRA man in Twinbrook. Your problem is you've never got a good fuck. We have two British soldiers here who will show you how it's really done.' I shouted, 'No, please!' and I heard the woman tell the Branch men to untie my feet from the chair and hold me across the table. I could hear men with British accents and I screamed like a madwoman as the Branch men untied my ankles and dragged me from the chair. I was fighting and screaming and they were pulling and dragging me until all of a sudden I was thrown down and I heard a door slam shut. I waited for a moment and then pulled off the hood and realized I was alone."

"So they didn't rape you?" Bernadette asked.

Martha shook her head.

"Thank God for that," said Eilish.

"The light was bright and after having the hood on for so long, I could hardly focus my eyes and I was just so dizzy," Martha continued. "After only a few minutes, I could hear them coming down the corridor for me again. They took me to the same inter-rogation room. But this time they didn't say even one word to me.

"They put me in the chair. The policewoman pulled my head back over the top of the chair and then one of the Branch men pushed a soaking-wet towel down onto my face. Not only couldn't I breathe, but I thought I was going to drown from all the water going into my nose and my mouth. "Just when I thought I was blacking out, he pulled the towel off and I screamed, 'I will sign the statement, I will sign the statement!' After I signed the statement, the police-woman read it, smiled at me and then slapped me across the face.

"I was put back in the cell, with the bright light going on and off, and left there for, I suppose, twelve or twenty-four hours. I was so confused I lost all track of time.

"Anyway, I was released this morning and Gerard was arrested. But, as Eilish told you, our solicitor rang just awhile ago and said Gerard was just taken in for harassment and was to be released very soon."

"So," Bernadette asked, "Gerard never signed a statement when you were being questioned?"

"Indeed, he didn't," interjected Alex. "I was with him in his house the whole time Martha was being held."

"I'm just so sorry," Martha said, "I let poor Mairead down. I let everyone down."

"Martha, don't be saying that," said Bernadette almost defi-antly. "You let no one down. You did all that any person could be expected to do. God love you."

Martha looked at her. The trembling had stopped. "Thank you, Bernadette." She finished her cup of tea. "I want to go home."

While Eilish walked home with Martha, Bernadette and

Alex sat, talking.

"The poor woman, she's been through hell," said Bernadette.

"Aye, indeed she has," replied Alex. "And there was no need for it at all. The Brits knew she wasn't a republican and had nothing to do with the Ra. If all they wanted was for her to sign a statement taking back the complaint, they could've gotten her to do it in less than fifteen minutes. But Jesus, they had to break into the house with the rifles and all that *craic*."

"What'll happen now to Mairead's case?"

"That's all over. I can tell you that. Oh, the peelers'll act as if they're conducting an inquiry, but at the end of the day, it'll be a whitewash."

"Just like it's always been!"

"Aye, just like it's always been. I'd expect, though, that for a while at least the Brits will ease up with the plastics. This was almost a public relations disaster for them. And they don't want to risk that again. Not while they're pushing the supergrasses the way they are."

Bernadette stood up.

"Do you have to go?" asked Alex.

"Aye, I promised Siobhan I'd fix a dress for her. Her wee friend Maggie's having a birthday party tomorrow."

"Let me call you a taxi."

"No, I'll walk."

"Jesus, it's miles from here to Andytown."

"Ah, it won't take me much longer than an hour. I may be older than you and Eilish, but I'm not so old that I can't walk!" she said with a smile. "Besides, there's something I must do."

"Be careful."

She smiled at him. "I will indeed, Alex."

CHAPTER FOUR

On Monday morning, Bernadette was at the Crum, talking to Dermot in the big room where the prisoners met with family and lawyers. She pulled a letter out of her handbag.

"Eilish brought this over before I left. It's a copy." She handed the letter to Dermot. He read it quickly.

Dear Mrs. Brady,

I have to inform you that the investigation papers relative to the death of your daughter have been studied by the Director of Public Prosecutions who has directed, "No Prosecution." Should there be any aspect of this investigation you wish to discuss with me, please do not hesitate to contact me so that a meeting can be arranged.

Yours faithfully,
G.R. Kensington
Detective Inspector

"Another triumph for British justice!" He handed the letter back to Bernadette. Dermot had spoken loud enough for the screw standing at the end of the table to hear him, and the warder now eyed him warily.

"Nothing to do with you," Dermot said as he smiled cynically at the guard. "Just some of your brave mates, who enjoy shooting wee girls."

"Any more of that talk," the warder snapped, "and I will enjoy terminating this visit."

Bernadette touched Dermot's hands. "There's far too much to talk about without worrying about the likes of that eejit," she said.

"Aye, you're right." He smiled at her. "And how are the children doing?"

Bernadette spent the next several minutes talking about the children. When she was convinced the warder was no longer paying close attention to them, she dropped her voice a level and looked directly at Dermot.

"You were right about me coming out of my depression."

"Ah, I knew you'd be fine," he said.

"What got me out of the fucking depression was thinking— a lot of thinking. Something I should've done long ago." Bernadette glanced almost imperceptibly at the screw. She could tell his mind was still elsewhere. Nevertheless, she lowered her voice some more and Dermot leaned forward.

"Rory and you, I should be doing the same as the two of you've done," she said.

Dermot looked right in her eyes. "And the children?"

"Mairead's mother was never involved."

"That's not a real answer."

"But it is. Involved or not, we're at their mercy. They set the rules."

"Aye." He smiled grimly. "Britannia waives the rules!"

"It's been in front of me for years. I just wouldn't look. Mairead and Martha McEntee made me see."

"You're certain?"

"Aye."

"Then I'll get word out."

"Grand."

"And tell Paddy I'm still waiting for those damned books," he said, his voice raised. The warder glared at him.

Bernadette smiled. She was at peace.

It was half eight on Thursday evening of the following week when the driver pulled his taxi in front of her house and beeped the horn. Bernadette opened the front door and gave a wave to let him know she'd be out in a minute. Maura was sleeping—for the night, Bernadette prayed—and Brendan and Siobhan were doing their homework.

"I don't want either of you going out tonight. Do you hear me now? Look after Maura, and if you've any trouble, ring your granny. I'll be in by eleven. Be good now," said Bernadette.

"Aye, Mommy, we will," said Siobhan.

"Cheerio, Mum," said Brendan.

Bernadette went out and got into the taxi. She asked the driver to take her to the Andersonstown Social Club.

"Aye," he said, "the P.D."

She had visited Dermot at the Crum the past Monday. It had been a week since she told him she wanted to get involved. In the middle of innocuous small talk he whispered, "The P.D., on

Thursday, nine o'clock."

The P.D., for "People's Democracy," was a longtime republican pub in a ramshackle old building in Andersonstown. The bands that played there, such as the Gael Force, which would be there tonight, played rebel music, and many of the people who frequented the P.D. supported the republican movement.

But just going to the P.D. wouldn't be particularly subversive in the Brits' eyes. Clubs like the P.D. did boost republican morale, and the Brits knew some of their proceeds were siphoned off for IRA weapons, but these clubs were also gathering places for "ordinary" people, particularly relatives of prisoners. So Bernadette didn't worry that her appearance at the P.D. would cause suspicion.

She paid the fare and got out of the taxi.

"Oh, Bernadette, you're looking beautiful tonight." It was AnneMarie Kelly, whose son was in Long Kesh. "And how is Dermot keeping?"

"He's great, and how's your Michael?"

"He's fine. I was at the Kesh just yesterday. It should be a good night tonight with the Gael Force."

"Aye," said Bernadette, "they're brilliant."

As they reached the gate that guarded the front of the P.D., the inside man recognized them and buzzed them in. They walked through the bar area and into a large room in back, where the band was setting up. Tables and chairs were tightly arranged throughout the room.

More than half the chairs were already filled. I bet there'll be more than two hundred people here tonight, Bernadette thought. There won't be an empty seat in the place. As she surveyed the room, she recognized just about everyone there. A number of the women smiled and waved toward her, asking how

Dermot was keeping. Just great, she smiled back, as she worked her way through the tables with no particular destination in mind.

Moving a chair out of her way, Bernadette almost bumped into Seamus Fitzpatrick. "Ah, Bernadette, it's so good to see you," he said, standing up as if to let her pass.

"And you as well, Seamus. It's been quite awhile."

Seamus Fitzpatrick was a language teacher in St. Columba's secondary school. He hadn't changed a bit in all the years she'd known him. Black curly hair, ruddy face, smoking a pipe, the rumpled tweed jacket. Never married. It seemed as if he was always writing his poetry and his essays. In Irish and French, as well as English.

She remembered being disappointed during the hunger strikes in 1981 when she'd heard that Seamus was one of only a few teachers in St. Columba's who wouldn't sign a petition supporting the hunger strikers' demands. She began to move around him toward a corner table where she saw some Sinn Fein workers.

Seamus, smiling broadly, touched her elbow and whispered, "I see Dermot gave you the message. Why don't we just sit over here?" he said, pointing toward a small table against the wall with three empty chairs.

Bernadette felt herself mumbling something and blankly followed Seamus to the table. Mother of God, she thought, Seamus Fitzpatrick. I never would have thought of him. Never. She nervously lit a cigarette as a waitress came to their table. "White wine," she said. Seamus ordered a pint of Guinness.

"Just look as relaxed as you can, Bernadette," said Seamus, still smiling broadly. "No one has any reason to be suspicious."

"I'll do my best," said Bernadette, forcing a smile. "It's just such a surprise."

"Life is full of surprises," Seamus grinned. "We know you want to get involved. We believe you're very serious about it. That you're aware of all the consequences and ramifications. And the top people believe you can be very helpful."

"I'm no starry-eyed romantic who wants to die for Ireland. And I don't want to spend the rest of my life getting strip-searched. But yes, I've decided I have to do something. Too much is going on now."

"Bernadette, I'm not able to give you the details, but what we want you to do is important and dangerous. But if everything is done the way it should be done, the mission will be successful and you will be safe." Seamus sat back in his chair and gave her a chance to let it sink in.

"Testing, testing, all right," the lead singer spoke into the microphone. "Please stand for the national anthem."

In an instant, all of them were on their feet, facing the Tri-Colour positioned in the center of the platform. The room was just about filled to capacity now. The people hushed as they listened to the band sing "The Soldiers Song," the Irish National Anthem.

Sitting down again and taking a sip of her white wine, Bernadette said, "Seamus, I gave my word I'd do what I was asked to do. Now tell me what's to be done."

"Next Wednesday evening at about seven o'clock, I'll meet you at the leisure centre. We'll have to drive for several hours for a meeting. Don't plan on being home until after midnight."

"And who'll we be meeting?"

"You'll find that out on Wednesday," Seamus said. "Why don't I have another pint and then I'll be on my way, and you can join some of your Sinn Fein friends so no one will start to think anything. All anyone has to know is that I'm getting Irish books for Dermot."

"Dead on, Seamus. And while you're ordering, I'll have another white wine."

Inhaling deeply on her cigarette, Bernadette listened to the band as it sang,

What good is youth when it's ageing?
What joy is in eyes that can't see?
When sorrow and sadness have flowers
And still only our rivers run free.

A few minutes later, Seamus was back with the drinks. "I know it's none of my business," Bernadette said, "but how'd you ever get involved? I'd just never have believed it."

"It's been for many years. And sometimes I wonder where it's all leading. But I just don't see any alternative."

"God help us all, Seamus. God help us all," said Bernadette. She finished her wine and Seamus put down his empty glass and stood up. He nodded to Bernadette and casually walked from the table to the bar area in the next room. He stayed there for a few minutes and then walked out into the night.

Days later, Bernadette was walking to the leisure centre to meet Seamus. Her mother had come by at six-forty-five to stay with the children. Bernadette was still amazed that Seamus Fitzpatrick was in the Ra. She had not been prepared for that at all. It made her think that the IRA might really have that hidden strength they always claimed to have.

It was a clear, unusually mild night for early summer, and by the time Bernadette walked the nine blocks, it was just after seven. She could see Seamus outside the door talking to some teenagers.

He seemed to be as carefree and affable as ever. Just as rumpled, yes, almost absentminded. Whatever they were to be doing that evening, it wasn't showing in Seamus's face.

"Ah, Bernadette, you're right on time," he said. "I have those books you wanted for Dermot. They're at the school. Why don't I drive you there now?"

Bernadette nodded. "Aye," she said.

He waved to the teenagers and led Bernadette to his car. Later, as they were driving out of Andersonstown, Bernadette asked Seamus whether he could tell her where they were going.

"We'll be crossing the border to Donegal. Don't worry, though, it won't attract any attention. I go there often to meet with other Irish language teachers. The Brits are so damned arrogant they couldn't believe that someone like me—educated and a teacher no less—would ever lower himself to get involved with the IRA."

"Will it tip them off if you're with the wife of a republican prisoner?" Bernadette asked.

"Not at all. Many of the prisoners get involved in Irish language studies and I spend a good bit of time with their families. I hate to disappoint you, luv, but you're really not that important—at least not yet." He laughed.

As they drove southwest through the north of Ireland toward Donegal, they spoke of mutual friends. Bernadette asked Seamus nothing at all about his precise function with the IRA. Nor did Seamus ask her anything about Dermot. She was fairly certain that Seamus was very much aware of whatever Dermot had been doing. A lot more aware than she ever was.

Seamus told her that their destination was just outside of Ballyshannon in the southern part of Donegal. He intended to stay on the main roads, so she wasn't too concerned about security. The shades of night were just beginning to fall by the time they reached Enniskillen, a town in Fermanagh about three miles from the border.

"Jesus, Seamus, I haven't been here since I was canvassing for Bobby Sands in 1981."

"Sometimes that seems like only yesterday—other times it seem like ages ago. But Bernadette, no matter how many years go by, the hunger strikes will never be forgotten. I believe that was the most important moment in Ireland since 1916."

"But what a terrible price to pay. Dermot knew Bobby and Joe McDonnell very well and, Jesus, I knew Kieran Doherty since we were wee children together. I don't know how the Brits could have let them die like that."

"For a while we thought they wouldn't. In fact, twice we came so close that—"

"You were involved in the hunger strikes! But I thought— "

"Yes, I was involved, but I couldn't say anything publicly. It would have taken away my cover."

Bernadette listened intently but said nothing. This was a world of intrigue she knew nothing about.

"Those were very delicate negotiations. They would have been difficult in any case. But with us we had to make sure that, except for the Sinn Fein people who were already public, the rest of us remained unidentified. We also had to maintain communication with the prisoners. The same with the Brits. They could never admit they were negotiating. So they had their intermediaries. But we were dealing with the highest levels of the British government—the very highest."

"And you say you came close to a settlement?"

"Aye, we did. But to be honest with you, we never believed we could save Bobby. It was almost as if someone had to die for both sides to prove their points. Probably no one understood that better than Bobby himself. But I can safely say that no one, on either side, ever thought ten men would have to die before it was finally ended. To this day I don't know what went wrong. I do know that in June and again in July, we all thought a definite agreement had been reached. Then both times at the last minute it fell through. Whether it was Thatcher herself I don't know. But it was someone in London, that I do know."

"Were any unionists involved in the talks at all?"

"No, not one, and I'm certain of that. It became obvious to us that the Brits didn't give a damn about them."

"Jesus, if Paisley ever knew that!"

"I truly believe that down deep they do know. Paisley, Molyneaux, McCusker—the whole lot of them. The Brits use them when they need them and ignore them when they don't. But the unionists never want to think about that because without the Brits, they've nothing. Not a damn thing. They've nowhere else to turn."

"Seamus, this is a mad country we live in. Absolutely mad."

They were approaching the UDR checkpoint just past Enniskillen. Seamus cautioned her to be as calm and unassuming as possible. The UDR man in battle fatigues, wearing his beret and cradling his M-16 in his arms, stepped out onto the road. Seamus whispered to Bernadette that off the road in the bushes and trees were at least four UDR men with their rifles aimed at his car. Seamus stopped the car and rolled down his window. The UDR man bent forward, first peering at Seamus and Bernadette and then searching the backseat with his eyes.

"Beautiful evening, isn't it?" the UDR man said.

"Ah, yes, it's grand," Seamus answered cordially.

"Where're you going to this evening, sir?"

"Just over to Donegal to visit some teachers," Seamus answered. "We'll be back later this evening."

"Have a safe trip. Carry on."

"Thanks very much indeed," said Seamus, rolling up the window.

He drove off along the darkened road to the tiny border town of Belleek and then into Donegal. Several hundred yards over the Donegal side of the border, two Irish soldiers manned a small lookout post.

"Bastards," muttered Bernadette as they drove past the post. "Doing the Brits' bloody work."

A few minutes later they were driving through Bally-shannon, a thriving town with shops and pubs. Leaving the center of town, they went first down one country path, then down another and still another until Bernadette had lost all sense of direction. Seamus looked carefully from side to side and then drove off the path and parked the car in a cluster of tall bushes whose leaves enveloped the car.

He turned off the engine and lights, and they got out of the car. The night had become damp and chilly. Whispering to her to be quiet, he took her hand and led her through the bushes and through a narrow clearing. A half moon floated in the cloudy sky. She couldn't see well in the dark, but she could make out a two-story farmhouse about five hundred feet away.

Neither of them said a word as they drew closer to the house. Lights were on in only two windows on the first floor. The curtains were thick and Bernadette couldn't see even shadows behind them. The back door opened slowly and deliberately and a man's voice whispered, "Seamus, come right in. But watch your step."

"Don't worry, Roddy. I didn't travel this far to be falling on my face," Seamus replied in a barely audible voice as he and Bernadette came through the door.

Standing in the dimly lit kitchen, Seamus introduced Bernadette to Roddy Marron.

"I've known Roddy for many a year and he's as sound as they come," Seamus said, taking off his jacket and placing it over the back of a chair.

"We're glad that you could make it this evening, Bernadette. We know it's a long run and you've the wee baby at home. But it's important," Roddy said to her. She looked at him closely.

"Yes, Bernadette, we met about ten years ago," he said, anticipating her question. "I was in the cages with Dermot for about four months and I'd see you when you came to visit him."

"Ah, yes," Bernadette said. "I knew I recognized you. Aren't you from the New Lodge Road?"

"Yes, I was. But once I got out of the cages in '75 I came down here, across the border, and I haven't been back to Belfast since."

Roddy had changed quite a bit. Not that she ever had ever known him that well, but she could tell the years had taken their toll. He probably wasn't more than forty, but his face was leathery and deeply lined. His brown curly hair was streaked with white. He was still tall and straight—about six foot—and his body was trim, but he appeared very tired, particularly in his eyes, which looked as if they had seen too much.

"Could I pour you a cup of tea?" Roddy asked.

"That'd be brilliant," said Bernadette, who was rubbing her hands together to warm up from the dampness. She'd unbuttoned her coat but still hadn't taken it off.

Bernadette and Seamus sat down at the kitchen table and Roddy gave them their tea. Saying he'd be back in a few moments, Roddy went into another room of the house, closing the kitchen door behind him.

Bernadette and Seamus drank their tea without talking. About ten minutes later, just as they were finishing, Roddy came back into the kitchen.

"I'm sorry to have kept you waiting like that, but you know how things are," Roddy said.

"Ach, think nothing of it at all, Roddy. Besides, it gave us a chance to stretch ourselves," said Seamus.

"Well, we're ready to start the meeting—if you'll just come with me," said Roddy.

Bernadette removed her coat and placed it over the chair. She and Seamus followed Roddy down the hallway into the second door on the right. As soon as they entered the room, Roddy closed the door behind them.

It was a good-sized room, illuminated only by a roaring fire, which was directly opposite the door. The one window in the room was on the right-hand side as you looked at the fireplace. The curtains were tightly drawn. In the center of the room was a round wooden table. Seated off to each side, several feet from the table, were two men. Each wore a dark cardigan. Each sat motionless. She could see that each had a pistol on his hip.

When Bernadette's eyes became accustomed to the darkened room, she focused on the man standing behind the table, directly in front of the fireplace. He wore a black sweater, his bearded visage emblazoned in the glow of the raging flames. Bernadette recognized him and felt the blood racing through her veins.

"My God," she heard herself saying, "Kieran McAloran. I'm very proud to meet you."

"Bernadette, it's my pleasure," McAloran said. "And how are you this evening, Seamus?"

"Just grand, Kieran."

"Please sit down," McAloran said, gesturing toward the chairs at the table.

Bernadette sat to McAloran's left and Seamus to his right. Roddy looked around the room and then sat down opposite McAloran.

McAloran looked just like his pictures, Bernadette thought. The black wavy hair, the piercing black eyes, the neatly trimmed beard. He had to be in his late thirties, but there was not a line in his face or even a fleck of gray in his hair.

Extremely intelligent and fearless—some would say ruthless—McAloran had been a larger-than-life military presence since the Troubles began in 1969, having led small but successful raiding parties into the most secure loyalist areas throughout the early seventies. He had also masterminded a series of successful ambushes of British army patrols, and by the mid-seventies was the most wanted man in Belfast.

Bernadette remembered the day in 1976 when McAloran was finally captured after a furious gun battle that left four Brits dead and two badly wounded. His capture had been front-page news, with the Brits hailing it as a "devastating blow to international terrorism." She also remembered that he had not been captured until the other three men in his unit were able to escape.

McAloran was left in Crumlin Road for ten months before he came to trial. A former seminarian, he was still devout and spent his free time writing poetry—poetry of the sky and the ocean, of rolling fields and mountain streams, of love and despair and of birds and children.

Charged with murdering the four Brits, McAloran had sat impassively at his trial for three weeks as each day went by and the case against him grew stronger. On the morning of the last day of the trial, McAloran undid all the Brits' plans for him. His hands in cuffs, he was being escorted by four RUC men through the tunnel under Crumlin Road that connected the jail with the courthouse. All at once he pulled a pistol from under his shirt and shot all four guards, wounding three and killing the other. Moments later, he was on the street and jumping into a waiting car, which sped him away.

Bernadette recalled that after the escape, McAloran became a mystery man. He was spotted in Belgium, then in Portugal. Others said he was with Basque separatists. The FBI had reports that he had been in the United States raising money for the IRA. Interspersed with all of these rumors were the recurrent stories that he had died, was severely wounded or paralyzed. Just as often, however, particularly daring IRA missions were credited to McAloran. "Aye, five Brits killed. It had to be Kieran," was the talk in the nationalist pubs in West Belfast.

Then word came out that he'd returned from Spain, where he'd spent nearly a year writing and thinking. He'd decided military actions had to be combined with political moves and, as a member of the IRA's ruling Army Council, became a strong advocate for Sinn Fein. And now he wanted Bernadette to help him.

"You've traveled a long way, Bernadette, and I know you have to get back to Belfast tonight," said McAloran in firm, deliberate tones, "so I'll get to the purpose of the meeting straightaway. We have decided—no matter that he's a Catholic—to take action against Harry Hamilton."

Bernadette had never met Harry Hamilton, but she had known of him since she was a girl. For years he had been the best-known Catholic politician in Belfast—a distinction he now grudgingly shared with Gerry Adams.

Hamilton had emerged on the public scene in the early 1960s when, as a young docker, he organized protests for better working conditions on the docks and demanded more jobs for Catholics. When the civil rights movement began in 1968, Hamilton demonstrated his courage, whether it was speaking at public rallies or leading protest marches. On two marches—the first just outside of Dungannon and the other in Strabane—he was attacked and beaten by loyalist mobs. Numerous other times he was arrested.

"No one, absolutely no one, during all the years of this struggle has ever let us down as badly as Hamilton," said McAloran bitterly.

"It was as if he changed overnight when he was elected to the City Council in 1971," said Seamus. "I had never heard him say even one word critical of the Ra before he got elected. And then the first week he's in office, he's telling the *Telegraph* that the IRA and the Brits are equally to blame for the troubles. That fucker."

"I've no doubt we could go on all night talking about what a disgraceful bastard Hamilton has turned out to be," said McAloran. "No one can forget what he did during the hunger strikes. He never stopped with his support of Thatcher. Telling her not to negotiate. Thatcher didn't need Hamilton to be telling her that, of course. But it gave her credibility. And the Brits used it for all it was worth. There was hardly a newspaper in the world that didn't quote Hamilton against us. Ten of our best men died, and I know some of them would've been saved if it weren't for Hamilton."

McAloran paused, looked at each person at the table, before continuing. "Ever since the hunger strikes I've detested Harry Hamilton. But what we learned about him in the past months is even more contemptible. And absolutely unforgivable. Hamilton is a fucking agent for the Brits. A tout. An informer. A fucking spy."

"Mother of God," Bernadette cried.

"When Hamilton lost his seat in the last council election," McAloran went on, "the Brits gave him that community relations job where he's supposed to help our people with their housing problems and their dole payments and all that sort of *craic*. Republican families will have nothing to do with Hamilton. But there's still a few of the old people who remember Hamilton when he was a barman fighting for the workers and when he was in the civil rights campaign. So even though they disagree with his politics today, they still have a certain affection for the man they think he used to be.

"And when they see him with their problem, he can usually resolve it for them. While he's meeting with them, Harry is all talk and smiles. And all the while he's getting information out of them. 'And how's your Sean? Does he still knock around with Tommy McCartney?' 'Is Mick at your house often?' And he gives every last bit of what they tell him to the Brits."

"Are you certain of this?" Bernadette asked.

"We are indeed. We've our own source who is dead sound. He's given us all the facts—the names, the places, the dates—and Hamilton is guilty. As guilty as fucking sin. Billy Cullen and Tommy

Curtin who were lifted in Ardoyne a fortnight ago—that was because of what Hamilton gave the Brits. That's why he must be stopped and stopped now. Our decision has been made for us, and Hamilton made it. He's signed his own death warrant."

"I assume," Marron said somberly, "by now there's no doubt in anyone's mind exactly what it is that we're talking about."

Sensing that the remark was intended for her, Bernadette glanced at the table before fixing her eyes first on Seamus and then on McAloran.

"I don't see how there can be any doubt," said Bernadette in precise and composed tones. "Harry Hamilton is to be executed. And I've also no doubt," she added with a hint of hesitation, "that I'm to be a part of this operation or you wouldn't have asked me to be here tonight."

"Yes, Bernadette," said McAloran. "Hamilton must be killed and it must be done soon, with maximum efficiency and minimum risk. And we want you to be the one to carry it out."

Bernadette was silent for a long moment. Then she said, "When I said I'd help and do whatever you asked me to do, I was thinking in terms of a support role—gathering intelligence or helping in a getaway, something such as that. I didn't think I'd be asked to kill anyone."

"It's precisely because you've never been involved that we've selected you," McAloran replied. "If you carry out the operation successfully, you'll not be a suspect. The Brits would have absolutely no reason to think you were involved. And we believe we have a plan which will virtually guarantee your escape."

"Let me tell you straightaway that if the Ra wants me to do it, I'll do it," said Bernadette. "I hate the ground that Hamilton walks on, and I felt that way before you told me he's a tout. It's just that I didn't think I'd be at the center of such a vital operation so quickly. But I'll do it," she said firmly.

"Thank you, Bernadette," said McAloran.

"You say you've a plan. How final is it?" asked Bernadette. "Can you tell me any of the details?"

"Yes, indeed. We know that sometime in the next month, Hamilton will be going to the Royal Victoria to meet with hospital officials as part of his job. The meeting will most likely be in the early evening. In any event, we have direct access to his schedule and will know the precise time he expects to arrive. His car is bullet-proofed, but he always travels to meetings such as this without a bodyguard. We feel he'll be most vulnerable just as he gets out of his car on the Falls in front of the Royal."

Bernadette grimaced but said nothing.

Seamus smiled at Bernadette and said, "You poor child. It's an awful lot that we're asking of you. Yes, Kieran and his mates have done all the planning. But you're the one who has to carry it out."

"And I will," said Bernadette in a soft but firm voice. "I will."

CHAPTER FIVE

For the first hour of their drive back to Belfast, Bernadette said nothing to Seamus as he maneuvered the car through the dark Irish night along roads that were wet and slick from showers that had fallen intermittently through the evening.

Finally, she broke the long silence. "Seamus, how do you explain someone like Harry Hamilton? I could understand if he'd backed away from us a bit. But to turn against us so. And to become a fucking tout. I just can't understand what must go on in his mind."

"I don't know if there's any simple answer to it all. But you know Hamilton isn't the first to have done this to us. And God knows he won't be the last," said Seamus. "I suppose the most likely explanation is what Sean MacBride calls the 'slave mentality.' The Brits are such a powerful presence. And I don't just mean the army. The Brits influence everything we do. They're all around us—television, radio, the cinema, fashions. They're everywhere.

"Take Harry. He was a barman who was usually out of work. Sure, he was out there fighting for us, and a good fighter he was. But then he's elected and he gets a wee taste of the power structure. And Jesus, the Brits go to work on him.

"They tell him how much they'd like to invite him to receptions and even give him top-level briefings, but he'll have to pull back from the Ra—just a wee bit, of course. And this goes on and on over the years, until Harry Hamilton the barman finds himself mingling with cabinet ministers and being treated as a statesman by the media all because he's 'broad-minded' enough and 'courageous' enough to condemn the Ra.

"After enough years go by and Harry keeps moving further and further from us, he finally becomes a Brit. And, Bernadette, I honestly don't know whether in his own mind Harry ever realized he'd become a Brit.

"But Jesus, think how he must've felt when he lost the council election last year. He was absolutely nobody again. But the Brits could make sure he was still somebody. They'd give him the job and the title and the pounds. And they knew Harry would take it. No matter what the price. And now he's their tout. He's a fucking Brit whore."

"Ever since we left Kieran," said Bernadette, "I've been thinking of Hamilton. And I've listened to you. And God help me, but I don't feel a bit sorry for him. When I think of all the torture and pain that our people are going through in the Kesh and Armagh and Castlereagh and him touting on us. I just have no sympathy or feeling for him at all. Maybe I would have at one time, but not now. I've seen too much."

"Jesus, Bernadette, we've all seen too much."

Back in Andytown, Bernadette made sure she went about her regular schedule. Visiting Dermot in the Crum, shopping for food, taking Maura to the doctor, calling on her mother and Eilish, going to the P.D. for a drink. She wanted to show as little change as possible from her normal routine.

When she stopped at the leisure centre one night, Seamus told her it would be next Thursday evening at half six that she would kill Harry Hamilton.

Bernadette was ready. For the past ten days she had gone through the plan time and again in her mind. She'd also walked past the Royal several times. Trying to look entirely casual, she committed every inch of road and footpath to memory.

Learning how to use the pistol was less difficult than she'd anticipated. First she spent several hours at Liam Morrissey's flat off the lower Falls where, with an unloaded revolver, he taught her the basics—hold the pistol with both hands, squeeze the trigger gently—and she got acquainted with the feel and touch of this instrument of death. Two days later, Seamus took her to a remote area in the Donegal countryside where an unidentified Provo with a pronounced southern accent taught her to fire live rounds. After four hours of intensive instruction and repeated firing, he finished the session. Rubbing a hand through his red wavy hair, he smiled and told Bernadette, "I don't know what you're to do. All I was told was it'd be close range. After watching you today, I'm sure you'll do very well. Good luck."

With each passing day, she felt more secure. Dermot, of course, didn't discuss the assignment with her other than to give her a knowing smile and say, "Thanks. It will work."

It had never entered Bernadette's mind that she would take a life. Now that had been asked to do it, she felt neither fear nor delight. Each time she visited Dermot or looked at Brendan, Siobhan and Maura, or saw the Brits patrolling her street, she knew she was doing what had to be done. She had depersonalized Hamilton as an instrument of the Brit machine who had to be removed.

It's all so much larger than Harry, she thought. Harry knew what he was doing. He had chosen his path. That path just won't be as long as he thought it would be.

Hadn't the nuns and priests taught her that every man is responsible for his own actions? Bernadette might not go to church anymore, but she remembered well about free will. And about having to account for the consequences of what you've done. Jesus, she laughed, I can almost say I'm doing this for Holy Mother Church.

Thursday afternoon was grim and gray. The rain had stopped by noon, but dark clouds still hovered menacingly. The warm air of early summer was heavy with humidity. Bernadette was in the back room of a bakery several blocks below the Royal and about seventy-five feet off the Falls.

"Here, luv, put these on. I'll be back in a few minutes to take your own clothes. They'll be waiting for you in Ballymurphy," said the elderly woman who owned the shop.

Bernadette took off her jeans skirt and powder-blue blouse and put on the loose-fitting tan skirt and brown jumper the woman had given her. She would keep her white running shoes. She fitted her long auburn hair under a short blond wig, put on tinted glasses and looked in the mirror.

"Mother of God," she said to herself, "if I didn't know better, I'd swear I was someone else. And I don't look too bad at all as a blond."

The shop owner took Bernadette's skirt and blouse, folded them neatly and placed them in a paper bag.

"Please God you'll be wearing these again in less than an hour," the woman said, looking at the clock. It was five-forty-five.

She turned to Bernadette. "Will you take a cup of tea while you're waiting?"

"I would indeed," answered Bernadette.

The woman returned with steaming hot tea and a tray of biscuits and began talking away the remaining minutes. "The weather never lets up, does it? I believe you've three children. How is the wee one? God love her. And your Dermot. His spirits are fine, I'm sure. They must be when he has such a wonderful wife as you."

Bernadette sipped the tea and ate four biscuits. She held the cup with a steady hand and gazed at the clock. It was six-fifteen.

She put down the cup, got to her feet and thanked the woman. They walked from the back room into the bakery, which was now closed for the day. A pram sat inside the front door. The woman went behind the counter, reached down and picked up a folded blue-and-white checked blanket. She placed it on the counter and opened it just enough for Bernadette to see the .38 tucked inside. Then she handed her flesh-colored gloves. Bernadette pulled them on and put the blanket in the pram where a baby's feet would be. Instead of a baby, a doll lay there, covered with a fluffy white blanket, the head on a soft white pillow.

The woman opened the front door, went out to the foot-path and looked up and down the street. Satisfied that all was clear, she motioned Bernadette to come out of the bakery.

"God love you," the woman said as Bernadette, pushing the pram, walked past her and turned right toward the Falls.

After turning left at the Falls, she walked slowly along and glanced at her watch as she approached Dunville Park. It was six-twenty-three.

Once past the park, she stopped for the traffic light at Grosvenor Road. Looking to her right, she saw the RUC station

terrible
Beauty

and glanced again at her watch as she crossed Grosvenor Road. It was six-twenty-seven.

The immense structure of the Royal began on her left and ran far up the Falls. The entrance where Hamilton would be arriving was within her sight. As she drew closer to the entrance, she looked over at St. Paul's Church standing mightily on Cavendish Street to her right. Parked on Cavendish in a hijacked gray Ford was Robby O'Connor, his usually cropped, light brown hair covered with a bushy, dark brown wig reaching almost to his shoulders. He nodded.

Bernadette was less than twenty feet from the entrance. No one else was walking on the Falls or on Cavendish Street.

It was six-thirty. No sign of Hamilton. She stopped the pram and reached in to adjust the pillow. She ran her hand along the checked blanket and felt the outline of the revolver.

Looking over the top of the pram, she saw a blue Opel coming down the Falls and crossing over toward the curb in front of the hospital. It was Hamilton. He parked the car near the entrance, with the driver's seat next to the curb.

She pushed the pram forward slowly. He was alone. She heard the motor stop. It was six-thirty-one.

As she came alongside the car, Hamilton opened the door. Bernadette took one more step and stopped with her back to Hamilton. She reached into the checked blanket and pulled out the .38. Grasping it with both hands, she turned and aimed the revolver at Hamilton's head as he leaned forward to get out of the car. Concentrating on the target, she squeezed the trigger slowly.

Blood sprayed out from above Hamilton's right ear and his glasses flew off. He lurched forward, crashed first against the car door and then onto the footpath, where he landed on the left side of his face. She fired two more bullets into his head. Blood flowed from the gaping wounds and gushed from his mouth.

Leaving the pram behind but still carrying the gun, she ran to the waiting gray Ford and got into the front seat. O'Connor pulled away while she was still shutting the door.

"You get him?"

"Aye, I did."

"Dead?"

"Aye."

It was six-thirty-two. The road was clear and in seconds they were passing St. Dominic's High School and St. Mary's College on their right. Then they heard a series of blasts behind them.

"Ah, Bernadette, there go the bombs in the town. I'm sure the others are going off as well. That'll screw the bastards up, so it will."

Bernadette said nothing as O'Connor turned right onto Beechmount Avenue and then veered left onto Beechmount Street through St. Paul's School. Ahead was the fence. No one appeared to be in the area. O'Connor stopped the car, took the .38 from Bernadette, and put it under his jacket and then under the belt of his jeans. They got out of the car and went through the opening in the fence.

They walked into the broken streets of Ballymurphy. At the first corner, O'Connor turned right and down an alleyway. Bernadette walked several more streets, turned left and went to the third house. As she approached the front door, it opened.

"Come in, luv," said a white-haired woman who appeared to be in her seventies. "Everything will be grand."

The woman took Bernadette into the bathroom. Her skirt and blouse were on the towel rack. Bernadette took off the wig, glasses, gloves, skirt and jumper and handed them to the old woman.

"I'll take these," the woman said, and then pointed to the sink, which was filled with hot soapy water.

"Wash your hands and scrub them with the brush before you put on your skirt and blouse. That should get the gunpowder off."

Bernadette scrubbed her hands, combed her hair and dressed. She walked into the living room.

The clock on the wall read six-fifty-three.

At seven-fifteen Bernadette got out of the taxi in front of her house. Brendan was waiting at the front door.

"Mommy, it was just on the radio. Harry Hamilton's been shot. They think he's dead."

"When did this happen? Did they say who did it?" she asked, feigning surprise and regretting the necessary deception.

"He was shot outside the Royal. It was just a short while ago, so it was. The peelers think it was the Ra, but no one's claimed it yet."

"Well, I don't want you or your sister to be going out of the house tonight. Do you hear me?" she demanded as she came into the house and stood in the living room. "God only knows what might be happening tonight after something like this."

Bernadette went upstairs where Siobhan was playing with Maura. "And how's the child, luv?" she asked Siobhan as she picked Maura up and squeezed her.

"She's been good, so she has. I was reading to her and then we played with the dolls. I think she's getting tired."

"Thank you, Siobhan. You're just great. Now would you fix your mommy a cup of tea while I get Maura ready for bed?"

"Aye, Mommy. Course I will."

Two and a half hours later, the children fed and Maura asleep upstairs, Bernadette sat on the living room couch with Brendan and Siobhan, her legs tucked under her, and sipped her cup of tea, waiting for the ten o'clock TV news. They were all dressed for bed. Except for the small lamp on the corner table, every light in the house was off. The blinds on all the windows were pulled tightly shut.

At last the news came on. "Tonight," the news reader intoned, "not just Belfast, but the world, mourns the tragic death of Harry Hamilton, the Roman Catholic political leader who was gunned down outside the Royal Victoria Hospital at approximately half six this evening. The Provisional IRA has claimed responsibility for the murder."

"I knew it," said Brendan.

"Shh," said his mother. "I want to listen."

". . . Mr. Hamilton was shot several times in the head at close range as he got out of his car at the Falls Road entrance to the hospital where he was to attend a meeting. An unconfirmed report states that a hospital worker saw a blond woman running from the murder scene to a waiting gray car, which then drove up the Falls Road. The RUC has confirmed that a gray Ford was found abandoned in the Ballymurphy area shortly past eight o'clock this evening."

Bernadette put the teacup down on the table beside her and stared at the TV screen. Her mouth went dry. She closed her hands so tightly that she could feel her fingernails breaking through the skin on the palms of each hand.

The news reader went on: "In admitting responsibility for

the murder, the IRA said that Mr. Hamilton was 'a cynical politician who betrayed the nationalist community to the British colonial forces.' In a dramatic charge, the IRA said that 'for the past several months Hamilton had been working as a paid British informer.' The IRA also admitted responsibility for a series of bomb explosions that occurred throughout Belfast this evening. No casualties have been reported."

"I heard the bombs, Mommy," Siobhan said.

"You did not," Brendan said.

"Shh, please. I'm listening."

". . . Mrs. Thatcher has denounced the murder as 'a particularly cruel and diabolical crime which proves again that the IRA has no regard for human life or decency.' DUP leader the Reverend Ian Paisley has threatened that 'Protestants will take the law into their hands' if the murderers are not quickly apprehended.

"In other news . . ."

"Brendan, why don't you turn off the television and then you and Siobhan get yourselves off to bed," said Bernadette.

"Will you be going to bed as well, Mommy?" asked Brendan as he turned the set off.

"Not right now, luv. I think I'll stay up just a wee bit longer. Don't worry about the bombs," she said to Siobhan. "They're far away from here." She kissed her goodnight, then kissed Brendan.

After they were gone, Bernadette sat for almost half an hour, clutching the empty teacup in both hands, looking blankly at the dim light from the table lamp. Then she got up, walked out to the kitchen and put the cup in the sink. Taking a bottle of Powers from the cupboard, she poured herself a drink, went back into the living room and turned out the lamp.

Sitting on the couch in the blackened room, she lit a cigarette, took a deep drag, then a sip of the whiskey. The barest hint of illumination from the amber street lamps reflected along the edges of the blinds.

After taking a last, long drag from the cigarette, she crushed it in the ashtray. She stood up and finished the whiskey. Walking through the darkness, she put the glass in the kitchen sink and then went up the stairs.

At the top, she turned right and went into the bathroom. Closing the door behind her, she turned on the light, took off her robe and let it fall at her feet, then she pulled her nightgown up over her head and dropped it to the floor beside the robe. For a long moment Bernadette looked at herself in the mirror.

She climbed into the tub, pulled the curtain shut and turned on the shower. The warm water streamed against her face and over her breasts as she stood with her feet apart and her fists clenched at her side. Reaching forward, she adjusted the faucets until the water was coming out as hot and with as much force as she could endure. Turning around, she folded her arms across her chest as the water beat down on her shoulders and back.

Images of Hamilton rushed through her mind. She was too drained and exhausted to resist any longer. Her body began to tremble and tears filled her eyes. In a moment she was sobbing uncontrollably.

"Oh, my God!" she heard herself saying again and again, as she went down first to her knees and then onto her right side with her knees pulled up toward her chest. She covered her face with her hands as her body shook with sobs and the blazing shower continued to beat down upon her.

CHAPTER SIX

Belfast was gripped with apprehension on Monday as the city awakened to face Harry Hamilton's funeral. It was to be at St. Peter's Cathedral on the lower Falls, but the Brits had intensified their forces throughout all the nationalist areas.

When Bernadette had walked to a shop on the Falls that morning to buy a carton of milk and the *Irish News*, the military presence was even greater than during the hunger strikes. Brits and peelers in riot gear patrolled the streets and lined the rooftops. Helicopters and spotter planes filled the sky and saracens motored up and down every road. Three times she was stopped by the Brits and asked to identify herself and state where she was going. Each time she answered their questions and was allowed to go on.

Bernadette spent the rest of her morning at home tidying up. Maura was playing contentedly and Brendan and Siobhan were at school. At noon she turned on the television to watch the funeral on the news. The streets around St. Peter's were an armed camp. If it was the IRA that worried the Brits, she thought, the worry was unnecessary: The IRA wouldn't attack the funeral. The loyalists, of course, might launch an attack so it would be blamed on the IRA.

St. Peter's was filled to capacity with mourners. Among them were Prime Minister Garrett Fitzgerald, who had come up from Dublin with his foreign minister, Peter Barry; James Prior, the British secretary of state for Northern Ireland; and George Barrett and William Wells, two unionists from the City Council. Outside, however, except for Brits and peelers, the streets had been empty as the funeral cortege proceeded from Hamilton's house to the cathedral. The procession was headed by Hamilton's two sons and two brothers carrying his coffin. Following the coffin walked Hamilton's widow and her two daughters, who helped her along. As the camera closed in on Margaret Hamilton's face, Bernadette recognized the Valium-induced stare common to so many Belfast widows. She remembered that she had refused any medication when her Rory died. Still, she thought of what Margaret Hamilton and her children must be going through. Bernadette realized she'd done what had to be done, but that didn't make it any easier to accept. She would never forget the look on Hamilton's face. But she'd go on.

When it came time for the eulogy, Bishop McIntyre ascended the pulpit. Since childhood Bernadette had had trouble listening to sermons. She blanked out after the Bishop stated, "Harry Hamilton was a true son of Ireland and a true follower of Christ. Just as Christ died on the cross so that mankind could be saved, Harry Hamilton gave his life for the cause of peace in Ireland." But she heard him when he said, "There can be no tolerance of anyone who would commit murder. There can be no closing our eyes or looking the other way when there are such cruel murderers in our very midst. Unless each of us does all that we possibly can to find these murderers, then we must bear the same guilt and shame as if we ourselves pulled the trigger that destroyed the life of Harry Hamilton and brought such anguish and heartache to his dear family."

Bernadette's face stiffened when the Bishop said "heartache." All the Brits have ever given us is heartache, she thought. And the Church says nothing about that. Nonetheless, she sympathized with Hamilton's wife. My God, that poor woman has some dreadful days ahead of her, Bernadette said to herself. Some dreadful, desperate days.

By the time the evening news came on at six o'clock, the story of the Hamilton funeral was followed by coverage of a monster loyalist rally in the city center. Tens of thousands of people—including hundreds of hooded paramilitaries—filled the streets as speaker after speaker demanded that "justice be done."

Ian Paisley held a hangman's noose aloft in his right hand and bellowed, "Perhaps the time has come for the God-fearing unionists of Ulster to take it upon ourselves to impose our own form of justice!" It was an old act, but he was a virtuoso performer and he never failed to bring his feverish multitudes to a frenzy.

Paisley's skill at manipulating the media was confirmed on the eleven o'clock news when the news reader went to alternating clips of Paisley issuing his threats and Chief Constable McAndrew scrambling desperately to assure the unionists that Hamilton's murderers would be apprehended. "No stone will be unturned," said McAndrew in a tone that was not entirely convincing. He pleaded for calm and said that the burning-out of two Catholic families from their homes earlier that evening—one in Lisburn, the other in Ballymena—"would only play into the hands of the IRA."

Seamus had told Bernadette the other day that the Brits hadn't a clue who had shot Hamilton. What the hell will happen next? she asked herself. Now that Paisley had set the loyalists in motion, there was only so long even he would keep them under control. And if the loyalists keep burning out Catholics, the Ra will have to strike back hard. My God, she thought, those poor families that were burned out tonight! She turned off the set and went to bed.

On Tuesday night after the funeral, there was heavy loyalist rioting on the Shankill Road as masked paramilitaries hurled petrol bombs at the RUC, who then fired plastic bullets over the heads of the rioters. Jesus, if that had been us, the bullets would have been between our eyes, thought Bernadette, as she viewed the fiery events on her television screen.

The rioting on the Shankill resumed Wednesday evening, and later that night the UVF claimed responsibility for the murder of a Catholic old-age pensioner who was found in a North Belfast alley with his throat slit from ear to ear.

Early Thursday morning, an off-duty UDR captain was blown to pieces outside his home in East Belfast when he turned his key in the car ignition and detonated the bomb the IRA had wired to the engine during the night.

The twelve o'clock news that day reported that two men and a woman were killed in Poleglass when bombs they were storing in a house were accidentally detonated. And in Lisburn, two Catholic teenage boys were attacked and beaten by a loyalist mob. They were in hospital in serious condition but expected to live.

Later that afternoon, Bernadette was in the living room, ironing the wash that had accumulated over the past several days and half listening to the radio, when the three o'clock news came on.

"There has been a dramatic development in the investigation into the murder of Harry Hamilton, who was shot to death one week ago today."

Bernadette froze and stared into the radio, the iron in her hand poised over her powder-blue blouse.

"In a statement made just moments ago, RUC Chief Constable Robert McAndrew has identified Marie McElroy, one of the terrorists killed in the bomb factory explosion in Poleglass this morning, as the woman who shot Mr. Hamilton."

Bernadette set down the iron and listened intently when she recognized McAndrew's voice. "We can say with certainty that Marie McElroy was the murderer. In addition to information provided by intelligence sources, the RUC uncovered significant incriminating evidence while conducting a search of Miss McElroy's flat today. That evidence included photographs of Mr. Hamilton, maps of the murder scene with the escape route marked off and a blond wig. While forensic tests are not complete, traces of hair particles found inside the wig are similar to Miss McElroy's hair. Miss McElroy was known to be a member of the IRA. She was released from Armagh Prison last year after serving four years for weapons charges."

"Mother of God," said Bernadette in disbelief. She clicked off the radio, picked up the phone and dialed.

"Seamus?" she asked.

"Yes, Bernadette, I heard. We should meet this evening. Can you be at the Hunting Lodge at half nine?"

"Aye."

"Very well, I'll see you then."

She went back to her ironing.

After dinner, Bernadette took a taxi to the Hunting Lodge, a popular pub in Lenadoon, which was a key nationalist stronghold in West Belfast. The IRA was active there, and the Brits approached its streets with trepidation.

When she arrived at the pub, Seamus was already at a small table near the back. He was drinking a pint of Guinness, and a glass of white wine was waiting for her.

"Thank you for the wine, Seamus," she said with a smile as she sat down.

"Always thinking of you, luv." He smiled back.

As Bernadette lighted a cigarette, Seamus handed her a book of Irish poetry. "For Dermot," he said.

"Jesus, another Irish book!" she muttered through a forced smile. Dropping her voice, she continued, "Seamus, I couldn't believe the radio this afternoon. What the hell is McAndrew doing? Is this really the end of it?"

He nodded. "The Brits and the peelers knew straightaway they hadn't a clue who did it. And with Paisley carrying on the way he was, you can see why they took advantage of poor Marie's death."

"Did you know Marie?"

"Indeed I did. She was a wonderful woman, so she was. She had nerves of steel and was as determined as anyone I've ever known."

"And the two men who were with her, Tommy Malone and Jim Turner?" she asked.

Seamus shook his head. "I understand they were only twenty. God help them. Tommy's two brothers are in the Kesh—doing life, I believe. And Jim's father was killed by the orangies in the early seventies."

"Their poor families," she said.

"Their poor families, indeed. But as for McAndrew, he can accuse Marie of killing Hamilton and never have to go to trial."

"And Paisley and the loyalists?"

"You can be sure Paisley knows full well that Marie McElroy had nothing to do with Hamilton. But this way he can go to his people and say he was the one who forced the peelers to solve this case."

"Seamus, after all that's happened, I can't believe that it's over. Just like that. So fast."

"I understand how you feel, but everyone—on all sides—wants it to be over. So it will be over. Now, Jesus, watch what you do and say, of course. Don't ever mention even one word to anyone. Not a soul. But as sure as you can be of anything in this mad place, Harry Hamilton's death is part of the past."

"It may be, but it'll always be part of me. I don't think I'll ever be able to put it out of my mind."

The waitress came toward the table.

"Not for me," Bernadette said. She put out her cigarette. "It's getting late. Maura has had a bit of a cold the past two days. I have to be getting home."

"Fine. I've my car. I'll give you a lift."

"That would be dead on, Seamus. Thank you."

"Have you been to see Dermot?" he asked as they left the pub.

"Aye, I saw him yesterday. He was trying to put up a good front, so he was, but he looked more anxious than I've ever seen him."

"I can just imagine. All this going on. So much pressure being on you. And him locked in the Crum not being able to help you at all. He must be going mad."

"I'll be in to see him again tomorrow. I'm sure by then he'll have sorted out today's events and will agree all should be well for me now."

"If I know Dermot, he already has everything sorted out," said Seamus with a knowing grin.

"Ah, I'm sure he does."

As Seamus put his car key in the door, Bernadette hesitated for a moment and then said in a low voice, "I want you to know what a help you've been to me. I don't know what I would have done without you. You were the only one I could talk to, and you always seemed to know what to say and how to say it. You kept me together these past few days."

"Thanks for the kind words. But I think you'll always keep yourself together. Still, if anything happens at all, be sure to ring me straightaway."

"I will indeed," she said.

"And if I have to see you for any reason, I'll tell you I have some more Irish books for Dermot."

"Seamus," said Bernadette, with the widest smile she had managed in weeks, "to hell with your Irish books!"

Two months had passed since Marie McElroy's death. Bernadette had finished her cleaning in the kitchen and had sat down to read through the *Irish News*. Maura was taking her afternoon nap and Brendan and Siobhan were outside playing, enjoying the last weeks of their summer vacation from school. Just as she finished reading the front-page story about a bombing in Tyrone that had badly wounded two UDR men, the phone rang.

"Bernadette, it's Seamus. How've you been keeping?"

"Very well indeed, Seamus. How's yourself?"

"I've some good news for you. I was able to locate those two Irish books Dermot was asking for. Do you think you could come by the centre tonight so that I could give them to you?"

"That's awfully good of you. Dermot will be delighted. Will half seven do?"

"It will indeed. I'll see you later."

Bernadette put the receiver down, walked into the living room and sat down in the old wooden rocker. Looking out through the window at the afternoon mist, she wondered what it could be that Seamus had to tell her. It had been weeks since she'd had any contact with him.

After dinner, Bernadette walked to the leisure centre. There was a light mist in the air, so she wore her raincoat but didn't bother to button it. She breathed in the late-summer air and thought of Dermot in his damp, cramped cell.

At the centre she spotted Seamus, who was talking with Billy Sweeney, an unemployed joiner who helped coach the hurling team.

"Ah, Bernadette, I'm so glad you could make it," said Seamus. "You know Bill Sweeney, I'm sure."

"I do indeed. How are you, Billy?"

"No so bad, Bernadette. And how's Dermot keeping?"

"He's doing very well, thanks. His spirits are wonderful."

"Ah, he's a strong man. But the Brits are right bastards with their supergrasses. Jesus, no one is safe the way they've been going lately," said Billy.

"No, but all we can do is our best and see what happens next," Bernadette said.

"Well, I must be off now. Good night, Seamus, and God love you, Bernadette. And tell Dermot I was asking for him."

"I will indeed. God bless," said Bernadette.

"I've the books for Dermot," said Seamus in a voice loud enough for onlookers to hear. "Why don't you come out to the car with me and I'll get them for you."

When they reached the car, Seamus unlocked the front door and pulled two hard cover books out from under the driver's seat. He handed them to Bernadette, smiled and said, "Dermot will certainly be an Irish scholar by the time we're finished."

"And God knows what condition I'll be in," she smiled back, putting the books into the handbag draped over her shoulder.

"Bernadette, luv, the weather seems to have cleared. Why don't we just walk along quietly and I'll tell you what we're thinking of doing."

"Seamus, that's all I've been wondering about since you rang me today."

"It's the supergrasses. They're hurting the movement more than we ever anticipated. It's not just the Army but Sinn Fein as well. Christ, before this is over, it could be worse than internment."

Bernadette pushed her hands deeper into her pockets and nodded.

"Understand one thing, though: The supergrasses won't break the movement any more than internment did. But it will knock us back and too many good people will be hurt unless we can end it and end it soon."

"Seamus, I can tell you it's had a dreadful impact. And not just the men who've been lifted or their families, but the whole community. Jesus, you don't know who it's safe to talk to anymore. Your next-door neighbor could be a tout for all you know." Bernadette sighed.

"Remember, everything the Brits have ever tried against us we've turned around on them and we've ended up with more support than ever. Internment, Bloody Sunday, the torture at Castlereagh, the H-Blocks—we were able to use them to expose the Brits before the world for what they are. And that's what we want to do this time. And we'd like you to help us."

"Tell me what you have in mind."

"We want you to go to America on a speaking tour and attack the supergrasses."

"Go to America!" she said, her voice rising to a shriek. "For Jesus' sake, I've never even gone as far as Dublin."

"Calm yourself, luv. It's not as difficult as you might think."

"But you want me to speak in front of people in America! I've never made a speech in my life. And I have the three . . . Jesus, Seamus, Maura's not even two years old yet. I—"

"Bernadette"—Seamus smiled at her—"if you would just stop your shouting and let me speak for a wee minute."

"I'm listening."

"We have to arouse Irish-American opinion. We need someone who knows what's happening with the supergrasses and someone the people will listen to. Obviously, with Dermot in jail you can tell the people firsthand what the supergrasses are all about. And while doing that, you can also describe what it's like in Belfast for a wife and a mother who happens to be Catholic."

"Seamus, I just don't see how . . ."

"And besides all that, you're such a beautiful woman that you'll just be magic. The Americans will love you."

PART TWO

HER EXILED CHILDREN
IN AMERICA

*Having organized and trained her secret revolutionary
organization, the Irish Republican Brotherhood, and through
her open military organizations, the Irish Volunteers and the
Irish Citizen Army . . . and supported by her exiled children in
America . . . she strikes in full confidence of victory.*

—FROM THE PROCLAMATION OF THE IRISH REPUBLIC,
EASTER MONDAY, 1916

CHAPTER SEVEN

Jack Tierney drove the car out of Kennedy airport and onto the westbound Belt Parkway. Bernadette, seated in the back with his wife, Brigid, looked in wonder at all the cars and trucks. The Tierneys had told her the rush-hour congestion had started earlier than usual this afternoon. The traffic was barely inching along.

"I'm sure there's nothing like this in Belfast," said Brigid, "but after you live in New York for a while, you get used to traffic jams."

"Do you actually live in New York City?" asked Bernadette.

"Well, we prefer to say we live in Brooklyn and leave it at that," said Brigid with a broad smile and a slight Irish accent. "But yes, Brooklyn is part of New York City."

"I'm not so sure about that," said Michael Garvey, who'd come with the Tierneys to pick up Bernadette at JFK. Garvey was in his mid-thirties, well-dressed and efficient-looking. He ranked high in the Northern Irish Republican Aid Association (NIRAA), the New York–based organization that was coordinating Bernadette's tour. "I live in Manhattan, and we think that's the real New York."

"Get on with you," Brigid said, playfully tapping him on the shoulder. "The real people live in Brooklyn."

"I can tell that you and Jack are both from Ireland," said Bernadette. "How long have you been in America? If you don't mind me asking."

"Not at all, not at all. And with the traffic moving as slowly as it is, I just might end up telling you so much you'll be sorry you asked."

"Bernadette," interjected Jack, "you've just made your first mistake. Never ask Brigid a question like that because now you're going to hear her life history, the family history and only God knows what else."

"Pay him no mind at all," said Brigid. "His job is to do the driving and, as you can see, he's getting us nowhere. Anyway, to answer your question, I came over here from South Armagh as a teenager in the late 1930s. It might surprise you, but even though I was raised in Crossmaglen and my mother and father were strong republicans, I had no interest in politics when I was home."

"Wasn't it as bad in those days?" asked Bernadette.

"Ah, indeed it was. I remember when I was only a wee child—barely eight years of age—my father was interned for a year just for making a speech at a republican rally. But—and this may be hard for you to understand today—I thought that was the way life was meant to be for Catholics in Northern Ireland. I never gave any thought that the system could ever be changed. I wanted no part of that life at all, so I came to America to become a millionaire."

"And did you become a millionaire right away?" she asked with a warm smile.

"I'm still waiting for that to happen. But I was lucky enough to get a job—a clerical job with the telephone company—a few days after I got off the boat."

"Wasn't it a lonely life for you?" asked Bernadette, who had already concluded that Brigid was a sound and genuine woman.

"Not at all. So many young people were coming over from Ireland in those days, there was always something to do. Just about every Saturday night there'd be a dance at one of the local churches. In fact, it was at one of those dances that I met Jack Tierney himself."

"God must've been looking over you that night," quipped Jack.

"Are you from Armagh as well?"

"No, Jack is from Monaghan," said Brigid. "And to give the devil his due, Jack was political from the start."

"I always believed," Jack said, "that the people in the south who lived along the border were the most republican people in all of Ireland. We were close enough to the border to realize what the Brits were doing. As far back as I can remember, our home was a safe house for the boys coming back and forth across the border."

"And when was this?" asked Bernadette.

"I'm talking about the late twenties and into the mid-thirties. Now, I don't want you to be thinking I was in the IRA or was any sort of a hero. But I always did whatever I was asked to do. Stash weapons. Deliver messages. Take wounded volunteers to friendly doctors. That sort of thing."

"You've a lot to be proud of," said Bernadette, who sensed the commitment and intensity beneath Jack's good humor.

"Well, it sounds much more dramatic than it was. Besides, we could do a lot more in the south in those days. Oh, the Free

State would crack down when things got out of hand, but nothing like what goes on today."

"These are the times when I see no difference between the British Army and the so-called Irish Army," said Bernadette.

"The Irish Army does for the Brits what the Polish Army does for the Russians," said Michael. "They do their dirty work for them."

"I'm afraid what you're saying is the truth," said Jack, "the very sad truth. And while it wasn't as bad in the thirties, it was my luck to get in trouble nonetheless. I had just turned seventeen and was tipped off that the Gardai would be coming to question me about a post office just across the border in Armagh which the IRA had blown to smithereens. Mind you, I wasn't involved in it, but I knew more about it than I should have. So I went on the run. After a few months, I got word that all was clear and I could come home. But being away for those months made me realize there was nothing for me in Monaghan."

"Bernadette, I hope you notice who's doing all the talking now," laughed Brigid. "I wish you could make as much progress driving, Jack, as you do talking."

"Actually, it looks as if the traffic is lightening up a bit," said Jack, changing lanes and moving faster. "We'll probably be home before I have a chance to tell Bernadette all the fascinating details of my life."

"Even though we're always talking at home about a united Ireland, I've met almost no one in my life who didn't come from Andersonstown or Ballymurphy," said Bernadette. "So, Jack, please go on."

"Well, I decided to emigrate to America with the money in my pocket and not much more than the clothes on my back.

Once I got here, I rented an apartment in the South Bronx with three of the lads I'd met on the boat. For the first few years I worked on the docks. The work was tough but the money was good. But after Brigid and I decided to marry, I needed a job that had more security and better hours. I was lucky that a cousin of mine was able to get me started at Con Edison, the utility company, and I've been there ever since."

"When did you first get involved over here with the north? Was there much activity in America then?"

"Almost nothing at all," Brigid said. "Of course, there were county organizations, but they were mostly social and traditional. Jack and I didn't join any Irish-American organization until the 1940s, after we'd been married a few years. But they had nothing to do as far as the trouble in the north. Remember, this was during the war and England was America's main ally against Hitler. It just wouldn't do for immigrants such as us to be criticizing the Brits when they were fighting and dying alongside American boys."

"That's something to keep in mind, Bernadette," said Jack. "The Irish who came over in my time loved America. I know that sounds melodramatic, but it's the truth. Brigid and I, for instance, became citizens as soon as we possibly could. During the war I tried to enlist three times but was rejected because of a bad knee, which I'd injured back home. So, as strongly as we felt about the north, we didn't want to say or do anything that would hurt America. And after the war, things didn't change very much as far as the organizations were concerned. Most of them were very close to the Free State consulate and all they were interested in was promoting tourism, teaching step dancing and that sort of thing."

"One thing changed, though," said Brigid, "and that was my thinking. From listening to Jack and some of his friends who'd come by to talk now and then, I started to read and study everything that I could about Irish history. I finally realized how cruel the Brits were to our people. And when I realized it, I became angry at the Brits for all they'd done to us, but even more angry at myself for ignoring it for so many years. And when I saw all that we enjoy over here, I just couldn't bear to think of our people suffering at home."

"What she's trying to tell you, Bernadette, is that she became a more fervent republican than I ever was," said Jack.

"About all we could do was try to steer some of the organizations in the right direction, mainly by asking questions or suggesting topics about the north for discussion."

"How long have you been collecting people like me at the airport?"

"For the past twenty-five years at least," Brigid said. But it's our pleasure. By now it's become like second nature to us."

"Twenty-five years! My God," said Bernadette, "I was just a wee child then."

"We were a lot younger then ourselves," Jack said, smiling.

"They first approached Jack and me in the late fifties during the border campaign. They asked us to raise money for food and clothes. Things were desperate then."

"From what I remember," said Bernadette, "there wasn't very much fighting in Belfast during those years."

"No," said Brigid, "it was primarily in the country and along the border areas. It was terrible in Fermanagh, for instance."

"Why did they come to you and Jack?" asked Bernadette.

"Ah, it's no great mystery. It was just that so few were doing anything at all. So it was natural they would come to us."

"Look ahead, Bernadette, that's the Verrazzano Bridge," said Jack. "Every good tourist should see it."

Bernadette gazed at the great pylons and the massive silver span over the entrance to New York Harbor. "Mother of God, look at the size of it," she said. "It's brilliant, so it is."

"We should be at the apartment in ten minutes," said Jack.

"Then I'd better hurry with my story," said Brigid. "It was in '68 and '69 that things seemed to go mad altogether. It seemed as if there were peaceful marches one day and then a bloody war the next. We were told to raise money as quickly as we could."

"Aye, there was a war all right"—Bernadette sighed—"except we'd no guns to fight it with."

"Ah, but it's become a much tougher game now," said Brigid. "Sometimes it seems the FBI has nothing else to do but go after the IRA. Anyway, Jack and I have been out of that part of it for years now. That's a job for the younger people. But we do what we can and we're always happy to help out when people like yourself are visiting over here."

"Well, I'm happy for that," said Bernadette, smiling and wondering just how much Jack and Brigid really were "out of that part of it."

They finally reached their exit, and as Jack drove from the Belt Parkway onto the streets of Brooklyn, Bernadette felt overwhelmed by the suffocatingly large buildings. "My God, Brigid, how can you even breathe in these streets?" she asked, looking skyward.

"These are nothing at all. They're just apartment houses. Wait until you get to Manhattan," Brigid said with a smile.

Jack and Brigid lived in a four-room apartment on the third floor of an apartment house off Shore Road. The apartment was comfortable and quietly decorated. A Celtic cross on the living room wall and a wooden harp handcrafted by a Long Kesh prisoner, which was on the desk in the living room, were the only Irish arti-facts in the apartment.

Brigid showed Bernadette her room and left her alone to freshen up. Bernadette was delighted with the room. The bed was firm when she tested it, the closet big enough for her needs, and the dark wooden dresser had empty drawers. She unpacked some of her clothes so the wrinkles would hang out and then joined the others in the living room. Brigid had a tray of tea and sandwiches waiting on a table. She handed Bernadette a cup of tea and a ham sandwich.

Bernadette took a deep drink of the tea. "Ah, that tastes like home," she said, and bit into the sandwich.

Brigid smiled and passed around a tray. The others helped themselves.

"Bernadette," said Michael, "we certainly don't want to work you to death while you're over here, but we do want to make your trip as worthwhile as we possibly can. The major event will be at the Acropolis Manor in Queens on Friday night. We're expect-ing a crowd of eight or nine hundred."

"When I agreed to come over, Michael, I agreed to do whatever had to be done. So whatever your schedule for me is I'll do it. I hope I do a good job."

"You'll have three days in New York, going to the Bronx, Queens and Manhattan. Then you'll be on to Albany, Boston, Philadelphia, Long Island, and then next Thursday night you'll be flying back to Ireland."

"Jesus," said Bernadette, "I really will be the eight-day wonder, won't I?"

"You'll be exhausted is what you'll be," said Michael. He stood up and put down his empty cup and plate. "Listen, there's no point in me taking up any more of your time. You need to get some rest. I'll come by about six o'clock tomorrow to take you to the Bronx and Woodside. If you need to get hold of me in the meantime, Jack and Brigid know how to contact me."

After he left, Bernadette lit up her first cigarette and inhaled deeply. "Brigid," she said, "it's hard for me to believe I'm here in America, and I still don't know what the hell I'm doing here. Michael certainly seems to have everything sorted out, though, doesn't he?"

"Ah, Michael's the best we have over here. He's dedicated, he works hard and, most of all, he gets things done. Believe me, we've an awful lot of people who talk a good game, but Michael's the one who gets results."

"He's very young to have such an important position," said Bernadette. "That was a good sandwich, thank you." She sat back in her chair and put her feet on the hassock in front of her.

"That's right, make yourself comfortable," Brigid said.

"Officially," Jack said, "he ranks fourth or fifth from the top in NIRAA, but as a practical matter he's the top man and, yes, he did move up quickly—but he got there on his own without anyone pulling any strings for him."

"I've come to know Michael very well during the past few years," said Brigid. "He's a second-generation Irish American who graduated from Fordham University and St. John's Law School. There's such a difference between his generation and ours. Wouldn't you agree, Jack?"

"I certainly would," replied Jack. "He just doesn't feel he has to explain himself to anyone or worry about what anyone thinks of him. I suppose that's the surest sign the Irish have arrived in America, when they can speak up for Ireland and not have to worry about their loyalty being challenged."

"Is he always so serious?" asked Bernadette.

"No, indeed he's not," said Brigid. "He's serious enough when there's work to be done, but when he gets a few minutes to relax, he's pleasant and friendly. The most important thing, though, is he knows what he's doing. With Michael taking care of all the details, you can be sure you'll be getting the most out of your trip."

"Jesus, Brigid, with all the questions I've been asking you, I haven't asked you a word about your children. Those pictures on the wall—they must be your children and the wee ones your grandchildren."

"Yes, Bernadette, there's Jack Jr., and our daughter, Kathleen. Thank God they're healthy and all the grandchildren are well. We've been very lucky."

"I'm sure that's because of you and Jack," said Bernadette.

"I don't know about that, but I do know you must be terribly tired indeed. Why don't you get a good night's sleep for yourself?"

Even though it was only eight o'clock, it was one o'clock in the morning Belfast time. Bernadette hadn't realize how exhausted she was until she lay down in the bed. Her thoughts drifted homeward. Once again she gave thanks for her mother, who had moved in to stay with the children. Her mother had been excited at the thought of Bernadette's visiting the United States, but asked her almost nothing about it. Unlike their grandmother, though, Brendan and Siobhan were full of questions. Some were typically juvenile: Would she see the set where *Dallas* was filmed? Would she meet Bruce Springsteen? Would she meet Ronald Reagan? Others were particularly perceptive: Would she be safe? Would this help to get their daddy out of jail? They were happy for her and knew the Yanks would love her. Mother of God, she thought, they certainly are making it easier for me. God love them.

She turned onto her side and pulled the pillow under her head. When she'd gone to see Dermot, she could tell right away, from his smile, that he knew all about the trip. He had sat down, kissed her and said, "I don't believe I've ever been visited in jail by a world traveler before. This is indeed a great moment."

"Don't be so smart now," she retorted. "It's because of you I'll be dragged from one city to another, being worn into the ground, while you're here in a comfortable room, getting three meals a day. If you ever go to confession again, you can put this at the top of your list of sins."

The two of them broke out laughing and Dermot squeezed her hands. "Ah, Bernadette, I'm so proud of you. And all the lads here are proud of you as well."

"Dermot, for too many years you had to do it alone. You've always known what dirty fuckers the Brits are, and you always did what you had to do while I was always changing my mind. But now, for as long as it takes, we'll fight them together."

" 'Together! Together!' she says. I'm rotting in jail and she's being wined and dined all over the United States and she says we're together," he exclaimed with a rueful smile.

"Dermot, my love, I suppose all I can say is that war is hell." Once again they broke into loud laughter. The warder standing nearby looked at them quizzically.

While Bernadette explained the plans for the trip, she found herself speaking with confidence and assurance. Dermot questioned her and listened intently to her answers. She felt closer to him than she had ever been—and more needed.

And with that thought, Bernadette turned on her other side and fell asleep.

It was half seven when she awoke on Thursday. A bright fall sun was shining through the curtains. Also coming through the windows were the discordant sounds of the buses, cars and trucks making their way along the Brooklyn streets. The noise was not overly clamorous or insistent, but it was considerably more than she'd anticipated in a residential area and much more than she'd ever heard in Andersonstown.

After breakfast, Brigid and Bernadette took a short, relaxing stroll through the neighborhood. Bernadette studied what to her was the curious interspersing of sturdy one-family homes with large, formidable apartment houses and felt very far indeed from Andersonstown. Look at the wee children playing, she thought, and not a Brit or a plastic bullet to be seen anywhere. Her own children—what were they doing now? she wondered. She was sure they missed her. But no need to worry. They always got on well with their granny, and Bernadette would ring them on Sunday to let them know they still had a mother.

And Dermot. If only he could be here with her. Jesus, she thought, if the two of them could ever just have a normal life. I suppose you don't realize how bad a fucking war really is until you're out of it.

"Brigid, tell me more about your children," said Bernadette, trying desperately to take her mind away from Dermot, sitting in his cell.

"As I was telling you last night, we've been fortunate indeed. The oldest is Jack Jr. He went to Fordham University and is a lawyer. He and his wife Peggy have two beautiful daughters and live up in Westchester County. Kathleen went to St. John's University and is a high school teacher. She and Tom have two sons and live on Long Island."

As they turned the corner onto Fourth Avenue, Bernadette said, "My God, it's two different worlds we're living in. I don't see any future at all for my children in Belfast. Our Brendan will be out of secondary school soon enough and it's either the dole or an odd job here or there. That's the most he can look forward to, if he's not getting knocked about by the Brits. And it'll be the same for Siobhan when she's finished with school in a few years. And God only knows where we'll all be by the time Maura's a teenager."

"It must be very depressing."

"I try not to let myself think about it too often. But sometimes it overwhelms me and I feel so helpless. There seems to be no end to the suffering. Our whole life is going on the dole, fighting the Brits, visiting the jails and going to funerals. Sometimes I wonder why we even have children. I wonder if it's fair to bring a child into the world in Belfast. Because what the hell kind of life can we give them? But don't worry," said Bernadette with a large smile. "I don't think that way too often. I enjoy the children, I enjoy Dermot—even when he's in jail—and I enjoy my friends. I suppose we make the most of what we have. Or maybe it's just that we're not smart enough to realize that we don't have anything." She laughed.

"It's incredible how you and the other republican women are able to keep going in spite of it all."

"I suppose it's either that or blow our brains out." She stopped in front of a variety store. "Maybe you can help me pick out some presents for the children," she said. She and Brigid went into the store.

It was a long drive from Bay Ridge to the Bronx. Eastbound this time on the Belt Parkway. Up the Van Wyck Expressway, across the Throgs Neck Bridge. Over to the Cross Bronx Expressway, then to the Major Deegan and finally to Gaelic Park at the very north end of the Bronx.

The names of the roads and highways meant nothing to Bernadette, but she was awed by the buildings and the lights, by the view of the Manhattan skyline from the Throgs Neck and by the seemingly endless stream of cars and trucks.

Gaelic Park, Michael Garvey explained as they drove through the streets of the North Bronx, was an antiquated and dilapidated structure built years ago to accommodate the athletic passions of the Irish immigrants flocking to New York. As recently as the 1950s there was never an empty seat for the Sunday hurling matches. But when immigration stopped during the sixties and the Irish accelerated their migration to the suburbs, Gaelic Park became a forgotten relic to all save a few die-hards. Now, with the recent upsurge in immigration, Gaelic Park was getting a new life.

"Where exactly will we be meeting tonight?" asked Bernadette.

"At the bar right next to Gaelic Park. They have a large meeting room in the back. This is a joint meeting of several Hibernian divisions, men and women. For the most part, they're old-line Irish who stayed in the Bronx."

"Are the Hibernians connected with NIRAA?"

"There's no official connection. Some of the best NIRAA people, though, are Hibernians. On the other hand, there are a lot of Hibernians who follow the Free State line."

"How will it be tonight?" she asked.

"I'd guess it will be a real mix. Some of them will love you and support everything you say. Others will be dead set against you. And a few will just be noncommittal. I do know some of the women are annoyed that you've been invited tonight. But don't worry. I'm sure most of the crowd will be with you."

Michael parked the car up the block from the Gaelic Park Casino. As they walked down toward the bar, she saw a number of people entering the front door.

"It's always great to see people arrive," said Michael. "Nothing's worse than coming to give a speech and walking into a room that's almost empty."

"Maybe it will empty once I begin speaking." She laughed.

"Not bloody likely. They want to hear what's happening from someone like you."

As she walked through the bar and into the back room, Bernadette saw that almost all the folding chairs were filled and a number of people were milling about in the rear. There must be well over a hundred, she thought.

She could sense that almost everyone was looking at her as Michael led her toward the front of the room. Michael was right: Belfast women are quite a curiosity, she thought. He introduced her to the four men and two women who were seated at the rectangular table at the front. Each one greeted her warmly. As soon as she sat down behind the table, the chairman gaveled the meeting to order.

The people at Families for Legal Justice, the Belfast-based organization sponsoring the trip, had written a speech for her, but they'd told her she could ad-lib as necessary. She was ready with the speech, but she wondered how she could amend it to reach the crowd facing her.

For the most part they were middle-aged, conservatively dressed and appeared friendly. But she was sure she had spotted several women who weren't particularly pleased about her being there. These must be the type Michael had told her about, what he called "the Biddies." Bernadette could not tell their ages, but they looked as if they'd always been old. They sat primly with their legs neatly crossed and their arms firmly folded. Their eyes glared out from drawn faces.

Talk about body language, Bernadette said to herself. She turned her attention to the chairman, who had begun his introduction.

"A woman of courage and integrity who is in the United States to let the American people know the truth about what the British government is doing to our brothers and sisters in Northern Ireland. She is on a busy schedule, and we are delighted that she was able to take the time to be with us this evening—Bernadette Hanlon of Belfast."

As she got up from her chair and approached the microphone, Bernadette felt no anxiety or tension. Standing at the lectern, she found herself calmly adjusting the microphone to her height and, in a clear voice, thanking the Hibernians for inviting her.

It was to be a short talk and she'd decided to give bits and pieces of the speech she would deliver at the Acropolis Manor tomorrow night: supergrasses, police raids, plastic bullets. As she got into the talk and began to weave one topic into the other, she could sense that the audience was attentive and that most of them were with her. The Biddies were still resisting, however. Their arms were just as firmly folded, their legs as neatly crossed and their eyes as piercing. Their jaws jutted under their pursed lips.

When it was time to conclude, Bernadette said with an irony that only she—and probably Michael—could appreciate, "I must give a special word of thanks to all the women in America who understand our struggle and do so much to support us."

"As women, you understand what suffering it must be to see your husband dragged from his home by soldiers in the middle of the night while your wee children scream hysterically. You understand what sorrow it must be to sit in your neighbors' home and try to console them after their wee daughter has been killed by a British soldier who blew off the top of her head with a plastic bullet. You understand what agony it must be to visit your friend who doesn't know why she's in jail, but does know that she's being strip-searched every day.

"Yes, you understand the special suffering the women in the six counties must endure, just as you understand that you could be going through that same suffering yourself if you were not fortunate enough to be living in America.

"So, I beseech all of you—but most especially the women— to continue to give us that same strength and support which you've always given us over the years and which binds us together as one. Thank you all very much."

Almost before she had finished, the audience was giving her a roaring ovation. Many were on their feet applauding as loud as they could. Even the Biddies were standing and applauding, albeit politely and self-consciously.

The chairman finally restored order and said there would be time for just two questions because Bernadette needed to be off for her next stop in Woodside.

From the right side of the room, about halfway back, a man in his fifties asked, "Mrs. Hanlon, what do we have to do to get the Irish consulate to tell us the truth about what's happening in Ireland? They have the staff. They have the money. But I'm sorry to say, they do nothing to help the people in the north. Thank God for people like you, Mrs. Hanlon, but—and excuse me for saying this—but what the hell is wrong with the Dublin government?"

Many in the audience cheered, but Bernadette could see

that others appeared to be uneasy about such a direct attack on the Free State government.

"I must say that the gentlemen has asked a question that I cannot answer. I cannot answer how a government that calls itself Irish can allow its own people to suffer as they do in the six counties and do nothing about it. I will never understand why an Irish army protects a border the British created. I will never understand why the Irish Army and the Gardai harass and arrest republicans in the twenty-six counties but say nothing about British oppression in the six counties. I will never, never understand how Charley Haughey and Garrett Fitzgerald allowed Bobby Sands and his brave comrades to die on hunger strike and do nothing about it. The Irish government, or the Free State government as we prefer to call it, does not even allow its people to know what's happening in the north. How many of you know, for instance, that Ian Paisley is permitted to appear on television and radio in the Free State and Gerry Adams isn't?" She stopped and looked around the room.

"I'm sorry if I've gone on too much, but I feel so strongly about this. The Free State government has sold out its own people, and I'd hate to think that Irish Americans would ever be taken in by those British lackeys."

The crowd applauded strongly, but some were still holding back. I can't blame them, she thought, for not realizing what collaborators the Free Staters are.

From the second row, on the left side of the room, a woman with bright red hair— definitely not one of the Biddies —stood up and said in a strong voice, "Mrs. Hanlon, before I ask my question, I want to say you're a brave and beautiful woman, and your husband and your children must be very proud to have you as a wife and mother."

The crowd once more broke into loud applause. Bernadette nervously touched the microphone, looked down at the lectern and moved back and forth from one foot to the other.

When the clapping stopped, the woman continued speaking. "How about the American government? No matter what happens in Ireland, they always do what Thatcher and the Brits want them to do."

Bernadette knew she had to tread carefully with this question. "First of all," she said, "thank you very much indeed for your kind words. As for the American government, I don't believe it would be good form for me to come to this country and criticize your government. What I would do, though, is ask Americans how they can say they support freedom everywhere in the world, but not in the north of Ireland. I remember when I was a teenage girl in 1968 and the pictures of the Soviet troops with their tanks on the streets of Prague. And I remember how outraged the Americans were and how strongly they condemned the Russians. So when the Brits rampaged through the streets of Belfast and Derry just a few years later, we waited for the American government to say something. And we're still waiting.

"And for all these years we've lived in a police state. We're not safe in the streets or in our homes. We've no jobs and we've no rights. And America still says nothing.

"I can only say that what's wrong is wrong. And if Americans think it's wrong for the Russians to persecute the people of Czechoslovakia, then it's just as wrong for the British to persecute the nationalist people in the north of Ireland."

As the audience once again broke into loud applause, Bernadette raised her arms to quiet the crowd. The room fell silent and she said, "You certainly have made this a memorable occasion

terrible
Beauty

for me, and I would love to stay with you for the rest of the evening. But Michael tells me I'm already late for my next meeting in Woodside. So I have to be on my way. Thank you very much indeed."

As she made her way toward the exit, Bernadette shook as many hands as she could. The door closed behind her and Michael, and they stepped into the Bronx night. She could still hear the echoing of applause.

CHAPTER EIGHT

"I was absolutely delighted, so I was. The people in the Bronx were magic. I know some of the Hibernians may not always be as strong as you'd like them to be, but the group last night couldn't have been nicer. I honestly felt most of them were with me," said Bernadette, still on an emotional high from the night before.

"Let me pour you more tea," said Brigid, "and you should eat some of that bread. I made it myself."

"Ah, Brigid, you're far too good."

"Now, tell me about the NIRAA meeting in Woodside. How did that go?"

"They were the most genuine people. God love them. Michael and I were delayed because there was an accident on the bridge we were taking."

"It must have been the Triborough."

"Aye, that's the one. Anyway, we were over an hour late by the time we got there, but no one was doing any complaining at all. Every seat was taken, and people were standing around the back and the sides of the room. Michael said there were more than one hundred fifty people there. They cheered everything I said and, afterwards, we stayed for well over an hour. So many of the people wanted to talk or just say hello. I was over the moon, so I was.

It must've been well past midnight when I got back. I hope I didn't wake you up."

"Don't bother yourself about that. I was awake reading, but Jack was sound asleep, and since it was almost one o'clock, I was afraid we'd wake him up if we started talking then. But we've some time now, so tell me what Michael thought about it all."

"Ah, Michael is sound. He helped me so much. He told me what I should expect at both places. He was dead on. It was so reassuring to have him with me. And he did seem very pleased with the way things went. One bit of advice he did give me, though, was not to say 'comrades' when I'm talking about the Ra. He said it sounds too 'communistic.' "

"Well, we can't have people calling you a 'Red'," laughed Brigid. "It's bad enough you're a terrorist. Now, you'd better be getting yourself ready to meet all those lawyers."

The law offices of Hurley and McMahon were on the tenth floor of a solemn building located on lower Broadway. Tom Hurley was the president of the Irish-American Lawyers Association. Michael had told her during the drive into the city that Hurley often used his firm's conference room for meetings. Sitting at the head of the long mahogany table, Bernadette admired the dark wood paneling of the room.

Michael had also told her that, like so many Irish-American organizations, the Lawyers Association had come into existence during the hunger strikes in 1981. Its membership had grown to about one hundred lawyers, most of whom were in their thirties or forties. The association had issued a number of position papers critical of the Northern Ireland court system and had also defended Irish Americans and Irish nationals charged in

America for offenses related to Northern Ireland, usually gun-running.

Even though there had been short notice and the meeting was during business hours, more than twenty lawyers had rearranged their schedules to meet Bernadette, and Hurley had said he was pleased with the turnout.

As Bernadette sipped her tea and began talking, she soon realized by their comments and their questions that the lawyers were knowledgeable about the legal system in the six counties. They listened with rapt attention to everything she said.

"Bernadette, my name is Joe Flynn," said one of the lawyers, "and I know I'm speaking for everyone who's here today when I tell you how worthwhile it has been for us to have the opportunity to listen to you. Most of us are familiar with the facts and details of the Diplock courts and the supergrass system. But it wasn't until you came here today and described it in human terms that we realized how cruel and devastating this has been to the nationalist community."

"I know you haven't received very much good news lately," Hurley said. "So it may brighten your spirits a bit to learn that our association has voted to send an American lawyer to Belfast to attend your husband's trial as an observer. The Brits may have no regard for due process or justice, but we're hoping they have some regard for international opinion."

"My God, that is great news," Bernadette said, stunned. "I can't begin to tell you how much this means to me and, of course, to my husband and children. I wish we'd more lawyers in Belfast who would show the same concern and interest for the nationalist community that you people here in New York do. Thank you. Thank you very much indeed."

terrible
Beauty

On that happy note, Bernadette and Michael left the law offices and headed for the McMurray Towers on Lexington Avenue and 50th Street.

Side by side over the entrance of the hotel, the Stars and Stripes and the Irish Tri-Colour waved furiously in the breeze that surged through the cavernous haunts of Midtown Manhattan. As they walked through the revolving doors into the hotel lobby, Bernadette asked Michael if the McMurray Towers always flew the Tri-Colour.

"Yeah, one of the owners, Jack Joyce, is a very active Irish American. A really solid guy. He got himself into quite a row with the Free State consulate during the hunger strikes. When Bobby Sands died, Joyce lowered the flags to halfmast and the consulate was raging. Fair play to Jack, though, he wouldn't back down and the consulate has snubbed him ever since. Here, Bernadette, look at this," said Michael, pointing at the bold white lettering on a black felt message board in the center of the lobby: NOON—2:00 P.M.—PENTHOUSE SUITE—COCKTAIL PARTY—IRISH-AMERICAN LABOR FEDERATION—BERNADETTE HANLON.

"It's not quite Broadway," said Michael, "but you're definitely on your way to stardom."

Bernadette smiled and said quietly, "They'd never believe this at home."

There must have been at least fifty union leaders, many more than Michael had expected, and after just a few minutes, she lost track of who was who.

"Tommy McMahon, president of the Steamfitters. It's a pleasure to meet you, Bernadette."

"Ah, it's my pleasure."

"Augie MacBride, business agent of the Carpenters. I'm certainly pleased to meet you."

"Thank you very much."

"Jack Kilbride, president of the Tunnel Workers. It's great to meet you."

"Pete Lenahan, vice president of the Transit Workers. I hope you're enjoying New York."

"I am indeed, thanks."

"Jimmy Boyle, president of the Firefighters. How're you holding up?"

"Just fine, I think."

"Eddie Ward, vice president of the Longshoremen. Can I get you a drink?"

"A coke would be lovely, thanks."

Finally, at about one-fifteen the bar closed and Paddy Young, president of the Irish-American Labor Federation, led Bernadette to a microphone in front of a floor-to-ceiling window overlooking Manhattan. What a breathtaking view, she thought.

When Young began speaking, the room fell silent as the labor leaders gave him their full attention. Bernadette stood several feet to Young's right, with Michael farther off to the side. Traces of Young's Tipperary accent could be detected as he spoke.

"From the days of James Connolly, the American labor movement has proudly supported the Irish people in their struggle for freedom.

"Down through the years, the voice of labor—including such giants as Mike Quill, Teddy Gleason, John Lawe and Bill Treacy—has condemned the British government for exploiting the suffering nationalist people in the six counties. And today we stand in solidarity with those courageous Irish men and Irish women who are fighting for the freedom of their country."

Young waited for the applause to stop before concluding. "We're honored to have with us today a woman who is as beautiful as she is brave, a woman from Belfast whose husband is at this very moment locked away as a political prisoner in a British jail. She has the spirit and the will which the British have never understood and will never break. I'm honored to present to the Irish-American Labor Federation—Mrs. Bernadette Hanlon."

After an ovation that went on for more than a minute, Bernadette began her talk. "Mr. Young, I must thank you very much indeed for inviting me to be with you here today and also for such a very kind introduction.

"I must admit to you, however, that I was not listening to every word that you said. Because while you were speaking, I found myself admiring this beautiful window. And as I admired the window and looked out over this amazing city, I began to think of all the Brits I'd like to throw right through that window."

The crowd roared its approving laughter.

"But you know and I know that the struggle against the Brits is much more difficult than that, and we also know, even though we always try to keep our sense of humor and enjoy the craic, that there's nothing at all funny about what the Brits have done to our country and to our people.

"My three children have never known one day of peace in their entire lives. There's never been a night they could go to sleep without the fear that British soldiers would break into their home in the dead of night and arrest their mother and father. For fifteen years my husband's been denied the right to a job, the right to support his family, just because he happened to be baptized Catholic.

"As Mr. Young said—yes, Paddy, this I listened to—no matter what the Brits do to us, they'll never break us. Yes, they may kill the revolutionary, but I swear to God they will never kill the revolution. We will win because we're right and because we've the help and support of good people such as all of you."

The labor leaders rose to their feet and shouted their support. She thanked them, and when they would let her leave, Michael took her arm and led her to the elevator. They had more engagements to keep that day.

Bernadette's next appointment was on the West Side at the WABC radio studio. The midafternoon Friday traffic was brutal, which gave her and Michael a chance to talk about the meeting as they drove across town.

"Those labor people are so genuine," Bernadette said. "It was a pleasure to meet them. They must be a great help to you."

"They are genuine. That's true enough. And they do help. But not as much as we'd like. Labor unions are subject to a tremendous amount of federal regulation—to keep out the mob and to make sure no one's stealing the pension funds. But that gives the government a hell of a lot of leverage. They can look at the books of these unions whenever they want, even if the union is entirely clean and innocent, and investigate them from top to bottom. If the feds want to find something, they can. And even if they don't, the union has to spend too much time and money defending itself."

"So what you're saying is that if the unions give us too much support, the government could come after them—'squeeze them', as you Yanks say."

"That's exactly the problem. Still, with it all, they do pretty well for us. Especially Paddy Young. When we really need help, we can always turn to Paddy."

By the time they arrived at the studio it was five minutes before air time. Tommy Wilson, the interviewer, seemed to be a friendly enough sort. He greeted Bernadette as if they were old friends. "How are you, Bernadette? I was afraid the Brits might've lifted you."

He brought her into the glass-enclosed sound studio and had her sit next to him. Michael remained in the outside room but within her view. Wilson told her all she had to do was answer his questions and those from the callers. "Speak naturally," he said, "and forget about the microphones." He pointed to an overhead monitor. "Those are the first names of the callers who have been screened and are waiting to speak." The monitor also specified whether the callers were "for" or "against" Bernadette. She gave a quick look and, seeing it was flashing five "for" and three "against," thought it shouldn't be too hard to get through the interview.

Wilson began to speak. "For the next ninety minutes our switchboard will be lighting up because we will be discussing Northern Ireland. The IRA—are they terrorists or freedom fighters? The British Army—are they peacekeepers or a brutal army of occupation?"

Bernadette opened her mouth to speak, but Wilson signaled her to be silent.

"My guest today is Bernadette Hanlon of Belfast, Northern Ireland. Her husband, Dermot, is sitting in a Belfast jail awaiting trial. The British authorities say he is a vicious murderer, a terrorist who should spend the rest of his life in jail. Mrs. Hanlon says he is an innocent man, a political prisoner. Mrs. Hanlon is in the United States on a speaking tour to bring attention to her husband's case and to what she says is the unjust legal system in Northern Ireland. Welcome to the Tommy Wilson Show, Mrs. Hanlon."

"Thank you, Mr. Wilson. I'm delighted to be here."

"Mrs. Hanlon, before we go to our callers, I have one question. Your husband is charged with murder. The British government has said—you can't deny this—that he'll receive a trial. If he's innocent, as you say he is, why doesn't he prove that at his trial instead of letting his wife come to America to get sympathy for him?"

"Mr. Wilson, my husband *will* get a trial. But he'll not get a *fair* trial. What he'll get is a show trial, a trial which is a cruel farce. And that's why I am in America. I want the American people to know that the British don't give fair trials to Irish political prisoners."

"How can you say your husband will not get a fair trial?"

"Well, for one thing, he's not allowed to have a jury. He'll be tried before a judge who's been appointed by the British government and who in most cases is either a former unionist politician or a British Army officer. Most Americans don't know that political prisoners in the north of Ireland are denied jury trials.

"Most Americans also don't know the type of false evidence that's used to convict these political prisoners. In my husband's case, the only evidence against him will be the statement of an admitted perjurer and criminal. There's no corroboration whatever. But what are my husband's lawyers to do? There's no jury they can make this argument to. The entire case depends upon whether the judge says he believes the testimony of the perjurer, or the 'supergrass' as we call them."

"Would you explain the term 'supergrass'?"

" 'Supergrass' comes from 'snake-in-the-grass.' It means a desperate liar who cannot be trusted or believed. But let me say one more thing, Mr. Wilson. I'd ask your listeners to keep in mind that the British government spends millions of dollars in propaganda in the United States every year. I'm over here to attempt to counter that. I'm just one Belfast woman. I've no university education. I've no government training. I'm not asking you to believe everything I say. But please don't believe everything the British tell you, either. Keep an open mind. Study the issue. And then make your decision."

"Thank you, Mrs. Hanlon. And now to our callers."

"Hello, my name is Robert, from Westchester," said the first caller. "British soldiers fought and died side by side with Americans in World War II. How can any American support killing British soldiers in Northern Ireland?"

Bernadette was ready for that one. "America was allied with the Soviets in World War II, but that doesn't mean Americans should support the Soviets in Afghanistan. Besides, America fought in World War II to defeat tyranny. There is tyranny in the north of Ireland today, and the republican movement is fighting that tyranny."

Wilson signaled her to stop, and she did.

"Hello, Bernadette," said the second caller. "I'm Erin, from Seaford. Are plastic bullets still being used?"

"Indeed they are. Plastic bullets are lethal weapons. British soldiers and RUC fire them at civilians. My neighbor's daughter was murdered by a plastic bullet earlier this year. The soldier who shot her was never charged."

Again, a signal from Wilson. My God, Bernadette thought, he hardly lets me finish a sentence.

Then she realized why. The calls were pouring in, according to the lights on the switchboard. "George, from Old Brookville. Aren't you and your husband members of the IRA?"

"No."

"Isn't the IRA a terrorist organization?"

"No. The IRA attacks military targets just as George Washington did. Civilians are killed because of tragic mistakes, which regrettably are part of every war. British rule in Ireland is state terrorism."

With about twenty minutes remaining in the program, she glanced through the glass and saw that Michael had left. She was on her own.

"Vito, from Staten Island. Is the war in the six counties a religious struggle?"

"No. It's an Irish-British struggle. For economic and historical reasons most Protestants side with the British. Protestants should realize they're manipulated by the British and have more in common with us than with the British."

"Would you welcome Protestant support?"

"Absolutely."

She continued to field questions as fast as they came in. Then she saw Michael come back into the outside room. He looked worried, Bernadette thought.

"Mrs. Hanlon," said Wilson, "we have only a few moments left in our show. But you've been a most interesting and articulate guest. I don't pretend to have a magic solution to the Troubles in Northern Ireland, but I'll say the British government is making a big mistake if it underestimates the determination of people such as Bernadette Hanlon. Mrs. Hanlon, thank you for being on the Tommy Wilson Show, and I wish you and your family peace and happiness."

"Thank you very much indeed," she said.

Michael was waiting at the door with her coat over his arm. It seemed to Bernadette as if he were trying too hard to appear calm.

"Bernadette was a great guest," said Wilson. "You people have found yourself a natural this time. Do you have time for a cup of coffee downstairs?"

"I'd love to, Tommy, but we're running late. Thanks for the offer and for the show."

As Michael and Bernadette walked down the hallway to the elevator, he grabbed her left elbow with his right hand. When they got to the elevator, the doors opened and three people were inside. Michael stared straight ahead as they descended to the main floor, squeezing her elbow all the while.

"Just keep walking," he said, as they strode through the lobby and out of the building. Once on the street, they headed for the garage.

"I apologize for the dramatics. That's not my style. But I had to get you out of the building before the story came across the wire."

"What story, Michael? What are you talking about?" He was walking so fast she had trouble keeping up with him.

"About a half hour before the end of the show, my office called me with a message from Belfast."

"My God, is it Dermot or the children?"

"No, but there's been a tragedy. The Ra ambushed a foot patrol in the Markets this afternoon. Three Brits were killed, but backup support came in for them and five civilians got caught in the crossfire. Four are dead, including a mother and her infant son. One elderly man's in critical condition."

"Oh Jesus, Michael. Were any volunteers killed?"

"No, none were killed and none wounded or captured. They all got away safely—for now at least. You can imagine what kind of manhunt is going on."

"Mother of God, I can indeed."

They walked into the garage, and Michael gave his receipt to the attendant. Moments later they were back in the clogged Friday afternoon traffic.

"Bernadette, I don't want to seem overly callous, but our immediate problem is your pre-dinner news conference at the Acropolis Manor in less than three hours. We don't have to worry about reporters turning out for this one. They'll be there in droves, looking for your blood."

Bernadette had been euphoric since she arrived Wednesday afternoon. Everything had gone so well—too well, she thought now. She should've known. The Markets shootings were a brutal reminder that her life was not meant to be euphoric. She was surprised, and quietly gratified, however, to find that after the initial jolt, she was able to think logically and dispassionately about what had to be done.

"Michael, what information will we have by half six? Will we have the statement from the Army?"

"Between the phones and the telex, we should have the statement from the IRA, the wire service reports and probably the statement from the Northern Ireland Office."

"Once we get all the details," said Bernadette, "we can work out exactly what I'll say. But based on what we know now, I think all I can say is that this was an attack on military forces. The IRA never intended to injure civilians. Certainly I deeply regret the civilian casualties, but this is the kind of terrible incident that occurs in every war."

"They won't be satisfied with that answer. What they want is a confession of guilt, your mea culpa, and they'll keep after you trying to get it."

"You can be sure of one thing. They can ask me their questions all fucking night, but I'll never apologize for the IRA."

"I never thought that you would." Michael grinned at her.

"And don't worry yourself," said Bernadette. "I'll be as calm and sweet as I have to be."

As the car crossed First Avenue and onto the 59th Street Bridge, she thought of the four dead civilians and their families, of the men and women who would be dragged to Castlereagh that night. And she knew that was where her world would always be.

It was quarter to five when they drove into the parking garage of the Acropolis Manor. He reached into the backseat and removed the garment bag that contained Bernadette's dress for the evening. They walked into the lobby, and Bernadette looked at the mirrored walls and glass chandeliers while Michael went into the manager's office.

"Okay, here's the story," he said, as he came out of the office and handed her a key. "The manager has set aside a room for you so you can rest up and get dressed."

"That's dead on, Michael. No problem."

The small room on the second floor had a cot, a small desk, a toilet, a mirror and a sink. There was also a radio.

"Bernadette, the news conference will be down the hall and is scheduled for seven o'clock. I'll find out whatever I can about what happened in the Markets. I'll come back here about six-thirty to tell you what I've learned and to get ready for the news conference. In the meantime, why don't you turn on the radio to see if anything comes across?"

She turned the radio on and Michael adjusted the dial to 880.

"CBS is an all-news station," he said. "They'll probably go with the story as soon as they pick it up off the wires."

"Sound. I'll lie down for a while and I'll see you at half six."

Bernadette kicked off her high-heeled shoes, lay down on the cot and stared at the ceiling as she half-listened to the newscaster. There was more fighting in Lebanon, inflation was down again, a fire was being brought under control in the Bronx and there was a bank robbery in Brooklyn. As far as New York was aware, nothing had happened in Belfast today.

Bernadette thought of Dermot. Certainly the boys in the Crum knew all about the Markets attack, maybe even before it had happened. She knew Dermot would be wondering what effect the incident would have on her in New York. But she also knew Dermot would be smiling to himself: "Ah, fuck. My Bernadette'll handle herself well. Indeed, those Yanks'll be no match for her at all." She missed him dearly.

She missed the children as well. She looked forward so much to talking to them and decided she'd call them tomorrow rather than Sunday.

When Bernadette opened her eyes, she looked at her watch and saw that it was ten minutes before six. She got up from the cot, walked over to the sink, looked in the mirror and threw water on her face. The newscaster said that Mayor Koch was in another row with black ministers, and the police had arrested two major drug dealers in a lower Manhattan housing project.

Bernadette took off her powder-blue blouse and dark blue skirt and placed them on the cot. She washed her hands and face and then brushed her teeth with the toothbrush and toothpaste from the traveling kit in her handbag.

She opened the garment bag hanging on the back of the door and removed the white knit dress with long sleeves and a high collar, which she and Liz McCloskey, who'd helped her with the

terrible
Beauty

arrangements for the trip, had picked out in Belfast. Putting on the dress, she stepped back from the mirror to get a good look at how it fit. Bernadette had been denied many things in life, but God had endowed her with a beautiful body. Pleased to see that this dress did justice to God's work, she smiled and brushed her long, dark auburn hair.

As she reached for her makeup, WCBS radio switched to Washington, D.C., for the six o'clock national news. "Our lead story this evening is from Northern Ireland, where the Irish Republican Army has killed three British soldiers and four civilians in a terrorist attack in Belfast. The dead include a twenty-four-year-old mother and her ten-month-old son. Two soldiers were seriously wounded, and a seventy-six-year-old man is in critical condition and not expected to live. Prime Minister Thatcher has denounced the attack as a 'cowardly and dastardly act of terrorism.' In a statement issued in Dublin, the IRA has admitted responsibility for the killings."

Bernadette clicked off the radio and applied light makeup and lipstick. She reached into her handbag again and took out fifteen carefully numbered index cards on which she had printed the key points she wanted to make in her speech tonight. She made sure they were in proper order and read through them until she heard Michael knocking at the door.

"Bernadette, you look just beautiful. If looks mean anything, the news conference should be a breeze."

"Thanks, Michael. Were you able to get any information? I heard the radio report."

"The wire service stories had nothing we didn't already know. But here are the statements from the Northern Ireland Office and the IRA."

Bernadette took the telex papers from Michael and read the NIO statement first.

"The brutal murder of civilians and security personnel by the IRA in Belfast today is a cowardly act of terrorism. It is becoming increasingly clear that the IRA is resorting to such vicious acts in a desperate attempt to prevent the achievement of a just and equitable political solution in Northern Ireland. The government of Prime Minister Thatcher, however, will never yield to terrorism, nor will it diminish in any way its ongoing efforts for peace in Northern Ireland."

Bernadette's face froze in anger. "What lying bastards they are. Well, let me read what the Ra has to say." She read intently.

"The Belfast Brigade of the Irish Republican Army today carried out a successful attack upon a British Army foot patrol in the Markets area, killing three members of the Crown Forces. As the IRA Active Service Unit began its planned withdrawal after the attack, Crown Force reinforcements arrived and fired indiscriminately in the direction of the ASU. Several shots were returned by the retreating ASU as it successfully withdrew from the area. All volunteers returned safely to base.

"The Irish Republican Army deeply regrets that four innocent civilians were killed and one critically wounded in today's action and sends its sincerest condolences to the families of these victims. The responsibility for these tragic civilian casualties rests entirely with the British Crown Forces. The IRA launched this attack only after assuring itself that civilians would not be injured. It was the hail of bullets fired by British Army reinforcements that caused the crossfire which resulted in the civilian casualties. So long as British Crown forces continue to occupy Irish territory and patrol Irish streets, they will be subject to attack by the Irish

Republican Army." The statement was signed by P. O'Neill of the Irish Republican Publicity Bureau in Dublin.

Bernadette gave Michael the papers, and the two of them headed for the room at the other end of the hall on the second floor. It was overflowing with reporters, photographers and camera crews. Michael cleared the way for Bernadette so she could get into the room and up to the lectern.

Adjusting her eyes to the glare of the television lights, she looked at the swarm of microphones that had been affixed to the rostrum: News 88, WINS, Channel 2, Channel 7, Channel 9, Channel 11, Channel 4, WYNY, WMCA, WABC, WOR, AP, WFUV. She could hear cameras clicking and see the reporters jockeying for position as Michael introduced her and she stepped to the microphones.

The first reporter introduced himself as Marty Meehan from the *Daily News*. "Do you have any comment on today's terrorist attack by the IRA?" he asked.

In a firm voice Bernadette answered, "The IRA attacked a military occupation force, not civilians. The civilian casualties were tragic, not intended by the IRA, and were caused by the British. It's the British, not the IRA, who attack civilians. My heart goes out to the families of the casualties."

"Jack Rosen, *New York Post*," said the second reporter. "If the IRA had not attacked, four civilians, including a mother and infant son, would still be alive."

"And if the British Army was not occupying our country, they wouldn't be attacked," Bernadette countered. "I repeat, the IRA makes every effort to avoid injury to civilians."

Jim Slade from Channel 2 was the third questioner. "How can you expect Americans to support a terrorist organization that murders innocent women and children?"

"I'll say it again. The IRA is not a terrorist organization. It is fighting against an occupying army."

"Were the civilians killed when the IRA attacked or when the British reinforcements counterattacked?" asked Maureen McCartney from Channel 11.

Good question, Bernadette thought. This reporter did her own research. I had better take advantage of the opening.

"All the civilians were killed while the IRA was withdrawing and the Brits were counterattacking. It was the indiscriminate shooting by the British forces which caused the civilian deaths," she replied.

Bernadette held up her hand. "Before the next question is asked, I want to point out that many Irish civilians have been killed and wounded by the Brits, but it is not reported in the United States. The British are state terrorists."

Bernadette sensed the mood begin to shift.

"Mike Armstrong, Channel 4. What is your precise purpose for being in the United States?"

"To alert the American people to British injustice. My husband's in jail for a crime he did not commit. The only Crown witness is a paid perjurer. My husband will be denied a jury trial."

"Gene Turner, Associated Press. Will you be raising any money for the IRA while you're here?"

"No. I'm here to alert the Americans to the denial of human rights in British courts in the north of Ireland."

"Carol Burke, WINS. How long have you been in New York?"

"Two days."

"How do you like it so far?"

Bernadette relaxed and smiled. "Just grand."

"Rosemary Wiedl from News 88. How many children do you have, and do you miss them?"

"Three children. I miss them very much. I doubt if they miss me." Laughter. She had them with her now.

"Richie Neal, Channel 7. Are you nervous about your speech tonight?"

"After this news conference, everything else will seem very easy indeed."

The cocktail party for the dignitaries who would be on the dais was already under way when Bernadette and Michael came into the room. Word of her stellar performance at the news conference had worked its way through the Acropolis Manor. It took only a moment for the people to realize who she was and to break into applause.

Smiling, she again endured the ritual of introductions, handshakes and small talk. The supportive congressman. The Fenian priest. Heads of NIRAA units, Hibernian divisions, Emerald societies and Irish county associations. Labor leaders she thought she'd already met earlier that day. They all greeted her warmly and offered congratulations.

After about ten minutes, Bernadette politely excused herself from the maze of faces and walked with Michael toward the least crowded corner of the room. She looked around the room and said nothing as she sipped from a glass of white wine.

"You were superb at the news conference," Michael said. "What impressed me most was how well you stood your ground when they hit you with the hard questions and how deftly you turned them away."

Bernadette smiled at him. For the moment her person had become a duality of calm serenity and fast-flowing adrenaline.

She wanted to fully experience this moment.

A loud voice began to bark names and line up the dais guests, who would march from the cocktail party room to the main ballroom where more than a thousand people were awaiting their entrance.

Michael told her there would be a three-tiered dais and that she'd be sitting on the top level just to the right of the lectern. She and Michael would be the last to enter the ballroom.

From the hallway she could hear the sounds of bagpipes being tuned. "The Pipe Band of the New York City Police Emerald Society," said Michael. "They'll lead the procession of dignitaries into the ballroom."

Bernadette could see that it'd be at least several minutes before everyone was lined up in proper order and ready to march in. She took the time to go over to the doorway and look at the Pipers just outside. They were big and brawny and seemed in good spirits as they finished tuning their pipes.

She noticed that each was wearing a hip holster containing a revolver. Jesus, she thought, at home the cops are shooting at us and over here they're leading our parade. She went back into the room and took her place in the dais lineup, which appeared at last to be in proper order.

The pipes blared, the television lights glared and the crowd roared as dignitaries filed into the packed ballroom. As Bernadette worked her way to the top dais and looked at the people standing everywhere, she thought that she could never have imagined such a mass of humanity.

The anthems were sung, first the Irish and then the American. The Fenian priest said grace, concluding with, "We ask you, O Lord, to protect and guide those brave patriots who are fighting to free their native land—the men and women of the Irish Republican Army. We ask this through Christ our Lord, Amen."

Michael was the master of ceremonies. He welcomed everyone and thanked them all for being there. When he introduced each of the people on the dais, Bernadette received the loudest and most prolonged ovation. Michael told the crowd Bernadette would speak after dinner.

Bernadette read through her index cards a number of times. She barely picked at the dinner of roast beef, potatoes and string beans. To make sure she'd be thinking clearly during the speech, she substituted Coca-Cola for white wine. She was dimly aware of the many eyes in the room focused on her. She found it oddly amusing that the dance floor was filled with people dancing cheerily to the saddest of Ireland's patriotic songs, such as "Take Me Home to Mayo," about an IRA hunger striker's dying wish that his body be returned to Mayo for burial. Leave it to the Yanks, she thought.

After the tables were cleared, Michael, seated just to the left of the lectern, leaned over and asked Bernadette if she was ready. She nodded.

His introduction was warm and forceful, and Bernadette's face glowed in appreciation as she came to the lectern and arranged her index cards in front of her. The crowd fell silent.

"When I was asked by Families for Legal Justice to come to the United States and speak on behalf of the relatives of republican political prisoners in the six counties, I'd no idea how strongly you support the republican movement. I'd no idea how strongly you oppose British rule in Ireland and how strongly you support a free and united Ireland. In the few days I've been in America, so many people have opened their hearts to me, and for that and for so much more I'll be eternally grateful. I speak to you tonight not in any political or official capacity but as a wife and as a mother. I speak to you as a woman who was born in Ireland and has lived in Ireland for every day of her life but has never been allowed to be Irish in Ireland.

"As a child, I saw my father and my mother and other members of my family treated like third-class citizens, being denied the right to hold a job or to vote. I saw my parents struggle to raise a family in a flat which often had no heat or hot water and feed us from the little money we got from the dole.

"When I was a teenage girl, I saw the people in my community peacefully demonstrate and ask for their human rights. And I saw the B Specials and the RUC and the British Army shoot them down in the streets. I saw brave men such as my own brother fight and die to protect the people of their communities. I saw my husband dragged from our house in the middle of the night to be tortured at Castlereagh. I saw my husband interned in prison camps and on prison ships, and I had to explain to my wee children why their daddy would not be coming home for a long time.

"I saw my neighbor's young daughter bleed to death in the street after a British soldier blew off the top of her head with a plastic bullet. And I saw the soldiers laugh at that wee girl as she lay dying in her mother's arms.

"As we're sitting here this evening, homes are being raided throughout the north of Ireland and men and women are being brutally interrogated at Castlereagh. As you and your families go about your daily lives, republican prisoners of war are being degraded in Long Kesh and our women are being strip-searched in Armagh.

"I've three children and not one of them has ever known

even one day of peace, not one day when there were not British troops patrolling our streets and helicopters flying overhead.

"And now my husband is once more in jail. No, it's not internment this time, but it's something even worse. He's in jail on the word of a supergrass, a paid perjurer. My husband is charged with a murder he didn't commit, and the only evidence against him is the uncorroborated, perjured testimony of an admitted liar and criminal. Based on that perjurer's testimony alone, my husband could very well spend the rest of his life in jail.

"What I've described to you tonight is not unique to me. Many families have suffered far worse than mine, and many women have been forced to endure far more than I have. What I've described to you is the life of a Catholic in the occupied six counties. It's a life of suffering, of oppression and injustice.

"No British tactic is more cruel than the supergrass system. Hundreds of innocent men and women are being victimized and their families made to suffer because of this cruel and monstrous system. We're turning to America for help because there's nowhere to turn in our own country. We've learned over the years that no one has the power that Americans have to influence world opinion.

"So tonight, I ask you to use that power to help the people of Ireland. Use that power to expose the corrupt supergrass system, which the British have so cruelly inflicted upon us. Use that power so that our people will receive at least a semblance of justice in their native land. And while you are doing your part, I want you to know that we'll be doing ours as well. The men and women of the republican movement are prepared to fight on until every last British soldier is driven from Irish soil."

The crowd, which had been as hushed as if it were in a cathedral, erupted in clamorous applause.

"We've no illusions about this fight. We know it will be long and we know it will be difficult. And we know that the day will indeed come when Ireland is united and free and a nation once again. *Tiocfaidh ár lá*! Our day will come!"

The crowd rose as one and deafening applause resounded throughout the room. At Michael's urging, Bernadette stayed at the lectern and waved her thanks to the audience, who continued to stand and cheer. Then, as she glanced at the lectern, she realized she hadn't looked at the index cards even once during her speech.

When the ovation finally subsided, Michael congratulated Bernadette and asked her if she'd go to the end of the dais, where a photographer from the *Irish Echo* waited to take her picture with several local politicians. She readily agreed and worked her way along the top level, receiving congratulations and handshakes all the while. Michael returned to the microphone to introduce late-arriving dignitaries and announce upcoming events.

The photographer helped Bernadette down from the dais and introduced her to Congressman Mario Biaggi and City Councilman John Breheny. They congratulated her on the speech. "Brilliant," said Biaggi. "Very moving," said Breheny.

The photo would be the traditional show of solidarity. Bernadette in the center, Biaggi on the left, Breheny on the right. Their hands joined together. The photographer took four shots, then asked for one more and thanked them very much.

"It was a pleasure to meet you," said Breheny. "Good luck to you and to your husband," said Biaggi as he touched her right elbow with his left hand. She smiled her thanks.

Bernadette was moving back toward the dais when, over the din of the crowd, she heard a voice ask, "How are you keeping, Bernadette?"

She turned and a tremor went through her.

He still had that ironic smile.

"Not bad, Dessie," she heard herself say. "Not bad at all. And yourself?"

CHAPTER NINE

Dessie Maguire was a part of Bernadette's life known only to themselves. It had been years ago. Bernadette just seventeen, and Dessie barely twenty. It had lasted only four months, but the memory remained.

She'd first met him when she was about sixteen. Dessie and her brother Rory played on the same hurling team and knocked about on the Falls Road together. Dessie also belonged to the local boxing club. He had an easy disposition and was always well-liked. At the same time, he was different from the others. It seemed as if there was nothing he didn't read. His interests were wide-ranging: religion, politics, philosophy, art, sports. He never made any effort to display his knowledge, but when asked, he would express a strong opinion, no matter what the subject, and would state his case well.

At first, Bernadette had paid no particular attention to Dessie and made no real effort to get to know him. She found him pleasant enough, but Dessie was in her brother's sphere, and besides, she had her own friends.

When their serious involvement did come about, it was almost by chance. Bernadette was at a local dance, which was what most seventeen-year-old Belfast girls did on Friday nights. Dessie happened to be there as well and they started to talk. He walked her home and asked if he could see her again. "Of course," she said. And he smiled a crooked but warm smile.

Soon he became her whole life. Not just dances, but the cinema and, more important, long walks. Almost every night they'd meet and walk, usually along the Falls, and they'd talk. Dessie would tell her about growing up in Clonard, where he had lived until his family moved to Ballymurphy when he was thirteen. He'd talk movingly of the poverty and the unemployment that were all around them and how Northern Ireland would have to change, and change soon, or there'd be a revolution. And God only knew what that would bring with it. If there was a God, that is.

But he spoke even more movingly of how beautiful Bernadette was and how intelligent she was. "It's just a shame you don't read more," he'd say. "You sound just like my brother," she'd answer.

And they'd laugh. He'd put his arms around her and kiss her. And they'd laugh some more in mock fear that some moral guardian had been peeking out the window and would report them to their pastor.

Then there was the afternoon they went to his mate's flat on the lower Falls. His mate was on holiday in America and gave Dessie the use of it.

Bernadette had never been a religious zealot and didn't believe everything the priests shouted from the pulpits or the nuns had lectured the girls about in the classroom. But she did consider herself to be a good Catholic, and she had never even contemplated having sex before marriage. Nor was it something that any of her friends ever discussed. As far as Bernadette was concerned, sex was to be left until after you were married, and it probably wouldn't be pleasurable.

That all changed the afternoon and evening they spent alone in the flat and Dessie brought her to womanhood. She had felt no shame or guilt and enjoyed pleasures she'd never dreamed possible. It went on for months. In bed with Dessie, everything was beautiful and natural. He was thoughtful and gentle with her, yet strong as well. She was responsive to his every touch and move and she felt entirely uninhibited with him. Nothing they did together could ever be wrong.

But she soon noticed that the more intense her physical pleasure became, the more a feeling of submission and dependence came over her and the stronger Dessie seemed to become. Later, after they married, she and Dermot would have a satisfying and gratifying sexual relationship. She'd feel the same intensity, the same responsiveness and lack of inhibition. But she'd never feel submissive or dependent, and she never knew why.

The affair ended when the civil rights movement was under way and Dessie went headlong into it. Writing pamphlets and newspaper columns. Giving speeches. Organizing demonstrations and marches.

Bernadette had increasingly resisted Dessie's growing involvement in the civil rights movement. Later, she'd realize how immature she'd been, but at the time she was forced to share her lover with a cause that made little sense to her, that could lead to trouble and sorrow for everyone involved.

When she gave him her ultimatum, he said no. This was Ireland's moment, he said. He loved Bernadette. He loved her deeply. But this was their opportunity to break free of the poverty and oppression that would rack their lives and their children's lives.

"Your movement is a dream," she said. "A dream you'll never reach. Can't you see that? Either you leave the movement or I'll have to leave you." She looked up at him, hoping. "I'm sorry it has to be this way," he said, "but you leave me no choice." He kissed her good-bye.

She'd see him occasionally over the next several years. Their conversations would be fleeting but friendly, with never a mention of what had gone on between them. He'd ask how Dermot and Brendan and then Siobhan were keeping, and then he'd smile and tell her she was as beautiful as ever.

She had never asked, but she'd sensed from Rory that Dessie had joined the IRA after the loyalists, the cops and the "B" Specials began their attacks on civil rights demonstrators.

About two years after Rory was killed, Dessie left Belfast. Bernadette never knew why, and there was no one she could ask. She never told Dermot she'd even known him. Dessie's parents had died and she didn't know his brothers and sisters well enough to ask them. All Bernadette did learn was that he was alive and that, whatever the circumstances of his departure, he'd left with IRA approval.

She'd thought of him often over the years. About their four months together. Where he might be. And what might have been.

Now he'd returned. And with eleven hundred people in the room, she was alone with him again.

"Dessie, I'd no idea you were here," she said in disbelief. "Here in New York. No idea at all."

"Not many people do, Bernadette. And after all these years, I don't think many people care where I am." The calm, strong voice. The smile, the casual shrug. They were all there, just as she'd remembered them.

"But when I heard you'd be over," he continued, "I had to see you. I had to say hello."

His blue eyes were just as penetrating, she thought. His sandy hair was barely speckled with gray.

"Mother of God, Dessie. I'm delighted you did. You know I am. I just can't think straight. I'm in shock. There's so much I want to ask you, so much to talk over."

"Well, there's no way we'll be able to do much talking tonight. You're a celebrity and you're in demand. They love you. Will you have any free time at all while you're in New York?"

"Yes, tomorrow afternoon I'm to give a speech outside the Brit consulate and then go to a pub called the Last Post, I think."

"Aye, the Last Post. It's over on Second Avenue. Not a bad place at all. Did they tell you when you can expect to be finished?"

"Aye, they said about four. The demonstration is to start at noon and we're to be at the pub at two o'clock."

"Well, nothing they ever do ever starts on time. It's almost as bad as back home for being late. But you should be able to be away by half four, anyway."

"Ah, I'm sure I will, Dessie."

"Bernadette, to make this easy for you, I'll be waiting in front of St. Patrick's Cathedral. That's on Fifth Avenue. You just walk five blocks directly over from Second Avenue. And if you should get lost, ask anyone and they will give you directions, so they will. I'll be there from four o'clock, but don't be hurrying yourself. Whenever you get there, you get there. And then we can get a meal for ourselves and talk over where we've been."

"Sounds good to me," she said with a smile, and saw Michael coming toward her. She had to go back to work.

The sky was clear and bright the next day. A warm breeze wrapped itself around Bernadette as she walked with Michael along 49th

Street toward Third Avenue. In the distance she could hear a woman's voice, chanting through a loudspeaker in a powerful Irish accent, "Who are the only terrorists in the north of Ireland?"

They turned the corner onto Third Avenue and saw hundreds of demonstrators, who had gathered at high noon on a Saturday outside the British consulate at 52nd Street and Third. People filled the avenue from 52nd Street down to 51st Street, carrying placards and banners and marching along the sidewalk and into the street behind the barricades set up by the police, who were out in full force.

"The British!" Bernadette heard hundreds of voices responding in unison, almost as if it were a Gregorian chant.

"Who murders the Irish people in the north of Ireland?"

"The British!" they shouted again, over the din of bagpipes being tuned.

"Brits out!" a woman's voice boomed through the sound system.

"Peace in," they chanted back.

The bagpipes were now tuned and the Armagh Pipe Band, ten strong and in full regalia, stepped in to lead the procession, intoning the same gripping ballads Bernadette had heard so often on the Falls.

As she crossed 51st Street, the demonstrators greeted her with cheers and shouts of recognition. "Give 'em hell, Bernadette," shouted a genial, burly, middle-aged man. "You were great on television last night," yelled a well-dressed woman in her sixties.

Bernadette smiled at the crowd as Michael guided her along the street. They edged along the outside of the barricades toward a flatbed truck near 52nd Street, where the speeches would be made. Two lanes on the east side of Third Avenue had been blocked off for the demonstration, and trucks and cabs and an assortment of other vehicles were whizzing perilously close to them as they worked their way up the avenue.

"I'm sorry, sir, but you'll have to get behind the barricade," said a police officer to Michael.

"Officer, this is Bernadette Hanlon. She's the main speaker today and I'm taking her to the platform."

"Okay, but watch yourself. These cab drivers don't care who you are." The cop smiled.

"Jesus, Michael," said Bernadette, "if that'd been on the Falls, I would've gotten a baton across my head, so I would."

The crowd was still arriving in droves, and Michael told her it'd be another forty-five minutes before the speeches would begin, because that was when most of the television stations said they could be there.

The wait was no bother at all to Bernadette. She stood on the sidewalk near the truck and embraced the moment as she felt it embracing her—the beauty of the fall day, the spirited chanting of the crowd, the blaring of the bagpipes cascading against the mountainlike walls of glass and concrete that lined Third Avenue. She smiled and enjoyed the breeze against her face and neck.

As the demonstrators filed past her, they reached out to shake her hand and wish her well. Many had been at the dinner last night. Others had seen her on television or heard her on the radio. God love them all, she thought. God love them all.

Michael was delighted with the media coverage Bernadette was getting. He told her that just about every radio and television station had not only covered her last night but had treated her fairly. And everyone was telling her how beautiful she looked on television and how well she was coming across.

After being introduced to several city councilmen and rally organizers, she happily gave interviews to the radio and television reporters who were on tight schedules and couldn't wait for the speeches. The questions were more of the same.

"The police estimate the crowd will be more than two thousand. Are you surprised by such a large turnout?"

"Not surprised. But very pleased. Very much so."

"Have you spoken to your children since you've been here?"

"Yes, I rang them this morning. They're just fine."

"What's your message to the American people?"

"The Irish people want what the American people already have. We want justice and the right to self-determination. We want the right to run our own country. To be Irish in Ireland."

At Michael's signal, she climbed up a stepladder with the other speakers onto the flatbed truck, careful not to catch her black high-heeled shoes. She stood quietly while a labor leader and a state assemblyman spoke briefly. Then Michael introduced her.

"Today we're gathered outside the British Consulate, 845 Third Avenue—the very symbol of British power and influence in our country. The very symbol of a cruel and willful government that spends millions of dollars to keep the American people from learning the truth about British rule in Ireland. But with all that money and all their propaganda, the Brits cannot defeat the truth, because brave people such as Bernadette Hanlon have the courage to come to America and tell the American people the truth about British tyranny in Ireland."

The demonstrators gave him a shout of approval, and Michael went on. "Those of you who attended our dinner last evening or heard Bernadette on radio or saw her on television know she has a message that is too powerful for the Brits. It is a message of freedom, a message of justice, a message of courage and determination. Ladies and gentlemen, Bernadette Hanlon!"

As she took the microphone from Michael, Bernadette could feel her hair waving in the breeze, which, stronger now, surged up the avenue. She buttoned her pearl-colored raincoat, covering her black skirt, white blouse and gray cardigan. The microphones were in place and the television camera crews were positioned. When the roaring ovation was finally over, she began to speak.

"I've only been in your country a few days, and I certainly don't pretend to be an expert on everything that goes on in America. But there's one thing I definitely can say: The New York City Police Department are not the Royal Ulster Constabulary."

As the crowd cheered and laughed its approval, several of the cops could be seen smiling self-conscious smiles of embarrassment and appreciation.

"One other difference I've noticed," she went on, "is that in Belfast, the British soldiers patrol the streets and arrogantly show off power and might. But here in New York, the British diplomats hide in their offices high up in this tall building. You almost wouldn't even know they were here. But they are here, spewing out lies and propaganda."

Another resounding cheer went up.

"As I stand before you today, I wish to God my husband Dermot could see all you people, all these wonderful buildings and yes"—she smiled—"even to see all these trucks and cars and taxicabs, which I'm afraid are going to kill me before this day is over."

Laughter rippled through the crowd, who had relaxed and were listening to every word she said.

"It's the Brits in this building, right next to us, who don't want the American people to know what's happening to my husband or to the other political prisoners. The Brits can spend all their millions of pounds and spread all their propaganda, but so long as thousands of good Americans such as yourselves are willing to come here today and are willing to expose them as the murderers they are, the Brits will never win!"

She paused while cheers echoed up the avenue.

"I don't know which floor the Brits have their offices on in this building, but I know they're up there. And I know they're looking at us, and listening to us, and photographing us and recording us. And I know it's driving them absolutely mad that there is absolutely nothing they can do to stop this demonstration. If it were Belfast or Derry, they could send in their soldiers and the RUC to beat us down and drive us away. They could have helicopters fly low to terrify the crowd. Or they could fire plastic bullets!

"We're in a war. And that war is fought on many fronts. It's fought with the armalite, it's fought with the ballot paper, and it's fought on the battleground of public opinion. You've stood by us on each of those fronts, and I know you'll continue to do so until our battle is won! Thank you very much."

As the crowd erupted into loud applause, Bernadette grabbed Michael's hand and stepped down the ladder into the street and a sea of well-wishers. Out of the corner of her eye, she could see the television cameras were getting it all.

Michael got her over to the Last Post at about two-fifteen. The sturdy, dark wood pub was already filled to capacity. He told her that the ten-dollar admission charge went directly to NIRAA and the bar owner kept the proceeds from the drinks. NIRAA would also be raffling a harp and a wallet handcrafted by republican prisoners in Long Kesh. He thought NIRAA would clear about five thousand dollars from the afternoon. "It'll keep us in business awhile longer," he smiled.

Bernadette worked her way through the crowd, trying to shake as many hands and meet as many people as possible. My God, she thought, if they're taking the time to be here and pay their money, the least I can do is say hello to them.

The noise of the crowd and the blare of the band playing rebel music made saying hello a little more difficult than she'd anticipated, but she persevered, drinking only a coke along the way.

After greeting just about everyone, Bernadette told Michael she'd have to leave to take care of private business. He merely nodded and asked her to say a few words to the crowd. He introduced her.

Speaking from the lead singer's microphone on the stage at the rear of the pub, she thanked them all and wished them all the best. By three-forty-five she was walking out of the dark, crowded pub into the afternoon, which had grown chilly.

Bernadette had no trouble finding her way as she walked westward along 50th Street and then turned right onto Fifth Avenue. Dessie was waiting on the front steps of the cathedral.

"By Jesus, you've become a real Yank, so you have. You're two minutes early," he said with a smile as he kissed her on the cheek.

"Ach, no problem. I surprised myself by getting over here on my own and without getting lost. Have you been waiting long?"

"No, not too long at all. I got here about half three."

"Jesus, Dessie, there's a bit of chill in the air. Were you cold at all?"

"No. Besides, I was in the church for part of the time."

terrible
Beauty

161

"Well, by God, that's a miracle if I ever heard one."

"Not as much of a miracle as it used to be," he said. "But we've a lot to talk over besides my religious habits. So, tell me now, do you want to eat in a restaurant, or would you want to go to my apartment and have me be the chef?"

"Mother of God, Dessie, what will it be next? First I find out you're going to church and now I find out you've learned to cook! You who could never even boil water back in Belfast. This is an opportunity I'm not letting go by. Is your flat far from here?"

"It's in Sunnyside, which is over in Queens. We can walk down to Grand Central Station in about ten minutes, get on the subway and be in Sunnyside in another fifteen minutes."

"Brilliant, Dessie. I just love walking on a day like this. It's clear. It's sunny. And there's no Brits to be seen anywhere!" she said, laughing as she pulled him by the arm from the church steps and they began walking down Fifth Avenue.

They caught up with each other's news on the way to Grand Central. She asked him how well he'd adjusted to America and, almost casually, how long he'd been here anyway.

"It isn't home," he told her, "but I've been here almost eight years now and I'm pretty much adjusted to it." Then he changed the subject and asked her about her family.

"Ah, sure, Dermot's doing fine, so he is. He knows what might be ahead of him. But he's dead on. Brendan—I worry about him. He's at that dangerous age. Siobhan is quiet and keeps a lot inside. And Maura. Ah, God love her. She's a beautiful child, so she is."

They turned east on 42nd Street and reached Grand Central Station.

"My God, Dessie, that's a beautiful building," she said upon entering the building. Bernadette was struck by the enormous height of the 150-foot ceiling and the light streaming through grand, arched windows onto the concourse below.

After walking down the long staircase to the concourse, they turned right and followed the signs to the subway. They went down still more stairs and came upon the fare booth and turnstiles. Dessie took two tokens from his pocket, and he and Bernadette each went through the turnstile and down another staircase to a platform, where people were waiting on either side of the tracks.

"Mother of God, Dessie, I feel as if we've gone down into the bowels of hell," she exclaimed.

"And we're not there yet," he laughed. He led her down yet another staircase and then along a winding, descending ramp, which took them to still another staircase.

"This will finally be it," he said as they descended the stairs and reached the platform just as a steel-gray train with the number "7" displayed on the front car screeched into the station and stopped. The doors opened, and they entered a car and took two seats next to a window. The train sped on, and Dessie explained to her over the roar that, if this'd been a weekday rush hour, there'd barely be room to move or even breathe—either on the platform or in the train. Of course, Bernadette had been on trains before. But only on brief trips in the North. There was none of the overwhelming noise of the subway or the impersonal blackness of deep tunnels.

After two stops, the train emerged from the tunnel, and as Bernadette looked out the window behind her, she could see they were going up a steady incline into the gathering grayness of late afternoon.

"I was in Woodside the other night. Thursday, it was. I'm losing all track of time, so I am. Is Woodside near you at all?"

"It is indeed. In fact, it's right next to Sunnyside."

Now that the train was out of the tunnel, the roar had diminished and it was much easier for them to hear each other.

"From what I've been told," Dessie went on, "Sunnyside and Woodside were both very much Irish-American neighborhoods until about twenty-five or thirty years ago, when a lot of the Irish started moving out to the suburbs to get away from the city."

"How is it now?"

"For the past few years, there's been a big turnabout and neighborhoods like these are in demand."

"Why so?"

"It's all these young and educated ambitious people—and, Jesus, there's a fierce lot of them. They work in Manhattan and they're on their way up. But they can't afford to live there and don't want to live far out in the suburbs. So places like Sunnyside and Woodside, being as close to Manhattan as they are, are ideal for them. The irony is that at the same time all these well-dressed young executives are moving in, thousands of immigrants are moving in as well. Bernadette, you wouldn't believe how many are over from Ireland—and staying here illegally. And most of them're living either up in the Bronx or out in Sunnyside and Woodside."

"Why did they choose those places?"

"Either they had relatives still living there, or they knew there's always been a hard core of Irish in those neighborhoods and they decided they were the best places to take their chances. Here's our stop: 'Bliss Street–46th Street.'" The train lurched and came to a stop. They stepped from the train onto the platform. Walking down the stairs to the sidewalk below, Bernadette and Dessie walked under the massive concrete el they'd just come down from, then waited for the light to change at the corner of 46th Street so they could safely cross Queens Boulevard.

"Do you see that bank over there?" asked Dessie, pointing to the Manufacturers Hanover building a block away. "That was the last bank Willie Sutton robbed before he got caught. Sutton was the most famous of bank robbers in the forties and fifties."

"Sutton!" She smiled. "By God, Dessie, you can always count on the Irish to make their mark!"

"One way or the other." He laughed, took her arm and led her across the street. On the other side, they turned left.

His apartment house was almost four blocks away, a sturdy, six-story structure on 44th Street between Skillman and 43rd. As Dessie maneuvered his key in the lock on a door on the second floor, she saw the name "Walsh" under the doorbell. He led her into the flat, which was comfortable and roomy. Kitchen, living room, bedroom, bathroom. And it was certainly far tidier than she'd expected. She wasn't surprised when she saw that the shelves lining the living room walls were tightly packed with books and magazines.

Dessie took her coat and hung it along with his in the closet in the small hall. She sat down on the couch in the living room and Dessie offered her a whiskey. She said a white wine would do her better right now. He brought her a glass of wine and started manipulating the VCR.

"When I came home from the dinner last night," he said, "I taped you on the one o'clock local news on Channel 4. You came across very well. Why don't you take a look at it while I prepare the feast in the kitchen?"

"Am I dressed well enough for such a dinner?" she laughed.

"You don't have to be too well dressed for what I'm

preparing. Burgers, potatoes and turnips." The VCR lights came on. "The tape is ready. Do you want to see it?"

"Aye, I must admit that I do. I know I should be more modest than that, but I'm curious. The Tierneys are having someone tape everything I do while I'm here, and they'll put it together on one video and have it converted so I can show it back home. But I'm anxious to see your video now." He handed her the remote and went into the kitchen.

Bernadette watched the video intently and then replayed it.

"Well, what did you think of yourself?" he asked later, coming in from the kitchen.

"They gave very good coverage. They did use that BBC footage from the Markets, with the dead civilians and all, but sure, they had to do that. And besides, they showed my answers to the attack. But what I'm most pleased about is how much they had of my speech where I criticized the supergrasses. Also, I thought the reporter was very fair—even a bit supportive."

"The average person watching the news has no way of understanding the details of the north. But they do go away with impressions. And the impression you gave was a good one."

"Ah, for goodness sake, Dessie."

"I'm not slagging you, Bernadette. You were brilliant."

"Thank you. Thank you very much," she said in a soft, subdued voice.

Dinner was ready shortly before six o'clock, and Dessie brought the television set out into the kitchen and plugged it into the socket over the sink so they could watch the evening news as they ate. "It'll help take your mind off the food," he said.

By switching the channels back and forth, they saw the three-minute segment on Channel 7 Eyewitness News at six-o-five and then caught the final minute of Channel 4's coverage. It was all there—the demonstrators and the bagpipes and Bernadette saying "The Brits will never win." Channel 7 referred to her as "Bernadette Hanlon from besieged Belfast," while Channel 4 called her "the wife of an Irish political prisoner."

"That was pure magic, Bernadette," said Dessie when he turned off the set. "What you're doing is humanizing the Ra. People watching you on these shows will be saying that if the IRA has the support of people like you, how can they be psychopaths and gangsters?"

"I hope you're right. I really do. But Jesus, I do know you've learned how to cook. This is a delicious meal, so it is."

After dinner they went back to the living room and Bernadette sat on the couch. "That whiskey would taste great now, Dessie."

"It would indeed." He smiled and poured each of them a Powers, then sat down in an armchair at the side of the couch. They sipped the whiskey and looked at each other. Bernadette lit a cigarette and Dessie handed her an ashtray.

"It's been so long, Bernadette, and so much has happened."

"It has indeed. You don't seem to have changed very much at all."

"Well, one thing has changed. For the past eight years I've been 'Tommy Walsh.' Tommy Walsh from Donegal."

Bernadette looked at her drink for a long moment. "Dessie, all I know is that about eight years ago you left Belfast. I never knew why you left, where you went or what you were doing. God forgive me for saying it, but there were times when I wondered if you were alive."

"Jesus, there were times when I asked myself if I was fucking alive," he said with a grim smile. He took a deep breath and went on. "I'm sure you remember Danny Donovan and Mick Hennessy."

"I do indeed. They were killed in a premature explosion near the Dunmurry barracks."

"Yes, Danny and Mick were killed and so was the wee four-year-old girl, Kathleen O'Rourke. That happened eight years ago."

"Mother of God, Dessie, but—"

"Yes, I was there. Not close enough to be hurt by the explosion. But I was the fucking lookout. And I saw it all happen in front of me. I escaped and the Brits and peelers never knew there was a third man on the operation."

"But surely it wasn't your fault."

"No, Bernadette, I'm not talking about fault or fucking guilt. And, dear God, it wasn't the first time people were killed in front of me—Brits and Ra. Jesus, no one was closer to me than your Rory."

"But to see Danny and Mick blown to fucking pieces and the wee child blown up into the air and seeing her mother running toward what was left of her body, screaming all the while, was more than I could take. Maybe it'd been building up over the years and I just hadn't been aware of it, but after that fucking bomb went off, I thought my fucking brain was going to explode as well."

Dessie took another sip of Powers. Bernadette waited for him to continue. She could think of nothing to say that would mean anything.

"I waited a few days and then went to Brigade," Dessie went on. "I told them I couldn't be of any help. That I had to get away from Belfast. I had to get away from Ireland. I had to get away from the fucking war."

"All I ever did hear after you left was that you were still on good terms with the Ra."

"Oh, aye. They were dead on. When they realized how serious I was, they did everything they possibly could to help me—with a new identification and a new country. I would be Tommy Walsh and I'd be on my way to New York. And they gave me all the papers I needed—passport, visa, birth certificate, driver's license. I don't know how they fucking got them, but they did. They also gave me a contact here in New York, and the week I arrived I had a green card, social security number, this apartment and a job in construction."

"Did you know anyone here at all?"

"No one, except for the contact. And I've never seen or heard from him since I was settled in." He paused and leaned forward. "Bernadette, during the past eight years I've found out what it means to live in the fucking shadows. Back and forth to work, talking to as few people as possible. Afraid to confide in anyone. Drinking in fucking pubs by myself, looking over my shoulder for the FBI or Immigration. Hoping I don't meet anyone from Donegal who'll ask me what town I'm from, how the folks are doing and all that *craic*."

"Do you talk to your family in Belfast often?"

"Aye, we talk, but not often. I'll ring them every few months. We set the exact date and time, and then I call from a public telephone here to a public telephone at home. And even then we speak in as much of a code as we can. But remember this is something I chose for myself. No one forced me to leave Belfast."

"Dessie, the war caused you to leave Belfast. That fucking war, those fucking Brits, they're destroying all our fucking lives," said Bernadette, crushing her cigarette into the ashtray until it fell apart.

"You can never get away from the war," he said. "Whenever I'd read something about home in a newspaper here or see something on television, the feeling would come over me just the same as if I were back there. Except there was no way to get rid of my anger or frustration. I suppose what I'm saying is, that I couldn't fucking go out that night and stiff a fucking Brit," he said with a grim smile.

"Jesus, I wish we could fucking stiff every one of those bastards," said Bernadette. She realized she and Dessie'd been talking for some time and had barely drunk any of the whiskey in their glasses.

"Bernadette, the most difficult time for me was the hunger strikes. Jesus, I knew all the lads from Belfast who died—Bobby, Joe, Big Doc—and here I was fucking helpless in New York. All the time I'd been here, I'd never even been to any NIRAA dinner for fear of being recognized or noticed. But during the hunger strikes I found myself going to the demonstrations at the consulate where you were today. Oh, I wasn't part of the demonstrations, but I'd stand and watch from a safe distance across the street or down the block. It made me feel as if I were at least a small part of what was happening. It was also during the hunger strikes that I started writing again—short stories and poems about home. I have got quite a few of them published in different Irish arts and cultural magazines. I've even made a few bob—under pseudonyms, of course."

"Jesus, I still can't think of the hunger-strikers without feeling sick inside," said Bernadette.

"There's one other thing I haven't told you about myself during the hunger strikes," Dessie said with a shy smile as Bernadette looked at him expectantly. "I went to church again."

"You're joking. But Jesus, you did say you were in the cathedral today."

"Don't worry. I'm not a Holy Roller or a religious fanatic, and I'm still not sure how much of it I believe. Maybe it's just that I'm so alone that I find a comfort in it. Anyway, you know I'd stopped going to church back in '69 or '70, right after the Troubles began. There wasn't a Catholic priest who was worth a damn in Belfast except for Dessie Wilson and Tom Slattery. I never thought I'd even go near a Catholic church again. But the Saturday after Frankie Hughes died in May of '81, I was up at the consulate watching the demonstration, and after a while, I started walking downtown. There's a church on 31st Street called St. Francis where Franciscan monks hear confessions all the time. I decided to go in."

Bernadette lit another cigarette without taking her eyes off Dessie, who was still leaning forward, his body tense.

"I sat in that church for almost an hour. Jesus, you wouldn't believe the characters who were there. Bums, laborers, businessmen, good-looking girls, old ladies. But I liked that. A church should be open to everyone. I'm sure you can guess what happened next. I was in line and then I was in the box, kneeling in the dark. Jesus, so help me, when the priest slid that window open, I thought my heart was going to jump through my chest. But then I just started to talk. I told him about the Ra. About the operations I'd planned and gone out on myself. About the dead Brits and peelers and about Dunmurry and Danny and Mick and the wee girl. I told it all."

Bernadette sat silently, looking at him. She could think of nothing to say.

"When I was finished, I just stopped and waited. And for what seemed like the longest time, the priest said nothing. I thought maybe some new prayer had come along which I was supposed to say but didn't know about. But then, I could hear him talking very slowly and calmly: 'My son, you've been through a great deal of suffering and torment in your life. You've endured a great deal and you've been forced to make some difficult decisions. I've never been in your position and I can't judge whether your decisions were right or wrong. But I think I can judge whether you made those decisions in accordance with the dictates of your conscience and whether you did what you thought was morally right. After listening to you, I think you followed your conscience and thought you were doing the right thing. For your penance say five 'Hail Marys' and five 'Our Fathers' and ask God to give you the peace of mind to which you're entitled. Go in peace.'

"Bernadette, I was almost dumbstruck. I remember when I came out looking for the name over the confessional box and saw it wasn't even Irish. It was a French name—Cartier. Now I know I could just as easily have gotten some bastard of a priest that day who'd have driven me from the Church altogether. But I didn't. And that priest, at that time of my life, put the Church in a different perspective for me. It gave me some consolation and, yes, some of the peace of mind the priest told me to pray for.

"Anyway, on a Sunday, I'll walk down the corner to Queen of Angels Church for Mass. And sometimes when I'll be walking along by myself, I'll just drop into the church and sit in the back for a few wee minutes. I suppose you never thought you would hear me talking like this, now, did you?"

"No, I didn't. But listening to you, I can understand the way you feel. After all, if the priests we knew at home weren't such bastards, a lot more of us'd be at church. But, best of all, you seem to've found some peace."

"I don't know, Bernadette. Someday, maybe, all this will make more sense to us."

"Maybe it will, maybe it will. But maybe it fucking won't

either," she laughed as she sipped the whiskey from her glass.

"There's a pub a few streets over, just off Greenpoint Avenue. It's usually pretty quiet, even on a Saturday night. Why don't we go over there for a while?"

"That's fine with me."

"And you don't have to worry about taking the subway back to Brooklyn. I've borrowed a car for the night, so I'll give you a lift."

"Ah, that'll be grand."

Dessie went into the bedroom. After a few moments he came out wearing a green cardigan. "Do you remember this?" He laughed, pointing toward a white-edged insignia on the left breast of the cardigan.

"'Oliver Plunkett Boxing Club,'" she read. "My God, you still have that after all these years! You used to wear it to the fights when you were boxing at the Dominick Savio Hall on the Falls."

"Jesus, you've a great memory, so you do. Let me just put the jacket on over this. It wouldn't do me any good for someone to recognize the crest and start asking questions."

They walked out the apartment door, down the stairs and onto the street. Neither said a word until they were on the sidewalk.

"What weight did you fight at in those years anyway?" she asked as they walked back up 44th Street toward Queens Boulevard.

"I was a middleweight—eleven-and-a-half stone. Happy to say, I'm still only twelve stone today."

"I don't suppose you've been able to do any boxing since you've been in New York?"

"No. Besides, I'm getting too old for that sort of thing. But I do try to run at least three times a week and I manage to work out quite a bit in different gyms."

The light turned green and they stepped off the sidewalk to cross Queens Boulevard.

"I do go to the fights when I get the chance. In fact, see that fast food burger place?" he said, pointing toward his left. "When I first came over, there was a boxing club there—Sunnyside Gardens they called it. I saw some good professional fights there before they tore it down."

Just then, there was a loud roaring noise behind them on the boulevard. They turned and saw a white vehicle with red lights flashing speed by.

"What was that?" she asked.

"An ambulance. They sound different here than they do at home. But an ambulance is an ambulance. You have lots of rows and accidents in New York on a Saturday night. Whoever he is, I hope they get the poor bastard to hospital in time."

As soon as Dessie mentioned "hospital," an image of Hamilton flashed before her, lying crumpled on the ground outside the Royal. Blood gushing from his head, with her racing off in the getaway car, leaving him to die like a wounded dog. She stiffened, stared aimlessly ahead and said nothing for several minutes. They crossed Greenpoint Avenue and turned left toward 45th Street.

"Dessie," she finally said, "the war has made us into persons we never thought we'd be, and made us do things we never thought we could do or would want to do. And I suppose we all have to live with what we've done."

Dessie said nothing. He could tell by her face that whatever Bernadette had done, she'd confront it alone. And Dessie was confident she'd prevail.

They entered the Wild Geese bar on 46th Street. It was dimly lit and about half full. Dessie led her toward a small table in the rear. He ordered a light beer, she a white wine.

"Dessie," she said, sipping her wine, "until tonight I'd no idea you were going through all this loneliness, all this isolation. I'm amazed you didn't go mad."

"I told you, I'm here by my own choice. There's a lot far worse off than me. Your Rory, the hunger-strikers, all the lads in the Kesh, the women in Armagh."

"Have you given any thought to coming home?"

"Aye, I know someday I'll have to come home. My heart and soul will always be there. But I've no idea when I'll be back. I have to be ready to go back and I want it to be on my terms. I don't want to be deported back as an illegal alien and get all the hassle from the Brits and peelers. But when I'll be ready, I just don't know. I don't know."

"Ireland needs men like you, Dessie."

"Ireland has good men and good women. A lot better than I am. But someday I'll be back."

Shortly after midnight they left the Wild Geese, walked around the corner to 47th Street and got into the car—a 1978 Ford—which Dessie's friend had left for him. Dessie drove to the Kosciousko Bridge, which would take them into Brooklyn. As they traveled across the bridge, Bernadette looked to her right toward Manhattan.

"My God, Dessie, this city is so alive and so bright."

"They say 'the city never sleeps,' and they're right."

"New York has been so exciting. And the people have been great to me. But I could never be happy away from Belfast. Even with all the troubles we have."

"Aye, I know what you mean."

They reached Bay Ridge just before one o'clock. Dessie

parked the car down the street from the Tierneys. Bernadette looked at him for a long moment and then touched his hand.

"Dessie, I know it's foolish and it gets us nowhere, but do you ever think of the wonderful lives we all could've lived if there'd been no war? Husbands and sons going to work and to school instead of to jail or to the graveyard? Being able to write books and poems instead of shooting armalites and planting bombs? Being happy for a child when it's born into the world instead of wondering if you've done it a terrible injustice?"

"Too many times. I've this thought of where you and I would be if the war hadn't driven us apart. But no matter what, I'll always be thankful for what you mean to me."

Dessie then fell silent and fixed his eyes upon her face. He gently put his arms around her and kissed her lightly on the lips. She put her hand behind his neck and he kissed her mouth.

Again she looked at him. She felt her eyes brim with tears as she kissed him on the cheek.

"You'd better be getting in before the Tierneys think you were kidnapped and call the cops," he said, forcing a smile.

"Aye, Dessie. Good-bye. And take care of yourself."

She kissed him one more time on the cheek, got out of the car and walked toward the apartment house. He waited until she was at the front door and then drove off.

She stood there and watched until she could see the car no longer. Then she bit down hard on her lip and tears flowed down her cheeks.

Sitting in the Aer Lingus terminal at Kennedy airport on Thursday evening, it was difficult for her to sort out the events of the past five days. There'd been Albany on Sunday afternoon and then

Boston, Philadelphia, Washington, D.C., and finally, last night, Suffolk County on Long Island. It was a mad scramble of meetings, press conferences, radio interviews, luncheons and dinners.

Though drained and exhausted, she was pleased she'd been able to get her message across and pleased with the warmth of the people she'd met and who'd helped her—particularly those families who opened their homes to her.

"If I'd known at the time what was ahead of me, I'd never have got off the plane last week," she said, laughing, to the Tierneys.

"But thank God you did," said Brigid. "Where's Michael? It's almost time for you to get aboard the plane."

"We should have all the newspaper clippings in the next few days, and we'll mail them on to you," said Jack. "The videotape will take longer, but as soon as it's done, we'll get it right over to you, so your children will see what a star their mother was!"

Michael came bounding up the staircase. "I'm sorry I'm late," he said.

"And I'm delighted I've the chance to say good-bye to you. You're doing a great job for us, and I'll make sure I tell them that when I get home."

"Believe me, Bernadette, it was our pleasure," said Michael. "Everyone is proud of you."

There were good-byes, embraces, promises to write and invitations to come over. Finally she was through the metal detector and on the ramp to the plane. The flight attendants gave her polite smiles and knowing looks of recognition.

The Dublin government was no doubt as unhappy as the Brits with Bernadette's American tour. Michael had told her she'd probably be under surveillance on the trip home by Aer Lingus personnel and possibly the Special Branch. Bernadette didn't give

terrible
Beauty

a damn who was looking at her or what they thought. She'd been sent to America to do a job, and she had done it.

As the jet lifted into the air, she turned and looked through the window to see New York once more. Then she leaned her back into the seat and closed her eyes. It was time to return to the brutal reality of Belfast.

PART THREE

MANY HEARTS ARE FILLED WITH ANGUISH AND WITH PAIN

Many homes are filled with sorrow and with sadness
Many hearts are filled with anguish and with pain
For Old Ireland now she hangs her head in mourning
For the men who died at Upton for Sinn Fein.

—FROM "LONELY WOODS OF UPTON,"
AN IRISH REBEL SONG

CHAPTER TEN

Belfast had changed not a bit while Bernadette was away. The gray dampness, Brits on patrol, graffiti-covered walls. It was all as it had been before she left and for too many years prior to that. Only now, she noticed it more now than she ever had.

But the warmth and caring of her family were also still there, and her homecoming was all that she could've expected it to be. Brendan, Siobhan and her mother greeted her with shouts of excitement and warm embraces. Maura smiled contentedly as Bernadette grabbed her up in her arms and squeezed her tight.

Brendan and Siobhan loved their sweatshirts—"New York Mets" for him, "I Love New York" for her—while Maura wasted no time striking up a quite involved conversation with her new Cabbage Patch doll. Bernadette's mother delighted in her new apron decorated with a large red apple and emblazoned with the initials "NY."

Eilish and Alex stopped by later, and the talking went on through the afternoon and well into the evening. They listened with rapt attention as Bernadette recounted her American experience. No detail was too small for them. They wanted to hear it all. And she told them all—except, of course, about Dessie. And she knew she never would. Not to anyone. Barely even to herself.

The next morning, Bernadette went to the Crum to see Dermot. She was thrilled to be with him again.

"Jesus, Bernadette, you look marvelous."

"Ah, you look as if you're keeping pretty well yourself."

"Everyone says you were just brilliant in America. There were some bits in the newspapers here and the news we got from the Yanks was they couldn't be happier."

"The people in America were great, so they were. They did everything they could for me."

"Could you ever fancy yourself living there?"

"Ach, no. It's too big and too fast. I'd be afraid that after I lived there for a while, I wouldn't even know myself anymore. They seem to rush about so much and worry about things we wouldn't even think of."

"Ah," smiled Dermot, "I suppose those are the problems that come with prosperity."

"Well, in that case we needn't worry about having those problems for a long time."

"Indeed not," he laughed.

"The one thing you haven't heard, which I'm just over the moon about, is that there'll be an observer coming over for your trial."

"Jesus, that's great news, so it is."

"There's a group of Irish-American lawyers who are interested in the supergrasses, and one of them will be coming over to stay at least a week."

"Brilliant, Bernadette. That's brilliant. That'll drive the Brits mad, so it will. Have you spoken to Paddy about this yet?"

"Aye, I rang him this morning. He was pleased as well and said he'll contact the head of the Lawyers Association straightaway."

"Did Paddy tell you anything else?"

"No," she said, a bit anxiously.

"He was here to see me yesterday. And I could tell he was a bit concerned by what he had to tell me."

"Jesus, is it that bad?"

"Well, it certainly isn't fucking good. But I don't know how bad it is. The Brits are going to try me and Mick together along with the Ballymurphy people."

"For Christ's sake, Dermot, there's more than thirty in the Ballymurphy case and that case has nothing to do with yours or with Mick's."

"Ah, from the Brits' view, they've everything to do with each other. Fucking McGrath is the supergrass in each of them and that's all that matters. Without McGrath there's no case against any of us. Also—this is the part that concerns me a bit—Paddy's been told that I'm the one the Brits want the most. And it'll be a lot easier for them to get me if I'm sitting in the dock with thirty people—actually thirty-four to be exact—rather than being on trial by myself. If I was alone on trial, the media would be able to focus on the evidence a lot more easily. With thirty-five of us sitting together, there'll be so many charges and Frank'll be telling so many stories about us all, that no one'll be able to understand what the fuck he's talking about and the judge'll be able to do whatever he wants to do."

"You mean whatever the *Brits* want him to do," she said.

Dermot was speaking in a voice loud enough for the warder to hear, but neither he nor Bernadette cared a damn.

"The reason the Brits are giving for this," he went on, "is that it'd be inconvenient to bring Frank back for more than one trial. They say there'll be enormous security problems protecting him for one trial, let alone two or three."

terrible
Beauty

"What a laugh," said Bernadette. "What you're charged with has nothing to do with the boys from Ballymurphy."

"What it'll be," said Dermot, "is a fucking big circus. A show trial."

"That'll have an effect on the date of the trial. What did Paddy say?"

"That's the other part of the story—the part which is not so bad. The Ballymurphy lads have already been held for almost eighteen months. So their case was due to come up next month. Now with me and Mick added to it, it's being knocked back a month. Which means that I'll be on trial at least a year earlier than I could've expected."

"Jesus, Dermot, two months! I thought we'd have more time than that to prepare."

"Calm yourself, luv. At least we'll get the trial over with. And, as for the preparation, there really isn't much more to be done. Frank's going to say I stiffed the UDR man. It's as simple as that. It'll just be his word, no corroboration. And I'm sure it'll be the same for the others as well. All the barristers can hope to do," he said, lowering his voice, "is show what a bastard McGrath is and how erratic he is."

"Well, that's the truth. He's a fucking header for sure," said Bernadette.

"That he is," said Dermot. "Paddy and Tommy Mullen are the solicitors for several Ballymurphy lads as well as for me and Mick. So they've been investigating Frank for more than a year now. And Paddy says they've found some damaging information on him."

"Does Paddy think they've found enough?"

"He thinks they've found everything that can be found, and if this were a real trial, it'd be more than enough to have the whole fucking case thrown out."

"But it won't be a real trial," said Bernadette.

"There you go," he said with a smile. "That's why we sent you to America."

"And I should've fucking stayed there and become a film star," she retorted. "But I suppose I have to save Ireland first."

"Jesus, that's very thoughtful of you indeed."

"Ah, I almost forgot to tell you about the present I got for you. A sweatshirt from the New York City Police Department and newspapers from all the cities I was in."

"For fuck's sake, a peeler's shirt?"

"Aye, with a big badge in the middle of it. The screws won't know what to say when they see you wearing that, so they won't."

"Christ, I'll enjoy wearing that. And I'll definitely want to read the papers."

"The visit's over," the warder interjected gruffly.

Dermot and Bernadette kissed one another. "I've to see Paddy in the morning," she said.

"Ah, that's sound," he replied. "Cheerio."

Bernadette met with Paddy the next day.

"I rang Tom Hurley in New York yesterday afternoon, Bernadette," said Paddy. "He seemed friendly and cooperative."

"Aye, Paddy, he was just great when I was over. Very genuine, so he was."

"He told me you were just brilliant. That the lawyers were impressed when you met with them."

"Ah, except for you and Tommy and a few others, those American lawyers know more about what's happening in the courts here than our own solicitors and barristers."

"I can believe that. Too many of our ones, once they start living on the Malone Road, they forget where they came from."

"But not you, Paddy."

"Jesus, I'm afraid of what you might do to me if I did." He laughed. "The lawyer that'll be coming over, they call him Terry Byrnes. He's from New York. He was a prosecutor for more than fifteen years and for the past ten years or so, he's been a defense lawyer. He's also been involved in Democratic politics for quite a while."

"Jesus, he appears to be very qualified."

"And Tom said he knows a lot about the north and is anxious to come over."

"When would you want him to come?"

"I expect this trial to last at least three to four months. Christ, with all those defendants and all those charges, they'll need a computer in the courtroom. Tom told me Byrnes can stay in Belfast for a full week. I think it's better he come at the very beginning of the trial when the media attention will be the greatest."

"Aye, I can understand that, but with the trial being so long, won't Byrnes be forgotten by the third month?"

"Ah, indeed he would—except I've an unexpected bit of good news for you."

"We could all use some of that, Paddy."

"There'll be a second American observer coming for the end of the trial. A congressman from New York—Michael Ashe—will be sending one of his senior staff members. Ashe is a Republican, which is good since Byrnes is a Democrat. It also helps that he's not a Catholic. Apparently, he has a good number of Irish Americans in his constituency and they've made him very knowledgeable on the Irish issue."

"Was this arranged through the Lawyers Association as well?"

"No, it was set up by an organization called 'The Committee for Irish Justice.' It's situated on Long Island, which I understand is very near to New York City."

"Aye, Paddy, I know. I was there," she said, laughing.

"Indeed"—Paddy smiled and continued—"I was talking to Liz McCloskey earlier on and asked her to make the arrangements for the observers. It's important that we have them staying in nationalist homes rather than in hotels. That way they'll get a truer understanding of what this war's about."

Liz McCloskey headed the Families for Legal Justice committee and had coordinated Bernadette's American trip. "You're dead right there," Bernadette said. "They could spend a week in the Forum and not even know there's a war going on."

"If we put them in West Belfast, they'll find out about the war soon enough. We must also be sure to have them meet as many people as possible whenever they're not in court."

"Who are you thinking of?"

"Certainly the prisoners' relatives and the solicitors. Also some men who've been in the Kesh and women who've been in Armagh."

"Then it won't just be about the supergrasses?"

"It'd be wise to make them aware of all the aspects of British justice. The strip-searching, the house raids, the plastic bullets. Which reminds me—we must have them meet Jerry O'Donnell and Mairead Brady's neighbors."

"God help her, Paddy. I'll never forget that day."

"I understand," said Paddy, "that Mrs. Brady is still not well; she cries all the time. And Colette Sweeney, one of the wee girls who was with Mairead, she's developed a nervous disorder. Her body is always shaking and she can't sleep for more than an hour at a time. And she refuses to leave the house."

"It was so desperate that day and poor Colette was in the middle of it all, so she was."

"Also, they should meet Father Slattery or Dessie Wilson."

"Have you given any thought to arranging a meeting for the observers with the orangies?"

"Yes, but that'll be a bit dicey. The problem isn't with our side. Even the hard-liners like Liz would visit with the loyalists if they had to. It would certainly be good public relations for us."

"But you think the loyalists are opposed?"

"Only some of them, but unfortunately they're very powerful. The relatives of the loyalist prisoners have shown a definite interest in meeting. But the UVF hard-liners, they can't bring themselves to even think of sitting down with Papists."

"What do you think the chances are?"

"Not too bad. The first loyalist supergrass trial starts next week."

"Joe Barker?"

"Aye, the Orange Butcher himself."

"Did it surprise you when Barker turned supergrass?"

"Not really. I never thought Barker had any political beliefs at all. He was strictly a brutal sadist. He used the UVF as an excuse to murder, so he did. And he was into extortion and robbery as well. He also raped several women from the Shankill. So when the peelers lifted Joe and showed him the evidence they had against him, he agreed straightaway to turn on his mates—or at least on some of them."

"Jesus, there won't be many at all in that trial," she said sardonically.

"No, Bernadette, there won't. Only seven. But even if it were only one, it's shocked the loyalists. Absolutely shocked them. They're now getting their first true look at what the Brits are capable of."

"And the Brits felt they had to do it?"

"To show a bit of evenhandedness. That's why they've scheduled it at this time. It won't last more than four or five weeks, so it will be over right before Dermot's trial begins. And if seven loyalists have to go to jail to make it easier for the Brits to get thirty or thirty-five of ours, the Brits feel that's a small price to pay. Very small indeed."

"You'd think this would show the orangies how expendable they are to the Brits."

"Some of them are starting to feel that way, and once the trial actually begins next week, some of the hard-liners will soften their position."

"So you think their relatives will start meeting with ours soon?"

"Yes, I do. They've already formed an organization called Loyalist Families for Fair Trials, which has had several meetings on the Shankill and has picketed the courthouse a number of times. Besides that," said Paddy with some hesitation, "there's also the possibility of meetings on another level. But we'll have to wait on that for a while to see what develops."

Bernadette very much wanted to ask Paddy just what other "level" he was referring to, but she could tell by his face that he'd said all he was going to say.

"Paddy, I know I don't have to tell you this, but I want you and Liz to know I'll be available to do whatever you want me to do for these trials. Whether it's the loyalist relatives, the American observers or anything at all."

"I never thought otherwise." Paddy gave her a warm smile.

It was late Thursday afternoon, the fourth day of the Joe Barker trial. Bernadette and Liz McCloskey walked into the lobby of the

Forum Hotel. Paddy was sitting where he said he'd be, on a couch against the wall.

"Have any of them arrived yet?" asked Liz.

"Not yet. There was a bit of a row in the court today, and they've been delayed."

"Was this the first time Barker testified?" asked Liz.

Paddy nodded. "He was to have begun this morning, but a peeler testified longer than was expected. So it was just after the court began again in the afternoon. Barker came into the dock and gave his name, when about thirty loyalist women in the gallery started shouting and throwing birdseed at Joe."

"Birdseed," laughed Bernadette. "Fair play to them. I wish we'd thought of that."

"I understand the peelers went berserk," Paddy continued, "swinging batons and dragging women out by the hair."

"Jesus, the loyalists aren't used to being treated like that at all," Liz said, smiling.

"We're still having the meeting this afternoon, though?" asked Bernadette.

"Oh, yes," said Paddy. "Several women were arrested, but the ones who were supposed to be here will come. I've the small meeting room in the rear. Why don't we go there now and wait?"

Bernadette had only been in the Forum once or twice. It was located in the heart of Belfast and was the largest hotel in the city. It was also famous and she knew a great deal about it. For one thing, it was where journalists assigned to cover the Troubles would stay—and drink. One of the complaints nationalists had was that too many of the journalists never left the hotel bar the whole time they were in Belfast.

The Forum was also acknowledged to be the most

bombed-out hotel in Europe since the end of World War II. And its name changed back and forth from "Forum" to "Europa" almost as often as it was bombed. Though the Forum's history of bombings provided the reporters a certain luster and air of bravado, it was a safe hotel. The bombings had all been commercial, and ample notice for evacuation was always given so there were no casualties. It was the ideal location for a meeting such as today's, being neutral and reasonably secure.

The meeting room was austere. The walls were painted a dull gray and the carpet displayed signs of wear. A pitcher of ice water and paper cups were in the center of the conference table. They sat down and Paddy poured some water for Bernadette and Liz. Someone knocked on the door.

Paddy went over and peered through a spy hole in the door and smiled. He unlocked the door and Bernadette recognized George Hopkins, who was standing there with a broad smile and extended hand.

"Come in, George," said Paddy, shaking his hand. "But don't be throwing any loyalist birdseed at us. Do you hear me now?"

"As usual," growled Hopkins, who had a craggy and pugnacious face, "I can hear you, but I'm taking no notice."

After he was introduced to Bernadette and Liz, he said, "Ferguson, I've three of the relatives in the lobby. Is it all right for me to bring them in?"

"Aye, George, we're looking forward to this meeting," said Paddy. Hopkins lumbered out the door.

Bernadette knew that George Hopkins was the leading UVF solicitor in Belfast and guessed he was in his early sixties. His drinking bouts were legendary in Belfast. He had been known on any number of occasions to finish a quart of Bushmills at night and then be the first to arrive at the courthouse the next morning. He was big and burly, and when in a bar would never hesitate to explode his fist in the face of anyone who would push him even a bit too far.

While George was out of the room, Paddy told Bernadette and Liz that George had a deep-rooted hatred of the Brits. "I first realized just how much he hated them during one of our late-night drinking sessions. I'd been telling George what Catholics had to endure when I was a kid in Ardoyne. The stifling poverty, the decrepit housing, the hopeless unemployment. George just sat there saying nothing."

"'Don't you understand?' I finally shouted. 'Catholics were second-class citizens. Fucking second class-citizens. And we still are!'

"'You're the one that doesn't fucking understand,' he said. 'It's the Presbyterians that are second-class citizens. Not you, you dumb bastard. You're third-class citizens. The Brits have been fucking both of us all along, while we're killing one another. You Catholics look upon everyone who's not one of yours as being Protestant. You think we're all the same. That's how fucking little you know. The Brits and their Church of Ireland—the Episcopalians, the Anglicans, whatever you want to call them—treat us like shit. They've nothing to do with us socially and they exploit us economically. Yes, the housing on the Falls and in Ardoyne was disgraceful. But I'm telling you it was only the slightest bit worse than what the Presbyterians had on the Shankill. Believe me, Paddy, we never had it better than you. You just had it worse than us.'"

Once, Paddy had asked George if he could ever see the day when loyalists and republicans would stand together against the Brits. Before answering, George had thought for a moment and then finished his glass of Bushmills. Waving his left hand toward

Paddy, he had said somberly, "I'm afraid there's not a fucking chance of that, Paddy. Maybe in 1798 with Wolfe Tone, but not today. Too much has gone by. Bad as the Brits are, they're all that my people have. If the Brits go, we'd be swallowed up in a united Ireland."

"It wouldn't have to be that way," Paddy had replied.

"You and I can't change the course of history," George had said sadly. "Maybe it's a curse on our people. This is the fucking way it was meant to be."

George returned to the room with three women. Bernadette and Liz reflexively rose from their chairs and walked around the table to greet them.

Except for her encounters with the RUC, Bernadette had never spoken to a loyalist before. Except for doctors and nurses and the RUC, she couldn't recall ever having even spoken to a Protestant—certainly not since 1968. Before she was fully aware of it, introductions were being made and hands were being shaken.

"This is Liz McCloskey and Bernadette Hanlon," she heard Paddy say.

"And this is Victoria Taylor, Elizabeth Wright and Brenda Johnson," said George in a gruff tone.

As soon as the handshakes were concluded, George said, with more than a hint of impatience, "Now that the greetings have been taken care of, perhaps we could get started."

"Ah, George," Paddy smiled, as he made sure the door was locked, "your charm is pure magic."

Bernadette and Liz flanked Paddy on one side of the table while the loyalists took the seats opposite them. Paddy poured cups of water for the newcomers.

Bernadette stared at the tabletop, glanced fleetingly at the loyalist women, then stared again at the tabletop. She could sense that Liz and the loyalist women were also uneasy.

"I understand you had quite a row at the trial today," Paddy said with a smile of support.

"The RUC are madmen," said George. "The way they reacted, you'd have thought it was petrol bombs being thrown instead of some birdseed."

Mrs. Wright, the oldest of the three woman, interjected, "Not just mad *men* but mad *women* as well."

"Ah, I've had my experiences with RUC women," said Bernadette. "I know just what you're talking about."

"How many were arrested?" asked Paddy.

"Seven," said George. "Seven housewives, who are getting their first taste of British justice."

"Did Barker begin his testimony?" asked Paddy.

"Yes, he did," answered George. "It took the RUC almost an hour to quiet the disturbance, and then Joe testified for about an hour and a half."

"He told more lies in ninety minutes," said Mrs. Johnson, "than ten people could tell in a lifetime. He said things about my husband John that were outright lies. And he said it all so calmly, in such a robotic fashion."

As Brenda Johnson spoke, she and Bernadette made eye contact. She seems genuine enough, Bernadette thought, not much different from any woman I'd meet on the Falls. Probably in her early thirties, her long black hair was stylishly combed and her makeup delicately applied. She had a tremor beneath her right eye, however, and Bernadette could see that her hands were trembling. Her husband, who had been charged with murder, was known to be a high-ranking UVF man.

"I met Joe Barker two times in my life," Mrs. Johnson continued, "and those two times couldn't have been for more than five minutes. And he was never in my house. Yet, there he was today telling about all the times he was to my house for tea, describing the wallpaper and the furniture, talking about each of the three children."

"He's learned his lines well," said Paddy.

"What disturbed me the most," said Mrs. Wright, "is that Judge Armstrong appeared to believe him."

This was the second time Mrs. Wright had spoken, and Bernadette knew straightaway she was intelligent. But there was something condescending about her, as if she'd sit with Catholics only if she had to.

Elizabeth Wright was almost sixty. Her son, Lenny, had been charged with two counts of murder. His pictures in the newspaper always showed him as unshaven and disheveled. For her part, Mrs. Wright was impeccably groomed. Her white hair was permed, and she was wearing a pearl necklace, gold earrings, an elegant watch and a stylishly tailored blue suit.

"My husband fought in the British Army in World War II," she said. "He fought to preserve the British system of government. And now the British are perverting that system to destroy my son."

"None of us is here today with any illusions," said Paddy. "We're all aware of the differences between us. But the supergrasses are causing great pain to both communities. If a person's rights are being violated, it doesn't matter whether that person is a Catholic or a Protestant. George and I have had many discussions about the supergrasses during these past few months, and we think each community can help the other."

"You can be certain, Ferguson, that we've no illusions at all," growled George. "But the cold reality is that we need each other to beat the supergrasses. Why don't we just call it a very temporary alliance of necessity?"

"George, as always, I'll defer to you and we'll call it whatever you wish," replied Paddy. "The important thing is that whatever we do together, we do effectively. Liz and Bernadette are here because Families for Legal Justice wants to find out which activities can be coordinated."

Liz spoke for the first time. "I'm the chairperson of the committee. As I'm sure you can imagine, there was considerable opposition within our community to this meeting."

Bernadette grimaced. There was no need for Liz to say that.

"But we voted and a majority authorized us to attempt to find areas of cooperation," she continued.

"You can be sure," Bernadette interjected politely but firmly, "that we'll do all we can to find those areas of cooperation. You have our word on that."

"Mrs. McCloskey," said Mrs. Taylor, her anger barely controlled, "if you think for even one moment that you're extending loyalists some sort of privilege by meeting with us, you don't know how wrong you are. There would be none of this trouble if it weren't for the Catholics. So if you're not happy to be sitting with us, you can be sure we're equally unhappy."

Before Liz could reply, Paddy touched her wrist with his hand. "I don't believe any purpose will be served if either side believes it's doing the other a favor by meeting," he said. "We're each doing ourselves a favor and that's that. We can understand the pressure you must be under, Mrs. Taylor, from people in your community. So I appreciate the leadership and courage you're showing."

Mrs. Taylor nodded and forced a tight smile.

Damn it, Bernadette thought, damn Liz for putting us on the defensive by opening her mouth like that.

Mrs. Taylor struck Bernadette as an inherently unpleasant woman. In her late thirties, her clothes were ill-fitting and she appeared incapable of humor; rather, every inflection and mannerism indicated she was a bigot. Her husband, Harold, had been charged with murder.

"We're here for politics, not love," barked George. "Let's decide on at least one or two actions we can take together. If not, let's go home."

Fair play to you, George, Bernadette thought. Let's stop making fucking eejits of ourselves and get something done.

"Do you have any pickets scheduled?" asked Paddy.

"There's one for Monday morning outside the court," replied Mrs. Johnson. "We understand BBC will be there filming for a documentary."

"It'd be brilliant if we could have a joint picket," said Bernadette. "We could each be carrying our own placards. Loyalist and republican. And we could march together."

"That would certainly attract attention and show that the British are losing the confidence of both communities," said Mrs. Johnson.

The fucking Brits never had any confidence to lose in the Catholic community, Bernadette thought. But she smiled in agreement.

"If we can arrange the joint picket for Monday," said Paddy, "then I believe we should schedule a news conference to be held during the picket. Each committee would designate a spokesperson, and they'd say that the loyalist and republican communities intend to continue to work together against the supergrasses until the security forces stop using them."

Bernadette appreciated how careful Paddy was to avoid any expression that might inflame or divide. He used "security forces" rather than "Brits" or "peelers." Yet, he never yielded an inch on principle. Good performance, Paddy, she thought. Good performance.

"Never did I think I'd see the likes of this," said Bernadette to herself, a broad grin lighting up her face. Standing a few feet from her were Liz and Mrs. Taylor, side by side. Behind them was the Crumlin Road Courthouse. Facing them were three television cameras, a battery of microphones, photographers jostling for position and reporters screaming out questions. The two women had answered all the questions with an ease that made them seem as if they'd been doing this all their lives.

Liz finished the session by saying, "I should make it clear that this picket is just the beginning of the joint efforts between our two committees. Our cooperation won't end after this morning. As for the British reaction, I'd hope they realize that unjust policies such as the supergrasses cause outrage in both communities."

Jesus, Liz was superb, Bernadette thought. All the practicing and rehearsing with Paddy over the weekend had paid off. Liz had said everything she was supposed to say. More important, she had said it just the right way, with no hint of anger or reluctance. And Victoria Taylor—fair play to her. She'd also done well.

The picket line stretched up and down the sidewalk in front of the courthouse. At least a hundred women were marching and carrying placards: "Loyalists Demand Justice." "Stop the Supergrasses." "Justice for Nationalists." "Barker Lies for Brits." "Stop the Show Trials."

Looking at the demonstrators, Bernadette judged there to be an equal number of loyalists and republicans interspersed with one another, giving an even stronger image of solidarity.

She knew that a number of the republican women had been reluctant to march with the loyalists. But after a few moments of unease when they started to gather this morning, the demonstration had proceeded in a spirit of civility and cooperation. The human side of the problem had displaced the political one, at least temporarily.

CHAPTER ELEVEN

Terry Byrnes was in his late forties, slightly bald and six feet tall. About two stone overweight, and wearing jeans and a gray sweater, he could as easily be a barman on the Falls as an American lawyer who'd arrived in Belfast barely an hour earlier.

After picking him up at the airport, Paddy drove him to Liz's house. The four of them—Liz, Bernadette, Paddy and Terry—were now in the dining room. "I understand this is your first trip to the north," said Liz as she poured him a second cup of tea.

Bernadette smiled as Terry picked up another sandwich. He showed no reluctance to eat whatever was put in front of him. She sipped from her cup and listened.

"Yes, it is," said Terry. "I was in the south on a vacation about ten years ago, but I never went any farther north than Dublin. Just the usual tourist spots, the lakes of Killarney, the Ring of Kerry, the castles."

"Ah yes," Paddy smiled, "peaceful, beautiful Ireland. Things are a bit different up here."

"I've already noticed quite a difference," said Terry, "during the ride in from the airport. I haven't seen that many soldiers since I was on maneuvers in the army. Are there always so many soldiers on the streets?"

"Not always," said Bernadette, "but the situation is particularly tense right now."

"Yeah, I was reading the British papers during the layover in London. I guess the past few days have really been bad."

"Jesus, they have indeed," said Liz. "The seven loyalists in the Barker case were all convicted last Wednesday and since then it's been hell, so it has. The orangies—thousands of them—were out on the Shankill Road demonstrating on Wednesday night. The peelers came in. Rocks and bottles were thrown. Then there were the plastic bullets. And then petrol bombs."

"Terry, you have to understand that the loyalists aren't used to this kind of treatment," said Paddy. "And they were raging."

Terry swallowed a mouthful of sandwich and nodded. "By the way," he said, "if I could just interrupt you for a moment, that was a terrific idea you had to work with the loyalists against the supergrasses. It got you great PR in America."

"Well, interestingly enough," said Paddy, "that's the reason for the massive security presence right now. Thursday noon, we had another joint picket—loyalists and republicans—outside the courthouse. There must've been almost three hundred picketing when the RUC charged the crowd."

"It looked as if the cops went crazy," said Terry.

"Christ, they went mad altogether," said Paddy. "I could sense from the start there might be trouble. But I'd no idea it would get as bad as it did."

"For Christ's sake. I picked a great time to come to Belfast."

"Ah," smiled Bernadette, "at least when you go home, you can say you saw the real thing."

"Do you expect more rioting tonight?" he asked.

"We think the worst is behind us," said Bernadette. "There might be the odd bus hijacked and burnt and some stone throwing, but it shouldn't be too bad."

"In that case, I'll stay at least one night." Terry laughed.

"Jesus, with all the talking we're doing," said Bernadette, "we're forgetting you must be exhausted from jet lag. Especially since you came through London."

"Actually, I'm not too bad," he replied. "I took a sleeping pill on the plane and got about five hours' sleep. I'll lie down for a while this afternoon and I'll be fine. Will I be staying here, Liz?"

"If that's all right with you," she replied.

"Sure, that'd be fine—if you and your family won't mind putting up with me."

"Not at all," said Liz. "My two young boys have been looking forward to having an American in the house and my husband's pleased as well."

"That sounds great. And I assume you have a lot lined up for me during the week."

"We do indeed," said Paddy, "but we'll ease you into it gently. This afternoon is free so you can rest, and then tonight we thought we'd introduce you to Belfast social life by taking you to the Felons Club."

"I'm almost afraid to ask," said Terry, "but what the hell is the 'Felons Club'?"

"I suppose the best way to describe the Felons Club," said Paddy, "is that it's a drinking establishment frequented by those who espouse the republican philosophy."

"In New York we'd call it an IRA gin mill," said Terry with a grin.

"Conditions require us to be a bit more circumspect and discreet," said Paddy.

"We think you'll enjoy the *craic*," said Bernadette. "The Irish Brigade band will be playing and they're just brilliant. Some relatives of the prisoners will be there as well, so you'll get a chance to talk with them."

"There'll also be a bit of a do for two of the prisoners released from the Kesh this week," said Liz. "Gerry Adams is to be the speaker."

"Gerry Adams," said Terry. "I was hoping I'd have the chance to meet him."

"Oh, aye," said Bernadette, "Gerry wants to meet you as well. You'll be able to speak with him tonight, but I know he'd also like you to come to his office during the week."

"Jesus, that'd be terrific," said Terry.

Bernadette smiled to herself at Terry's casual, unassuming manner. It was typical of so many of the Irish Americans she'd met in New York.

"Tomorrow afternoon, we'll take you to different areas in Belfast," said Paddy, "so you can get an idea what the day-to-day conditions are for us. And tomorrow night, there'll be a meeting of Families for Legal Justice at the Greenan Lodge. Monday morning we'll be at the courthouse for the McGrath trial."

"Bernadette," asked Terry kindly, "your husband is one of the defendants, isn't he?"

"Yes," she answered with a wry smile, "Dermot is one of the thirty-five defendants. No matter what else, he isn't suffering for lack of company."

"Didn't the trial just begin?" asked Terry.

"Aye, Tuesday last," said Bernadette.

"So far it's just been the preliminaries," said Paddy. "Police identifying evidence and that sort of *craic*. But Monday, McGrath takes the stand."

"That should be interesting," said Terry. "You got me here at the right time."

"Jesus, I'd love to just be able to get my hands on him," said Bernadette.

Terry looked for a moment at Bernadette before speaking. "You know, I mentioned briefly on the ride in from the airport that I'd seen Bernadette speak when she was in New York, but I have to tell you that she really did an outstanding job. I was at the NIRAA dinner and, Bernadette, you were just great. And from what I heard, you were great everywhere you went in America."

"Thank you very much," said Bernadette. "I'll have to buy you a pint at the Felons tonight."

"You might not want to admit it, Terry," Paddy said, "but you're about to fall asleep. Bernadette and I will leave now so you can get some rest. We'll collect you for the Felons at about half eight."

"That'll be great," said Terry, no longer able to suppress a yawn. "I'll see you tonight."

●

Unlike the P.D., the Felons Club was an imposing concrete structure. As they approached the entrance, Bernadette noticed Terry eyeing the large boulders along the curbside.

"That's to protect against car bombs," she said.

"Jesus," said Terry, shaking his head.

The entrance to the Felons was enclosed behind a heavy, chain-link fence. The three stood at the gateway for a brief moment until they were recognized by an inside doorman who buzzed open the gate. They stepped through the open gate, which then closed quickly behind them. The front entrance to the Felons was about ten feet beyond the gate. Paddy led the way inside and up a short flight of stairs to the second floor. Just inside the door, two men were seated at a table. Paddy put three one-pound notes down on the table.

"Thank you very much," one of the men said. "Enjoy the night."

"I'm sure we will," said Paddy.

The band had already begun playing, but a few tables remained empty. Paddy led them to a small table on the far left side of the room. The walls were a darkish wood. The only adornments were several portraits of Irish patriots, such as the nineteenth-century Land League hero, Michael Davitt. There was a Tri-Colour next to the bandstand.

"At least we'll be able to talk without the noise being so loud," said Bernadette.

Just after they sat down, a young waitress came over to take their order. Like the other waitresses, she was wearing a black skirt and a white blouse with a black string bow tie.

"Bernadette, how're you keeping?" she asked.

"Just grand, Kathy, and how's yourself?"

"I'm fine, so I am. I was at the Kesh yesterday to see Gerard. His solicitor thinks he'll get parole next month."

"That's great news," said Bernadette with a broad smile. "You must be over the moon."

"I am indeed. And I was to the doctor today with my wee Michael. His foot's just fine. He'll need no more operations."

"Kathy, this is Terry Byrnes," said Bernadette. "He's a lawyer from New York. He's over as an observer for the McGrath trial."

"That bastard tout. Jesus, Bernadette, I hate him. And poor Dermot. What McGrath is doing to him. Ah, Terry, you'll be seeing something when you see Frank McGrath."

"What we'd all like to see right now," said Paddy, "is something to drink."

"Jesus, Paddy," said Kathy, "it's always business with you." She took the drink orders. White wine for Bernadette. Pint of Guinness for Paddy. Pint of Harp for Terry.

"Such a young girl, and she's been through so much," said Bernadette once Kathy was out of earshot. "She was eighteen when her husband was lifted. That was just before their Michael was born. And before that—I believe it was '74 or '75—her brother, Mike, was shot dead by the Brits."

"And she still keeps going. How does she do it?" asked Terry.

"What the hell can she do but keep going?" replied Bernadette.

"Bernadette, Liz played a video for me this afternoon of a BBC show that you were on," said Terry. "You made the same point then. You were very effective. That must've had an impact on the average British person."

"I hope so," Bernadette replied. "But we never know what will work and what won't work. So we try everything."

"All these waitresses—are they like Kathy?" asked Terry. "Do they all have relatives in jail?"

"Aye, about all of them. Either in jail or dead," she answered. "It's a chance for them to make a few bob. It's important, you know, that we stick together."

"I'm sure it is," said Terry, listening to the Irish Brigade sing.

Armored cars and tanks and guns
Come to take away our sons
But every man must stand behind
The men behind the wire.

"The band is terrific," said Terry.

"Aye," said Paddy, "they're as good as anyone. They always give a great lift to everyone's spirits."

"I can see that," said Terry, looking around the room, watching the people clap their hands and defiantly sing the words of their rebel songs.

Paddy was paying Kathy for the third round of drinks when the program began. A man well into his sixties and wearing an aging tweed jacket introduced Gerry Adams to loud applause. Wearing a gray cardigan, Adams strode purposefully to the microphone. His opening sentences were in Irish. He then turned to English. The crowd was hushed. The waitresses stood still, looking toward the bandstand as Adams spoke.

"Tonight, we welcome home two comrades: Tom Sarsfield and John McCann. Two brave men who for the past six years endured the brutality of Long Kesh. Two brave men in their lonely H-Block cells who refused to be broken, who refused to be criminalized.

"Tom Sarsfield and John McCann suffered through the dark years of the blanket protest and then watched in agony when their ten brave comrades died on hunger strike. Tom and John each volunteered for the hunger strike and were waiting to be called when it was ended. The Brits will never understand men like Tom Sarsfield and John McCann. They will never understand the republican movement. They will never understand Irish men and Irish women who are ready to suffer and to die so their land might be free. They will never understand the spirit of freedom which binds the republican movement and sustains it in its darkest hours.

"No one expressed the essence of the republican movement more articulately than Bobby Sands when he said"—Adams paused for a moment, slowly rubbed his beard and then read from a sheet of paper—"'My body is broken and cold. I'm lonely and I need comfort. From somewhere afar I hear those familiar voices which keep me going: "We are with you, son. We are with you. Don't let them beat you." I need to hear those voices. They anger the monster and it retreats.' It is in that spirit—the spirit of freedom—that I introduce Tom Sarsfield and John McCann."

At the sight of the two men coming toward the platform, the crowd was on its feet erupting in wild cheers and applause. Adams shook the hands of the two men, then stepped to the side. It was several minutes before the clamor subsided. Tom Sarsfield was the first to the microphone.

"I did nothing more during the past six years than any of the republican prisoners did, not just in Long Kesh and Armagh but in the Free State and England as well. I was able to endure, and they are able to endure, because our cause is just and because we have your support. In our darkest days we thought of you and we knew you were there. Tonight, I ask you to never forget our brave comrades who are still suffering in their cells and also to never forget that our struggle must go on until the monster is defeated. *Tiocfaidh ár lá!*"

John McCann stepped forward and waited a few moments for the crowd to grow quiet. Then he said, "When I think of all my brave comrades in Long Kesh and when I see all of you here tonight, I know that we can never be defeated. And the Brits know it too. Tom said to you just now, '*Tiocfaidh ár lá:* Our day will come.

But I say tonight to the army of occupation: *Tá ár lá ag teacht.* Our day is coming! *Tá ár lá ann.*Our day is here!"

Their right fists clenched aloft, Sarsfield and McCann left the stage amidst a deafening din.

Bernadette stood and clapped, thinking of the many times she'd been at the Felons to welcome prisoners home. And she thought of Dermot in his cramped cell and, yes, of Dessie, thousands of miles away but imprisoned nonetheless by his conscience.

And she wondered indeed how long it would be before their day would come.

On Monday morning, Terry helped Bernadette and Liz out of a taxi. They'd just arrived at the courthouse. The air was clear and crisp and punctuated by the cadenced chants of the determined demonstrators: "McGrath is a liar. The Show Trials must stop. McGrath is a liar. The Show Trials must stop."

RUC were lined up along the Crumlin Road and on the courthouse steps. Some carried machine guns. Others, particularly those at the top of the steps, held rifles.

Bernadette led Terry to the demonstrators and introduced him to Victoria Taylor and Brenda Johnson. He told them he looked forward to meeting with their committee while he was here. Then Liz came over and told Terry several reporters wanted to speak with him.

The reporters were assembled just to the side of the steps. Bernadette was delighted. She recognized BBC, UTV, RTE, Downtown Radio. And the *Irish News*. Questions were fired at Terry.

"What is the purpose of your visit?"

"I hope to get an understanding of the supergrass system."

"Aren't you predisposed against the British court system?

He answered in a firm, clear voice. "I've always had great respect for British common law and system of justice. I do have various questions, however, about how the Diplock Courts fit into that system."

"Will you meet with Sinn Fein while you are here?"

"I'll be glad to meet with anyone who wants to meet with me."

"You were just speaking with the loyalist relatives. Do you have any meetings scheduled with them?"

"I believe I do, but you'll have to get the details from Mrs. McCloskey."

The barrage of questions ended at last, and Terry walked up the steps flanked by Liz and Bernadette.

"It went well," Liz said, and Bernadette agreed with her. The RUC eyed them warily.

Just inside the courthouse were two doorways. "Women to the left, men to the right," said a RUC officer.

Bernadette and Liz walked through the door on the left. A female RUC officer frisked her, while another went through her purse. She was then required to sign her name, her address and the name of the defendant in whom she was interested. Liz went through the same procedure while Bernadette exited into the rotunda. She went over to the right, where Terry was still being frisked and questioned.

"So you're the American lawyer who's over here to tell us what we're doing wrong," she overheard the RUC man say as he patted Terry down. "Not enough crime in New York for you?"

Liz joined Bernadette, and they smiled at Terry as he came toward them.

"Welcome to the Belfast Crown Court," said Bernadette.

"I don't believe it," said Terry, shaking his head. "And look at all the cops." At least twenty RUC were deployed around the rotunda, more than half carrying rifles.

Paddy was standing outside the courtroom on the right side of the rotunda.

"Terry, Patrick McClernan is waiting for you in the courtroom," said Paddy. "He's one of our most experienced solicitors, and he's arranged for you to sit in the jury box rather than in the public gallery. It'll give you a better view of what's happening. It's where the reporters sit."

"You can always be sure there'll be seats available in the jury box," said Bernadette.

Before they could go into the courtroom, they were searched again, including Paddy. He then introduced Terry to McClernan, a distinguished-looking, white-haired man in his late sixties. After whispering something to a court security officer, McClernan led Terry down to the jury box.

"You have your choice of seats," Bernadette heard McClernan say. "Thanks for coming over."

Bernadette and Liz walked up to the public gallery, which consisted of long wooden benches with no backs. Within minutes the gallery was filled with relatives and friends of the defendants. Before the trial began, she had known almost none of these people. Now, after just four days, she felt as comfortable with them as if they were old friends.

As Bernadette looked forward from her seat, she could see Terry below in the jury box. Directly in front of her against a backdrop of red velvet curtain was the judge's bench. The witness box where Frank McGrath would be testifying was to her right. Standing throughout the courtroom were at least forty RUC, more than ten of them women. Four of the RUC men near the judge's bench held rifles.

A moment later, the spectators fell silent. The first stirrings of muffled voices and clanging metal could be heard beneath them. The defendants were being brought from the jail through a tunnel that went under Crumlin Road and then into the courthouse. They emerged from a stairway onto the floor of the courtroom to the side of their barristers' table. Manacled and chained in groups of three and four, the defendants were then led into rows of seats behind their barristers. The area was enclosed in the rear and on both sides by heavy wood partitions. A low wooden railing was in front of them.

Bernadette strained until she could see Dermot. He was chained to Mick McAllister and to Liam Dwyer from Ballymurphy. Dermot looked up at her, and they exchanged fleeting but reassuring smiles. Once the chains and handcuffs were removed and Dermot sat down, she had to strain again to catch a glimpse of the back of his head.

Instructed to rise, everyone except the defendants stood up as Judge Harold Stafford, resplendent in red robe and white powdered wig, ascended the bench. He glanced toward the lawyers and then peered sternly at the gallery for a long moment before sitting down.

As far as Bernadette was concerned, Judge Stafford epitomized the worst in unionism. His father had been a unionist M.P. and was attorney general during the 1950s, a reign marked by severe oppression of nationalists. The Stafford family had extensive landholdings in north Down, and Harold and his brothers had been educated at elite schools and universities. After serving in the military, Harold was elected to his father's Parliament seat in the early 1960s and opposed any concessions to Catholics. In 1972 he was made a Crown Court Judge.

As Stafford looked through papers and discussed procedures with the lawyers, Bernadette tried to hear what was being said. Fifteen more RUC entered the courtroom, and the ten officers who'd brought in the prisoners were now taking positions between the prisoners and the witness box.

The door behind the witness box opened. A gasp came from the gallery and Bernadette's hands went to her face. For a few moments there was bedlam. The RUC shouted at the prisoner's relatives in the gallery, threatening to drag them out if they didn't keep quiet. Below, the defendants stamped their feet and yelled "Informer!" "Lying bastard!" The prison officers and RUC began to move toward them.

The courtroom fell silent and all eyes were on Frank McGrath. Four RUC men were at the front and side of the witness box, but by leaning forward in her seat, Bernadette was able to get a clear view of McGrath. Jesus, she thought, I would never recognize him. The long, straggly hair was close-cropped and parted neatly. His once bushy, walrus-like mustache was now trimmed and pencil thin. And the clothes. Mother of God. Him with the torn cardigan and frayed jeans. Now he wore a well-cut, dark blue, three-piece suit, a light blue shirt and red tie.

And his accent. Frank McGrath had always had a very severe working-class accent, complete with slang and faulty grammar. From his first words today, however, he sounded as if he were a BBC newsreader. The courtroom acoustics were dreadful, and during the first four days of the trial, Bernadette was barely able to hear what was said. But McGrath's voice cut through the courtroom with strength and clarity.

Unlike previous witnesses, however, who looked toward the lawyers, McGrath faced right as he testified, looking directly at the judge. Seated at such an angle and with RUC minders and prison officers positioned to his front and side, McGrath was insulated from any eye contact with the defendants.

The Crown counsel led McGrath through his story. "I joined the IRA," he began, "when I was eighteen because I thought I would be fighting for my country. I soon became disillusioned by the IRA's brutality, bank robberies and racketeering. I was afraid to leave the IRA for fear of reprisal . . ."

McGrath continued virtually nonstop through the first morning session. He said pretty much what Bernadette had expected him to. His style of delivery intrigued her, however. Not just the refined accent but also the deliberate and unemotional recitation, as if a machine were doing the speaking. And he never took his gaze from the judge, even when the prosecutor was asking him questions.

Walking out of the courtroom for the lunch recess, Bernadette saw that many of the relatives were shaking their heads in disbelief.

Bernadette and Terry left the courthouse and walked up Crumlin Road to the canteen, a small, temporary-looking building set up by a prisoners' support group for the families of prisoners on trial. Inside were a number of card tables, wooden chairs and a play area for children.

"Well, what did you think of McGrath's performance?" Bernadette asked, after they'd been served tea and cheese sandwiches.

"It seemed awfully rehearsed, and the security was incredible. I was sitting only a few feet from the witness box and I could barely see him—and at that, only the back of his head."

"I don't think Dermot and the rest could see him at all."

"No, they couldn't. When McGrath first came in, the men were twisting and turning from every angle trying to get his attention. But he wouldn't look anywhere near them. And once the RUC and the guards positioned themselves, McGrath was completely screened off. But what did you think of McGrath? You knew him."

"Just amazed, so I was. You were sitting there with all the reporters. What was the feeling among them?"

"I think they were embarrassed by it all. Especially with an American being there. They didn't know McGrath before either, but from what they were saying, they know that guys from Ballymurphy don't talk like him."

"Were you able to recognize Dermot?" Bernadette asked.

"Oh, yeah, right away. He was the fourth guy in. Looked just like the pictures you showed me. And he must've spotted me as a Yank pretty easily because as soon as he sat down, he looked over and smiled."

"The men are thrilled you're here. To have someone who is a politician and a lawyer sitting in the courtroom gives a great boost to their spirits."

"I hope their spirits aren't deflated when they find out I wasn't much of a politician. I was defeated after only one term."

"Ah, that was the people's loss," she smiled, "not yours."

"You should be a politician!" he said with a hearty laugh.

The chief prosecutor, Arnold Westgate, began the afternoon session by asking McGrath about Malachy Donnelly.

"I've known Malachy Donnelly since we were wee lads together," said McGrath. "We were in the same hurling club. I joined the IRA the same month he did. Malachy was the best man at my wedding."

Westgate then inquired about a meeting in Jack McNamee's house in the fall of 1979.

"I was in Jack McNamee's home in Ballymurphy. Malachy was with me. It was November 1979, soon after the Pope had been to Ireland. Jack and Malachy said they were to attack an Army foot patrol in Ballymurphy the next evening. It was to be a bomb attack. They asked me to be the lookout. I told them it would not be possible because I was to be at the leisure centre that evening and my absence would be noticed. The attack went ahead without me. Two soldiers were killed. I saw Malachy the morning after the attack. He told me—I will never forget this—'Those Brit bastards. We blew them to f—ing pieces. That's two more Brits in boxes.' And when I saw Jack that evening, he asked me if Malachy told me about 'the two f—ing Brits we stiffed.' I told him he had."

"Paddy, I just hope you weren't in McGrath's wedding party," said Terry, sitting comfortably on Bernadette's couch that evening and drinking a can of Harp.

"Thank God I wasn't," said Paddy, "but it shows they'll stop at nothing. Frank and Malachy were inseparable, and now Frank is doing this to him. By the way, Frank's wife left him years ago."

"Terry," asked Bernadette, "what was the expression on Malachy's face when Frank was saying all that?"

"That's what probably amazed me more than anything. He had absolutely no reaction whatever. None. He was as calm as could be, as if he were watching a television show. And it seemed to be real, not a put-on. He couldn't have been more casual."

"The boys have all been expecting the worst," said Bernadette, "so I suppose nothing would surprise them. And Malachy has been through so much. He was interned for two years and, Jesus, no one could keep count of how often he's been to Castlereagh. By now, I'm afraid, Malachy could keep a straight face no matter what he hears, even when he has to listen to Frank being so careful not to swear, as if Frank didn't have the foulest mouth in Belfast."

"Paddy, I've tried enough cases," said Terry, "to know you can't tell how a case is going to turn out after one day of direct testimony. But if McGrath keeps going the way he did today, he'll be destroyed on cross-examination. The inconsistencies are incredible. Here's a guy who says he was in the IRA for more than ten years. And even though he never carried out a mission, he knew the entire command structure, what operations were conducted and who carried them out. Christ, a kid just out of law school would tear him apart."

"Indeed he would," said Paddy, "but we go back to the same point: there's no jury. So long as McGrath sticks to his story and doesn't break, Stafford will not only convict anyone the Brits want convicted, he'll do so happily."

"Terry, I saw you taking notes when McGrath was testifying," said Bernadette. "Did the peelers say anything to you?"

"No, why would they?"

"We must've forgotten to tell you," said Paddy, "that only lawyers and reporters are allowed to take notes. The public isn't allowed to write anything. I suppose that, with you sitting among the reporters, they didn't want to create an incident."

"Jesus, if that doesn't show how afraid they are of the truth coming out, nothing does."

"Liz and Tom Mullen will be by to collect us at half eight

and we'll go to the Loyalist Sports and Social Club on the Shankill Road," said Bernadette.

"I have to be leaving," said Paddy. "Might as well go now."

"Ah, Paddy, luv," said Bernadette, "I'll see you at the court in the morning."

After Paddy left, Bernadette poured Terry a cup of tea.

Terry sipped his tea, then said, "I don't want to be probing, but before Liz comes by, I would like to ask you about Jack, her husband. She introduced me to him when he came in Saturday evening, and he was cordial enough. But since then he comes and goes saying nothing more than 'hello' or 'good-bye.' On the other hand, the two boys couldn't be friendlier."

"Jack was close to his older boys, Sean and Denis, who are both serving life sentences in the Kesh. He'd always been a happy and friendly man. Enjoyed his pint, enjoyed the craic. But when the boys were sentenced, Jack had a nervous breakdown, and after that you wouldn't have known him. He's a defeated man."

"Jesus, that's a shame."

"Indeed it is. I'm only surprised it doesn't happen more often," said Bernadette, thinking of her own encounter with the demons last spring.

CHAPTER TWELVE

"Christ, I feel as if I'm in a spy movie," said Terry as Tom Mullen, the wiry solicitor who was accompanying them, parked the car just off the Shankill Road.

"I don't fancy being here myself. You can be sure of that," said Bernadette, tightening her coat and girding herself for the damp chill of the late fall evening. This was the first time she had been to the dreaded Shankill. The street was empty except for two men in raincoats standing near a wall outside the glare of the street lamp.

"We've quite a welcoming party," said Tom in a low voice. He snapped open his seatbelt. "Bobby Cartwright and Eddie Spencer."

"We should have our fucking heads examined, so we should." Bernadette sighed. Before gettting out of the car, she turned and whispered to Terry, "It was Bobby Cartwright who proposed that the Brits cordon off nationalist areas with electrified barricades so that whenever the Catholics acted up, the Brits could activate the barricades. Any Catholic who tried to break through would be electrocuted."

"You're kidding," said Terry, opening the door and helping her out of the car.

"It got him elected," she said.

She'd never met Cartwright until the first joint demonstration at the courthouse; he'd been the only loyalist politician to show up. She'd expected the worst, but now, as Brenda Johnson introduced them, Bernadette was struck by his reserved, almost shy manner. In his mid-thirties, he was gangly and disheveled, and looked younger than he was. His speech bore the unmistakable tones of his childhood in Scotland. His awkward smile indicated he was still a bit disbelieving of his notoriety. Dermot had told her the Ra knew Cartright was close to the UVF but was not certain if he was a member.

There were no doubts about Eddie Spencer. He was a UVF commander from North Belfast. The hardest of the hard-liners. Reported to have a .60-calibre machine gun in his flat. His presence this evening would ensure against any attacks by freelance loyalist gangs. What else he could contribute, Bernadette didn't know.

As the four Catholics stood on loyalist territory, Cartwright and Spencer came forward from the shadows and shook hands with them. The two loyalists then led them along a narrow, puddle-covered side street to an alleyway, where they climbed a staircase to the second floor and entered the Loyalist Sports and Social Club. They walked quickly through the bar area to the back room.

Brenda Johnson greeted them cordially and introduced them to Sarah Williams from the Loyalists for Fair Trials Committee. They sat down at a round table, the four Catholics forming one semicircle, the four loyalists the other. Bernadette glanced about the room, which she thought wasn't too different from a nationalist club, except for the painting on the far wall of the Bloody Hand of Ulster adorned with the letters "UVF." A girl no older than eighteen poured tea, put a tray of sandwiches on the table and left the room, closing the door behind her.

"Mr. Byrnes," Brenda said, "we're pleased you could come here this evening. We in the loyalist community believe we're being used by the British government and that our rights are being violated. My own husband was convicted in the Joe Barker trial because of Barker's lies. My husband and six other men were found guilty of murder and sentenced to twenty years in prison. We realize you are a Roman Catholic and that you support the nationalist community but we—the loyalist relatives—believe that the supergrass issue seriously affects both communities."

"Well, it does affect both communities," said Terry, "and to be honest with you, it should affect everyone who believes in the rule of law. I was in court today and I've read the judge's decision in the Barker case, which Liz gave me. As far as I'm concerned, it's just another version of internment. This time, though, the Brits may have damaged themselves by alienating both communities."

"I can assure you they've alienated the loyalists," said Brenda, "but we don't know where to turn."

"Brenda is a wee bit more diplomatic than I am," interjected Sarah Williams. "What's happened here is that the working-class loyalists are not just alienated, they're raging over what's being done to us by the British government. After all, we're the ones who have been flying that damned British flag all these years, and this is the way they treat us. But where are our politicians? Except for Bobby Cartwright, they cannot be found. Paisley, McCusker, Molyneaux—where are they? You're a Roman Catholic lawyer from New York. And just by sitting here in this room tonight, you've done more for us than any of them."

Blond and blue-eyed, Sarah Williams couldn't be older than her late twenties, Bernadette thought, but by God she was a brilliant speaker.

"My husband, Andy, was convicted in the Joe Barker case as well," Sarah continued. "I've two wee ones, and they're going to grow up without a father at home because of Joe Barker. I've lived on the Shankill all my life, and I know the hatred that runs between the Shankill and the Falls. But if the IRA had attacked my husband, at least I'd know who the enemy was." She stopped and lit a cigarette.

Cartwright took his turn. "Terry, I hope when you get back to New York, you tell the reporters you met with me and I didn't try to electrocute you." He smiled self-consciously.

"Well, the night isn't finished yet," answered Terry with a booming laugh.

"Ah, you'll have no trouble," said Cartwright. His face turned serious, almost grave. "You can be sure of that because we're indebted to you. The unionist politicians have let our people down terribly, because we're expendable."

"If you don't mind me saying so," said Terry, "you've tied yourselves so closely to the Brits that when they use something like the supergrasses against you, you're defenseless. That's why, in this respect anyway, the loyalists are worse off than the republicans. Whatever disadvantages the nationalists have, they have strong support groups. Just a few months ago, Bernadette came to the United States to mobilize public opinion against the supergrasses. But you can't do that in the United States or even England. You can't do it anywhere. But I want you to know—and I'm saying this from the bottom of my heart—that when I get back to America, I'll speak on your behalf. As far as I'm concerned, there's no difference between Barker and McGrath. The evil is the same in both cases."

"Jesus, you and Cartwright got on well enough, didn't you?" said Bernadette once they were back in Liz's flat.

"Yeah, it was quite an experience," answered Terry. "Just as the meeting was finishing, he took me aside. 'For a few minutes,' he said. But by the time he was finished, it must've gone on for at least fifteen or twenty minutes."

"We know," Liz smiled. "We were waiting for you."

"Tell us, Terry," said Tom, "are you going over to the orangies?"

"No, I'm afraid you people will be stuck with me for a while longer. The main thing he wanted to explain was his remark about electrocuting Catholics. He said he hoped I wasn't offended by it, that it was just a figure of speech. All he'd meant by it, he said, was that he'd defend his people, the loyalists, against anyone."

"What did you say to him?" asked Bernadette.

"I didn't want to get into an argument with the guy, but I couldn't let him think I thought it was okay to go around talking about electrocuting people just because they happened to be Catholics. So I said I understood his explanation, but that he had to understand that a responsible political leader can't be using outrageous words like 'electrocute,' especially in a place like Belfast where emotions are so high to begin with. I also told him that remarks like that played right into the Brits' hands."

"He's a strange one, so he is," said Liz.

"Yeah, he is," said Terry, "but he's also very shrewd, very streetwise. Besides, let's be honest, he's got some guts. Here's a guy who built his political career on attacking Catholics, and now he's the only Protestant politician who'll meet with Catholics. And republican Catholics at that."

"So you think he's a skillful politician?" asked Tom.

terrible
Beauty

Terry nodded. "Certainly at the level he's operating at now. I don't know whether he has the ability to function in the international arena. Adams and Hume certainly can, and so can Paisley. I don't know how deep a guy like Cartwright is."

"Did you enjoy being in politics?" asked Bernadette.

"Oh, yeah, I really did. It's a tough business and can get pretty brutal at times, but I enjoyed the challenges. Being a district attorney for four years was a terrific experience."

"Do you think you might ever get back into it?" asked Liz.

"No, I don't think so. I had some good years, but once you lose, it's tough to come back. Especially in my case. I'm a Democrat in a Republican county."

"Are you active at all in politics anymore?" asked Tom.

"Oh, I keep my hand in it—supporting particular candidates that I agree with—but not enough to be a candidate again," Terry answered.

"Are the Democrats divided on the Irish issue?" asked Liz.

"No, I can't say they're divided because, unfortunately, despite what you might read in the papers over here, Ireland isn't a major issue with the Democrats or the Republicans. You have some good people in both parties who push the issue, but politically it's nowhere near as important as Israel or South Africa."

"Do you see any hope of that changing?" asked Tom.

"I hate to say it, but no, I don't. And there's a number of reasons. The first is the tight relationship between the American and British governments. And I don't just mean Reagan and Thatcher, even though that would be bad enough. But it's our State Department and their Foreign Office as well—the 'old boy' network—that permeates our entire Irish policy. Second, there's the Dublin government. Bernadette, when you were in America, I'm sure you realized what an obstacle they are."

"I did indeed," she said.

"Whenever we try to focus attention on the Brits, the Free State blames the IRA. It would be as if the Israeli government turned its back on Soviet Jews. Third, the media is strongly pro-British. Especially papers like the *New York Times*. Northern Irish Catholics just aren't a fashionable minority."

"Do we get very much support from the left in America?" asked Liz.

"No. Except for a few very notable exceptions like Paul O'Dwyer, the left is no help at all. To them Catholic is synonymous with 'reactionary' or 'right-wing.' But let me ask you a question about tonight. What was Eddie Spencer's role? He didn't say a damned thing except for 'hello' and 'cheerio'!"

"I was wondering about that myself," said Tom. "And I think his main purpose was to let us know that Cartwright speaks for the UVF leadership. And if that's so, it's very significant."

"How far do you think it might lead?" asked Terry.

"Jesus, it must be watched and analyzed very closely and very carefully," answered Tom, "because the one thing which must always be kept in mind is that Eddie Spencer is a murdering bastard. If he's serious about establishing contacts with republicans, it's entirely because he believes he has to, not because he wants to. He'll do nothing unless it serves the strategic and military purposes of the UVF. What he fears most right now is that to eliminate the Ra—by supergrasses and whatever else might come along—the Brits might well be willing to sacrifice the UVF."

"You mentioned the 'murdering bastards' in the UVF. Do you have any of these guys on your side?"

"Indeed we do. Any army—especially a volunteer army—is

bound to attract some psychos. But for the most part, the IRA is able to weed them out or keep them under control. But there is a splinter group that's broken off from the IRA. They call themselves the Irish People's Freedom Force—the IPFF—and no one can control them. God only knows what they might do."

"You seem to have a good feel for what's happening," said Terry. "Are you politically active at all?"

"I support Sinn Fein and I represent them in court, but I'm not a member. It would reduce my effectiveness as a solicitor. Everyone, including the judges, knows where I stand politically, but it would make it that much more difficult for me if I actually belonged to Sinn Fein."

"Tom isn't even from a republican family, so he's not," said Bernadette.

"Bernadette is dead-on about that," said Tom. "My mother and father and my brothers and sisters are all SDLP. Their politics are based entirely on selfishness and indifference. For the past thirty years my father has had a bookkeeping job with a well-to-do Protestant firm. At no time did I ever hear my father or my mother say even one word about all the Catholics who couldn't get jobs, and couldn't get them because they were Catholics. Instead, they insist on being anti-republican."

"When did you become a republican?" asked Terry.

"During the civil rights movement, in the late sixties, I first developed republican sympathies. But it wasn't until I became a solicitor and saw what was happening in the jails and the courts that I became a true republican."

Tuesday morning in court, Terry sat with Bernadette and Liz in the public gallery so he could view the trial from their perspective.

Again the prisoners were led in, Judge Stafford ascended the bench and McGrath appeared in the witness box to continue his story. Terry took out his pen and a notepad as Westgate directed McGrath's attention to Jack McNamee.

Two RUC men made their way down the narrow row, one from each end. "Put those away immediately or we'll remove you from the court," the one to his right said. Terry shrugged and slowly put the note pad in the right pocket of his jacket and the pen in his left breast pocket. The RUC men glared at him and walked away. When they reached the end of the row, they looked back at Terry to let him know he was in their sights. Terry returned their glares, then resumed listening to McGrath's testimony.

Facing again to his right and looking directly at Stafford, McGrath proceeded as mechanically as he had yesterday. "I very often went to Jack McNamee's home. His wife, Bessie, is my first cousin. I was very friendly with them and with their three wee boys. Jack kept paramilitary gear in his house. Ski masks, black gloves, as well as pistols. Rifles were stashed under the floorboards. Bessie would occasionally transport weapons concealed in the groceries. I became disillusioned with Jack after seeing how gleeful he was when he and Malachy Donnelly murdered the two British soldiers. Perhaps I should have realized this sooner, but I'm afraid I was blinded by my deep friendship with him." McGrath continued in this vein until lunchtime.

At the canteen, once again eating tea and cheese sandwiches, Bernadette told Terry, "Paddy's arranged for you to meet with one of the prisoners in the Crum tomorrow afternoon."

"Do you know which guy it'll be?"

"Sean King from the Short Strand. He's on remand in the Billy Archer case. He's dead-on, so he is."

"I don't mean to offend you at all, Terry," said Liz, "but I could've laughed myself to death this morning when the two peelers made you put away your pad and biro."

"I'm glad I provide so much entertainment for you." Terry laughed. "It would be funny if it weren't so tragic. A supposedly democratic government afraid to let people write down what they see in the courts. I expected it after what you'd told me yesterday, but I wanted to see it myself."

"What did you think of McGrath's testimony this morning?" asked Bernadette.

"It was basically the same as yesterday's. McGrath is going to go through the defendants one by one. First, he'll say how well he knew them and how much he liked them. Then he'll describe the terrible crimes they committed and how shocked he was."

"Jesus," said Bernadette, "did you hear Frank when Stafford would ask a question? 'No, my Lord,' says he. 'Yes, my Lord.' McGrath couldn't have been any more proper if he were Prince Charlie himself."

As Bernadette waited with Liz inside the courthouse for Terry, who was still going through the security check, she reflected on the pace of her life since he'd arrived. It had almost blocked from her mind what Dermot must be going through. Several times that morning, she had been able to catch fleeting glimpses of his face, which was drawn and tight. When he'd stood up at the close of the morning session to be taken back to the Crum, he looked up at her and smiled. She could tell it was forced. She had smiled back and waved her right hand before he was led out of her sight.

Terry finally walked up to Liz and Bernadette. "Jesus," he said with a broad smile, "when I get back to New York, I won't know what it's like to enter a courthouse without being interrogated and frisked."

"Ach, they can tell you're a dangerous one." Liz laughed. They headed for the courtoom. Two RUC officers stepped forward and stopped Terry.

"I'm sorry, sir, but I'm afraid we cannot allow you to enter the courtroom," said the older RUC man. "It's a matter of security."

"I don't know what you're talking about." Terry's voice was calm but strong.

"This is a very significant trial," said the younger RUC man. "Extreme security precautions must be taken to ensure that the defendants receive a fair trial and also to ensure the safety of everyone in the courtroom. Your attendance at the trial, quite frankly, is an intrusion. We've tried to accommodate you. Yet, you've taken actions which can only jeopardize security."

"I'm sorry," said Terry patiently, "but I still don't know what you're talking about."

"Mr. Byrnes," said the older one, "I'm certain you're very much aware of what you've done. This morning two of our officers had to order you to stop writing in the courtroom."

"And that violates security?" asked Terry in a tone that was both polite and incredulous.

"Mr. Byrnes," the older officer continued, "we cannot allow people to write down or sketch what security arrangements we have in the courtroom, how many officers we have and what their locations are. In a few days you will be back in the United States, but we will still live with the threat of terrorist attacks, including the possibility of one in this courthouse."

"I can assure you," said Terry with a hint of sarcasm, "that I had no intention of sketching your battle formations."

"With all due respect, Mr. Byrnes," said the older officer, "We don't have the luxury of being able to rely upon what you tell us your intentions are."

"Mr. Byrnes," said the younger officer, "I understand you're a lawyer in America."

"Yes, I am," replied Terry.

"Well, pardon me for saying so," the younger officer said, "but we don't consider it to be at all respectable for anyone—least of all a lawyer—to be engaged in transmitting signals to a terrorist murderer in the courtroom."

"Pardon me for saying so," said Terry, "but I don't know what the hell you're talking about."

"I'll find Paddy in the courtroom," interjected Bernadette.

"No, Mrs. Hanlon, you're not to go into the courtroom either," said the older officer. "You're the one who transmitted the signals."

"Mother of God," said Bernadette, "you're making no sense at all."

Liz left Bernadette's side and walked toward the courtroom. The RUC did not attempt to stop her.

"You know exactly what we're talking about," said the older officer. "You were attempting to signal your husband with your hand when he was leaving the courtroom this morning."

"You've got to be kidding," said Terry in a voice that was increasingly firm but still composed. "She was waving to her husband."

"Mr. Byrnes, this has gone on long enough," interrupted the older officer. "We have no obligation to be explaining ourselves to the likes of you. Besides, Judge Stafford is in fear with you in the courtroom. He considers you to be a threat to him. Yesterday, you sat in a location near the judge. A location where you were not authorized to be."

Before Terry could reply, Paddy appeared and positioned himself directly in front of the two RUC men.

"I would like an explanation,—and I'd like it now—why these people are being kept from the courtroom," he said sharply.

The RUC men recoiled in the face of Paddy's determined fervor but recovered immediately. The older man said in particularly deliberate tones, "Perhaps, Mr. Ferguson, this matter should be discussed between ourselves."

"That would be fine," said Paddy. He and the older officer walked about twenty feet away. Bernadette could not hear what they were saying, but could see how animated their hand movements and facial gestures were. The younger officer moved over several feet, situating himself so that no one could enter the courtroom without passing him.

"Liz, thanks for getting Paddy," said Bernadette. "This would've gone on all afternoon."

"Do you think we will get back in?" asked Terry.

"Ah, we will," said Bernadette. "This is all a show, so it is. They want the Yank to know who's calling the shots. All that's being discussed now is how they can let us in and save face. It's all part of the game."

"Some game," he said, shaking his head.

After several minutes, Paddy and the older officer walked back toward them.

"Mr. Ferguson has agreed with me," said the older officer, "that you're not to be allowed back into the courtroom unless we have your absolute assurance that you will write absolutely nothing while you're in the courtroom and that there will be no communicating of any sort with any prisoner in the courtroom. If either of you should violate either of these conditions, you will be removed immediately from the courtroom and taken into custody."

"I'm certain," said Paddy, "that Mrs. Hanlon and Mr. Byrnes will comply with these terms. They're reasonable people."

"We also attempt to be reasonable," said the older officer.

"Indeed," said Paddy smilingly. "Indeed."

Bernadette and Terry looked at each other.

"I'm pleased we understand one another," said the older officer. He and the other RUC man turned and walked away.

"Bernadette, you were right," said Terry. "It's all a game to them. A cruel mind game."

"Aye, and it's a deadly game as well. And they know the game won't be over until we've won."

"How'd you get on with Gerry?" Bernadette asked Terry the following morning. They were on their way to the courthouse with a driver from Sinn Fein. He pulled the car out from Sevastapol Street and turned onto the Falls toward Crumlin Road.

"He's a charismatic guy," said Terry. "Very astute. Very realistic as well. Nothing at all like the image the Brits try to paint of him in America."

"Aye," she said. "The Brits call him the 'IRA Godfather of Crime.' "

"I can see easily enough why the Brits don't want him in America. He'd come across as a thoughtful, assured intellectual, not the baby-killing bomber and lunatic they want everyone to think he is."

"Gerry's a natural leader. Dermot was interned with him. He said Gerry always stood out from the rest."

"I'm sure he stands out because of his ability," said Terry, "not his ego. I was with him for almost two hours and he didn't say a word about himself. And that office he's in! Christ, I was afraid the building was going to collapse any moment. It's amazing to think that a handful of people operating out of that run-down place have been able to outmaneuver and hold off the Brits for all these years."

"Ah, it's amazing all right," replied Bernadette.

"One weakness, though, which Adams seemed to acknowledge, is that Sinn Fein doesn't have a feel for what's going on in America. That's another way that the visa denial policy is so harmful. Americans can't listen to Sinn Fein, which is bad enough. But Sinn Fein can't meet with Irish Americans, either. I'm sure NIRAA does the best job it can keeping Sinn Fein up-to-date on what's happening in America, but there's no substitute for being there and seeing for yourself firsthand."

"I learned that when I was over," said Bernadette, "so I did.

"Well, what's the rest of my schedule?"

"Just a few more days, Terry, and you'll be home."

"Is the news conference still on for Friday?"

"Aye, at the Wellington Arms at twelve."

The car turned onto Crumlin Road and stopped near the courthouse. Bernadette and Terry got out and walked across the road, where Paddy was waiting for them.

"How was court this morning?" asked Bernadette.

"More of the same. McGrath is still going on about Jack McNamee. Frank's so programmed and robotic even Stafford was having a difficult time staying awake."

"Did the RUC miss Bernadette and me in court this morning?" asked Terry, laughing.

"Ah, Terry, the peelers were lost without you. Shattered, so they were. And when they learn you were with Gerry Adams all morning, they may not let you out of the Crum this afternoon," replied Paddy, feigning deep concern.

"First things first," said Terry. "How do I get into the jail?"

"First, you have to wait on the queue," said Bernadette, glancing toward the long line of visitors forming outside the jail. "That'll be at least half an hour, but it shouldn't be so bad. It doesn't look as if there'll be any rain."

"When you get inside, you'll be searched, of course," said Paddy, "but just show them your passport and tell the screws you're there to see Sean King. He put in the request for your visit and they've told him it was approved."

"You should get on well with Sean," said Bernadette. "He's from a strong republican family in the Short Strand and is politically aware."

"He's charged with murder?" asked Terry.

"Aye, Billy Archer says Sean stiffed a peeler on Newtonards Road two years ago," said Bernadette.

"I better get on the line before it gets much longer. Should I meet you in court after I'm finished?"

"Aye. That would be grand," replied Bernadette.

The monotony of McGrath's afternoon testimony was punctuated by a heated objection from one of the defense lawyers.

R. Lee Manning, a renowned barrister representing five of the Ballymurphy defendants, implored the judge to move the RUC men and prison officers, who were shielding Frank McGrath from his clients' view. "Defendants are entitled to confront their accusers, " he said. "My clients can hear McGrath, but the human wall of police makes it impossible to see him."

When Stafford replied, "It's a security matter," Manning asked, "How can the witness's security be imperiled by permitting the defendants to look at him? After all, he says he knows them all. So they must know what he looks like."

His annoyance transparent, Stafford brusquely denied Manning's request.

Bernadette was not at all surprised by the judge's ruling, but she was delighted Manning had presented his argument. She enjoyed Stafford's discomfiture. She also noted the stricken look that gripped McGrath's face when Manning was speaking. He was terrified at the thought of facing the men he was accusing.

The testimony continued for about another hour. Bernadette saw Terry enter the courtroom and look for a place to sit. It was crowded and there was no room near Bernadette or Liz. He finally found a place at the end of a row in the upper right corner of the room. She thought he looked out of sorts.

When the afternoon session had finished and Bernadette made her way from the courtroom, she saw Terry and Paddy talking in the rotunda.

"How was your visit with Sean?" she asked Terry.

"I was just telling Paddy," answered Terry, "that I never even got to see them. The guards said the visit was never authorized. I kept saying I thought everything'd been taken care of and there must've been a mistake in the system. They said they don't make mistakes."

"They're right about that," said Paddy, smiling. "They *don't* make mistakes. Everything they do is done intentionally."

"They did tell me," Terry continued, "that if I still want a visit and if King makes the proper application, it would probably be approved, but it would take at least ten days."

"That's very generous of them indeed," said Liz sarcastically, "since they know you must be leaving for America in three days."

"If they don't want you to have a visit, you're not going to have one," said Paddy in deliberate tones. "But we should try to get some public relations advantage out of this. We'll ring Downtown Radio straightaway. And the *Irish News* as well."

"Also," said Terry, "I'm supposed to call a *Newsday* reporter in New York to give him an update on what I've been doing. I don't know how interested he'll be, but I can tell him what happened with the visit and see what he does with it."

"If he does anything at all," said Bernadette, "Sean will be over the moon. Of course, Sean never had the same problem you had."

"What do you mean?"

"I mean, Sean has never had any problem getting into jail," laughed Bernadette. "It's getting out that has caused him considerable difficulty."

That evening, Liz and Bernadette took Terry to meet some more relatives of republican prisoners. Afterwards, as they were heading from the meeting back to Liz's house, they heard explosions. Within minutes the Brits and peelers roadblocked the Falls and helicopters filled the sky, beaming spotlights through the black Belfast night.

All the cars along the road were stopped and the drivers and passengers were taken out for questioning. Bernadette could tell from the way the Brits were carrying on that they must have suffered losses. "Get out of the fucking cars," they shouted, waving their rifles like madmen.

Bernadette was put over the front of Paddy's car and frisked roughly by a female RUC officer.

The contents of Liz's handbag were emptied onto the street, and one of the Brits stepped on her hand when she leaned over to pick them up.

When Terry showed them his passport, a Brit threw it back into his face, calling him an "Irish-American bastard."

Twenty feet or so from Bernadette, a man and woman had been dragged from their car for interrogation. Their young daughter—she couldn't have been more than five years old—was forced to remain in the car, and she began to scream, banging her hands against the car window. When the mother pleaded to be allowed to take the child from the car, a Brit put his rifle to her head. "Shut your fucking mouth, you fucking Irish whore, or I'll blow your fucking head off!" he yelled.

Another Brit pulled a pram from the boot of the car and kicked it across the Falls. Then the Brits jeered and laughed as the sobbing mother picked up the broken pram and carried it back to the boot. Her husband, held at gunpoint, could only look on helplessly.

This sadistic carry-on continued for more than an hour before the Brits lifted the roadblock and allowed the people to go.

It wasn't until they returned to Liz's that Bernadette learned what had happened. At about half ten, the IRA had attacked Fort Jericho, the main army base in West Belfast, killing three Brits and seriously wounding four others. Using RPG rocket launchers, the Ra had scored several direct hits, causing extensive damage to the massive fortress on the Upper Springfield Road, overlooking Turf Lodge and Ballymurphy. Most important, "all volunteers returned safely to base."

Bernadette was pleased not merely because the attack had been so successful but because the Falls roadblock had shown Terry how cruelly brutal the Brits could be.

Yes, she thought, the night had indeed been a success. But as she fell off to sleep, she kept seeing the wee child crying in the car and the looks of terror and rage on the faces of the girl's mother and father.

Steeling herself for another day in court, Bernadette got Siobhan and Brendan off to school. Her mother had already taken Maura to her house. She looked at her watch. It was after nine. Liz and Terry should've been here already. She went to the front window and looked in both directions. There was no sign of Liz's car. Bernadette lit a cigarette and sat down on the couch. Dragging heavily on the cigarette, she glanced through yesterday's *Irish News*.

After several minutes the phone rang. It was Liz. "Bernadette, there's been a change in our plans. We won't be able to collect you. Can you get a taxi to take you to the courthouse?"

"What's happened?"

"The bloody phone's been ringing all morning, so it has. First it was the Crum. The head warder said that it was all a mistake yesterday, that the papers had been misplaced and Terry can visit Sean this afternoon. Then the Brits rang from Stormont, saying they want to meet Terry and answer any questions he might have. That's been set for tomorrow morning before the news conference."

"What caused all this?"

"Apparently the Yank reporter Terry spoke to last night— Jake Short they call him—rang the Brits everywhere, in the embassy and consulate in America and here in Belfast as well, asking why Terry was denied the visit. And they must've panicked. This morning they were treating Terry as if he were royalty."

"Jesus, that's great news, so it is. And you won't be in court this morning?"

"No, I just got off the phone with Father Slattery, and he said it would be fine to bring Terry to Ballymurphy, this morning so the afternoon will be free for the visit at the Crum."

"That sounds brilliant. Then I'll see you tonight?"

"Aye, Bernadette. Terry and I'll collect you at half seven for the meeting with Mairead Brady's family."

"Grand. Cheerio, Liz."

On Friday morning, Bernadette and Liz were seated at a table in the rear of a small restaurant near the Wellington Arms Hotel. They were drinking their second cup of tea when Terry walked in and joined them.

"Well, how did it go at Stormont?" Bernadette asked, smiling. "Did they win you over?"

"No, they didn't win me over at all," replied Terry in a tone that was uncharacteristically grim. "To be honest with you, it was a very unsatisfactory meeting. There were three of them. I assume they were middle-level career diplomats. And they were reasonably polite. But we were just talking past each other. Sometimes I had the feeling that I was in India or some other British colony fifty years ago. They just assume they have the right to be here and the right to do whatever they have to do to stay here. So, to them, issues like the supergrasses or plastic bullets are incidental. Nothing to get excited about. Just more numbers and statistics."

Terry was obviously annoyed. He hadn't touched the tea she'd poured for him. "I could tell," he went on, "they have no idea what life is like in the nationalist areas. I doubt they ever leave

Stormont Castle. And they keep referring to the north as the 'Province,' which I suppose means they don't consider you to be Irish, but you're also not quite British either."

"Did you get to ask them any questions?" asked Bernadette.

"Yeah, but, as I said before, we were talking past each other. I spoke about Mairead Brady and how her death was so indefensible and how moved I was talking to her family last night, and they responded with a dissertation on riot control. I mentioned about the terrible unemployment in Ballymurphy and how I had gone to see Father Slattery and the work he is doing to help the people, and they agreed the economic situation was bad, but the economy couldn't improve until the IRA stopped its violence."

"Did you ask them why the government won't fund the community centre or the job retraining project that Father Slattery's started in Ballymurphy?" asked Bernadette.

"Yeah, sure. That was one of my first questions. They said the centre and the jobs project were both IRA fronts and that Father Slattery is a Provo priest. They very politely told me they could understand why I was sympathetic to Father Slattery—but that was because I didn't have the benefit of their intelligence reports."

"I can imagine what they said about the supergrasses," muttered Liz.

"Jesus, that was the worst. I told them what I've seen in the courtroom and about meeting Sean yesterday—he was a great guy, by the way. But they said they were using supergrasses as a temporary measure to preserve the court system. The only alternatives would be military courts or internment."

"I suppose they'd never consider justice to be a suitable alternative," exclaimed Bernadette.

"No, Bernadette, in all seriousness, I don't think they

would, because from their perspective, the situation in the north is a military problem, a question of control. And I honestly believe, whether they'll admit it or not, they consider the Irish to be inferior. That way, they can justify denying you rights they'd never think of denying to their own people. I guess it comes back to the colonial attitude the Brits have toward the Irish—condescending and racist. I felt like I was shadowboxing."

"Do you think the meeting was a waste of your time?"

"It was frustrating, but it gave me insight into the Brits' thinking. And let's be honest, now I can say I sat down with the Brits and heard their point of view." He paused momentarily and took his first sip of tea.

"This was just training for the real match you'll be having with the press in twenty minutes."

"Bernadette, you're right," said Terry, smiling broadly. "Let's get over to the news conference. I'll kill those bastards."

"Watch yourself," said Bernadette with an equally broad smile. "You can be arrested for saying things like that."

The wood-paneled conference room in the dignified Wellington Arms Hotel was filled with reporters: television, radio and print.

Bernadette and Liz were in the front of the room, standing off to the side. Terry sat calmly, alone, at the front table.

Sean Riordan, the Families for Legal Justice press liaison, was on the other side of the room from Bernadette and Liz. It was two minutes past noon. Sean took one look around the room. Satisfied that all the reporters had arrived and that the cameras and microphones were properly positioned, he nodded his head toward Liz that the conference could begin.

After glancing toward Terry, who also nodded his approval,

Liz walked toward the center of the room and said in a firm, clear voice, "I'm pleased to welcome all of you on behalf of Families for Legal Justice, and I'm privileged to introduce Mr. Terry Byrnes from New York." She went back to the side of the room, and the camera crews turned on their blinding lights.

Looking first at the microphones clustered in front of him and then at the assembled reporters, Terry began his statement by thanking Liz and her committee for inviting him and for their hospitality. He acknowledged his nationalist sympathies, but said he had tried to meet as broad a spectrum of people as possible.

"During the past week, I have not only attended the McGrath trial and met with defendants, lawyers, relatives and political leaders in the nationalist community, but I've also met with British officials at Stormont Castle and with loyalist relatives, a loyalist politician and an alleged loyalist paramilitary."

Bernadette could see many of the reporters looking at Terry in surprise. There had been speculation he would meet with loyalist relatives, but not even a hint of any meeting with loyalist politicians or paramilitaries.

"Based upon these observations," Terry continued, "I have concluded that the court system in Northern Ireland has become an extension of British military policy and that the supergrass trials are a modern version of the Stalin show trials.

"I realize the implications of what I've said. I'm a lawyer. The American legal system is derived from the British common law. Both our systems descend from the Magna Carta. During my twenty-five years of legal practice, as a prosecutor and as a defense counsel, I came to have an even greater respect for our two systems of justice, which are identical in so many ways.

"I was critical of British policy in Ireland, but I believed it was the political and military policies that were misguided. I didn't realize the extent to which the legal system had become a part of these misguided policies. But when the Northern Ireland legal system is looked at in its totality, there can be no other conclusion.

"The final bulwark of a free society is an independent judiciary. The sad fact is that the judges of Northern Ireland have allowed themselves to become accessories to British military policy. And I regret that the Lord Chief Justice would not meet with me. While the supergrasses have been directed primarily against the republican community so far, they are also being used against loyalists. The rights and freedoms of both communities are endangered, and I would urge republicans and loyalists to stand as one on this issue."

Terry had barely concluded when the reporters began hammering him with questions. Bernadette was not surprised when one of them zeroed in on Terry's contacts with the loyalists.

"What loyalist leaders did you meet with?"

"I can tell you I met with Bobby Cartwright. If you want any other names, I would ask that you get that from Mr. Cartwright."

"Are you aware that Bobby Cartwright is bigoted against Roman Catholics?"

"I'm aware that Mr. Cartwright has made a number of statements about Catholics that I would consider bigoted. I must say, however, that Mr. Cartwright was extremely gracious and friendly during our meeting."

"Do you trust Mr. Cartwright?"

"I only met the man once, but I did sense that he has a genuine concern for the working-class loyalist community. I also sensed that he was honestly opposed to the supergrasses. And looking at it objectively, it took political courage for him to meet with me. It should also send a signal to the British that their policies are becoming increasingly offensive to both communities."

Terry went on to field the rest of the questions with the same unerring accuracy and verve.

CHAPTER THIRTEEN

During the weeks following Terry's departure from Belfast, Bernadette's life became a routine. She was in court every day and visited Dermot whenever possible. Although she and Liz were preparing for another Yank, Jack Pender, who was coming to visit next month, she had time to spend at home and made the most of it.

The trial took its toll on the children. Siobhan grew moody and temperamental, slamming doors and losing patience with Maura. In fairness to Siobhan, Bernadette thought, Maura would try the patience of a saint the way she'd been acting lately. The wee child seemed to be whining all the time. Wherever Bernadette would go in the house, Maura would grab onto her leg. During the night she woke up crying and screaming.

Brendan troubled Bernadette the most, however. As soon as she came home each day, he'd ask her what had gone on in court. While she was telling him, he'd say nothing. When she was finished, he'd thank her, go to his room and close the door. He would come out for dinner but say nothing. After dinner he'd go back to his room and stay there until morning. Whenever Bernadette would attempt to talk to him, he'd reply with one- or two-word answers, erecting barriers she was unable to penetrate.

Bernadette's mother was, as always, a great help, but it was too much for her to be taking care of Maura every day. Luckily, Eilish agreed to mind Maura two or three days a week. Alex had the use of a car, and he'd either bring Eilish and Veronica to Bernadette's house or come and collect Maura and take her back to Twinbrook.

The Tierneys rang Bernadette every Sunday afternoon to see how she was doing and what was happening in the trial. She always felt so much better after talking with them.

And Dessie. Several days after Terry left, a letter arrived from Dessie. Bernadette had not expected him to risk writing to her, yet she knew in her heart that he would want to contact her. And that she wanted to hear from him.

Her name and address were typed on the envelope. There was, of course, no return address, and the postmark said "New Jersey." The letter—a brief note—was typed.

"Bernadette, Thinking of you and Dermot. And also of Rory. You were brilliant in New York. The Brits will never understand your courage. That's why they will never defeat us and our day will come. All the best."

The note was signed with a large "D" across the bottom.

Bernadette read and reread the note and placed it between the pages of a book of poems Rory had given her. Each night she found herself opening the book and looking at the note.

It was the trial that seized most of her time and attention. Each day McGrath would continue his monotonous drone. And each day she would see Dermot sitting stoically through it all.

It was midmorning on Wednesday in the fourth week of the trial that McGrath began to testify about Dermot. Bernadette became fully alert and Dermot sat straighter than at any time since the day McGrath had first appeared.

McGrath testified that Dermot Hanlon first joined the IRA in Ballymurphy. "But by the time I became involved, Dermot was in an ASU in Andersonstown. He was respected throughout the IRA in Belfast for his ability with pistols and armalites. I knew Dermot and his wife, Bernadette. We were not close friends, but we would always talk to one another whenever we would meet."

My God, thought Bernadette, what a liar!

"It was about four years ago that the Downpatrick IRA marked a UDR man for execution. The IRA had learned where he lived. It was in Killyleagh, a loyalist enclave just outside Downpatrick. They were afraid that one of theirs would be recognized, so they asked Belfast Brigade to send a Belfast volunteer to shoot the UDR man. Belfast Brigade agreed and selected Dermot Hanlon for the job. I remember Malachy Donnelly being concerned that it was a mistake to send an IRA man out of his area."

Bernadette shifted in her seat.

"After studying the maps and speaking with the Downpatrick people, Dermot decided he'd use a .45-caliber pistol. His Andersonstown unit did not have any .45-caliber, so the Ballymurphy unit gave him one of theirs. I was with Malachy when Dermot returned it two days after the UDR man was murdered. 'It worked so well,' he told Malachy, 'I hate to give it back. It was the easiest hit I ever made.' Malachy congratulated Dermot and said 'it took a Belfast man to get the job done right.'"

McGrath went on speaking in his robotic manner and concluded his testimony against Dermot about one hour into the afternoon session. His entire testimony against Dermot had gone on for two hours, two hours that could mean a lifetime in jail for Dermot. McGrath then launched into his testimony against Mick McAllister.

After the court was recessed for the day, Bernadette waited in the lobby for Paddy.

"Were there any surprises in his testimony?" she asked with some anxiety.

Paddy shook his head. "We knew there was a UDR man killed outside Downpatrick and we knew the forensic tests said he was killed with a .45. We just didn't know how Frank would connect Dermot to the shooting. But I thought they'd come up with a better story than they did. Jesus, if the Ra were that inefficient and careless, you can be sure the war would never've lasted this long. I know McEntegart is looking forward to the cross-examination."

"Ah, that's good to hear," she said.

"It is," said Paddy. "But we can't fool ourselves either. If Stafford wants to believe McGrath, he will believe him. No matter what McEntegart does."

"Paddy, I know as well as anyone what can happen, but let me go home tonight with at least some fucking hope," she said with a broad smile.

"Right you are," he replied with a smile just as big. "If anyone's entitled to a bit of hope, it's you."

It was a quiet night at the Felons Club. Seamus Fitzpatrick and Bernadette were sitting at a corner table.

"I read in the *Irish News* that Terry's already written a report about his visit," he said.

"Aye. And he's given it to some congressmen. Democrats and Republicans. They're putting it in the *Congressional Record*—I think that's what they call it."

"What really has the Brits raging is the meeting he had with the loyalists."

"Oh, aye. That went very well."

"That's why I wanted to talk with you. There's been a development. We're in direct contact with the loyalists."

The waitress came to the table and took their order. A pint of Guinness for Seamus, a white wine for Bernadette.

"I'll be meeting with Bobby Cartwright tomorrow night. And if it goes well, we'll probably keep meeting on a regular basis. The war could be entering a new phase, and we want to take every advantage we can of that new phase."

"But won't that bring you out in the open?"

"To some extent it has to. We're telling the loyalists, of course, that I've no involvement with the IRA or even with Sinn Fein. It's just that the republican movement trusts me as a nationalist intermediary to try to find some common ground with the loyalists."

"Do you think the orangies'll believe that?"

"I know they'll never believe it completely. They know the Ra would never authorize me to sit down with a UVF man like Bobby Cartwright unless I'd some involvement with the republican movement."

"Is the leadership united?"

"Yes. There's absolute unity. I was with Kieran the other day and he told me they're all of one mind. We have nothing to lose. If we make any progress at all, it has to hurt the Brits. If the talks go nowhere, we haven't sacrificed a thing. Besides, we'll be proving again that we're sincere when we say the republican movement is nonsectarian."

"Will the meetings be made known?"

"Well, we can't be publicizing them, but you can be sure the word will get out one way or the other. When that happens, the Ra and Sinn Fein will not only deny any involvement, they'll also deny they've authorized me to act on their behalf. However, they will say they welcome any contacts between the republican and loyalist communities."

"Do you have any agenda?"

"No, I don't. These truly are exploratory talks. And I'm looking forward to them. I'm a realist—Christ, after all these years, what else could any of us be?—but the possibility of even the slightest breakthrough is enough to get me going, so it is."

The waitress brought their drinks. Seamus swallowed a large mouthful of Guinness and smiled for a moment, savoring the taste. Bernadette sipped her white wine.

Seamus went on. "You mentioned Eilish earlier. How is Alex doing?"

"He's in great form, so he is. But," Bernadette hesitated for a moment before going on, "Eilish is worried. For the past few months now, Alex has been away from the house more than . . . well, more than at any time since he got out of the Kesh."

"How long has Alex been out?"

"Jesus, it's about four years. And Eilish says she doesn't know if she could go through that again. And you know the next time it would be longer."

"Eilish will be able to go through whatever she has to. Just as you have."

"There are times when I might not be doing as well as you think I am," laughed Bernadette.

"I'm sure of that. But at the end of the day, you've always been there doing whatever has to be done. And that's what counts. As for Alex, I don't know what he's doing, but we both know that most volunteers go back to their units. So I wouldn't be at all surprised if he was involved in operations again."

As Seamus paused to sip some more of his pint, Bernadette looked at him and realized that he had just told her indirectly that Alex was deeply involved again. Poor Eilish, she thought. God help her.

"The other American," asked Seamus, "when will he be over?"

"Next week. His name is Jack Pender. McEntegart expects to be cross-examining McGrath about Dermot when he's here, so the timing is good."

"How long will he be staying?"

"It looks like he can only be here for four days. He works for a congressman and apparently the Congress is busier than they expected so he can't stay as long as he'd like."

"Ah, Jesus, the way you and Liz are, I'm sure he'll see a terrible lot in those four days."

"God, we had poor Terry exhausted, so we did. Apparently the Lord Chief Justice saw the story about his report in the *Irish News*."

"Harold Ralston, that terrible bastard."

"When Terry was here, he wouldn't meet with him at all. But today his office called Liz and said he'd be delighted to meet Jack Pender."

"Jesus, they certainly are terrified of the bad publicity. Especially from America."

"Ah, Seamus, as you've so often said, this is a war that's fought on many fronts."

"It sure is, Bernadette. It sure is."

When Jack Pender got off the train in Belfast, Liz and Bernadette were waiting for him. They had never seen a photograph of him, but they spotted him straightaway. He was in his mid-forties, with sandy hair and glasses. "He looks like a Yank, so he does," said Bernadette, peering down the platform.

Wearing a heavy wool cardigan and a zippered down jacket, Jack lugged a suitcase in his right hand and held a garment bag over his left shoulder.

"Jack Pender?" Bernadette asked. "I'm Bernadette Hanlon, and this is Liz McCloskey. Welcome to Belfast."

"I'm glad to be here. I hope I can be of some help to you."

"We're sure you will," said Bernadette. "Did you sleep at all on your trip over?"

"I did get about two hours sleep on the plane to Dublin, but I was too scared to close my eyes on the train here."

"Jesus, you must be exhausted," said Liz. "And we have the rest of the day planned for you."

"Don't worry about it. Just as long as I don't have to carry this bag with me, I'll be fine."

"In that case," said Liz, laughing as they approached her car, "you can put your bag in the boot and we'll expect to hear no complaining from you while you're here."

"I think my rights just got violated." Jack laughed and put his luggage into the car.

Driving west toward Whiterock, Bernadette asked Jack if he'd been to Ireland before.

"This is my first time in Ireland, north or south. I suppose I shouldn't ask, but what's on today's schedule?"

"We're going to Liz's house first," said Bernadette, "where you can unpack and take a quick shower, if you like. We'll fix you something to eat, but then we've to rush you to the courthouse for this afternoon's session."

"Good. I'm eager to see what's going on. My boss, Congressman Ashe, met with Terry and read his report, and has written to the secretary of state asking for an explanation. A number of other congressmen have written to the secretary of state as well."

Liz and Bernadette smiled at each other.

Later that afternoon, Bernadette and Jack were at the courthouse. "So far it's just the way Terry said it would be," said Jack, as the two of them walked across the courthouse rotunda. "I can see how those security checks would intimidate people from coming."

"Oh, aye," said Bernadette. "Once you come here, your name and address go into the RUC computer, and if you didn't have problems before with the Brits and peelers, you will now."

Bernadette introduced Jack to Paddy and the assemblage of solicitors, barristers and relatives congregating outside the courtroom. Watching Jack meet and talk so easily with these people, Bernadette thought he would make a good impression.

Inside the courtroom, Jack sat next to Bernadette in the gallery. Liz joined them just before the session began. As the defendants were led in, Bernadette pointed out Dermot to Jack. In moments the judge was on the bench, McGrath was in the stand and Gerard McEntegart, wearing his white wig and black robe, was on his feet. Bernadette leaned forward and felt her face tighten as McEntegart's powerful voice boomed through the courtroom and the cross-examination began.

"Mr. McGrath, during this trial you have demonstrated astonishing powers of recollection, testifying precisely about names, places and incidents that occurred a number of years ago. Do you have any written records of these incidents?"

"No, my lord."

terrible
Beauty

"When these incidents were occurring, did you realize that someday you would be here in this court testifying about them?"

"No, my lord."

"Yet you are confident that everything you are telling us is accurate and factual?"

"Yes, my lord."

"How can you be so confident?"

"Because every night Jesus appears in my cell, and I tell Him what I expect to say in court the next day, and I ask whether it is accurate. So far, He has told me that all my recollections are accurate."

"Mr. McGrath, on any of these occasions when Jesus has visited with you, has he ever worn the uniform of the Royal Ulster Constabulary?"

"No, my lord."

The gallery erupted in laughter, and Stafford gavelled for order. After several moments, quiet was restored, and McEntegart proceeded to ask an extended series of questions regarding McGrath's personal encounters with Jesus. For the first time since the trial began, McGrath's voice betrayed traces of hesitancy and concern.

Then, without a signal, McEntegart altered his line of questioning. "Mr. McGrath, I believe it is your testimony that you left the IRA one year ago because you could no longer support its activities."

"Yes, my lord."

"And that you are testifying at this trial voluntarily?"

"Yes, my lord."

"And that no promises have been made to you?"

"Yes, my lord."

"Have you been charged with any crime?

"Yes, my lord. Membership in an illegal organization."

"And you have admitted membership in the Provisional IRA?"

"Yes, my lord."

"You have not been charged with any other offenses?"

"No, my lord. I didn't commit any other offenses."

"Mr. McGrath, isn't it a fact that when you first went to the RUC barracks, you did not go voluntarily but that you were arrested?"

"No, my lord."

"Mr. McGrath, are you familiar with the name 'Bessie Carney'? From Clonard?"

Bernadette looked toward prosecutor Westgate. He had been sitting calmly, almost stoically, throughout the cross-examination. At the mention of Bessie Carney, he moved his head and began stroking his chin with his left hand.

"I'm not certain, my lord."

"Mr. McGrath, you are a trained joiner, are you not? And you have done work for people in their homes and flats?"

"On occasion, my lord."

"Didn't Bessie Carney hire you approximately two years ago to do work in her flat in Clonard?"

"I'm not certain, my lord."

Even though her view was obstructed, Bernadette could see McGrath shifting uncomfortably in his chair. His voice was unsteady, almost quivering.

"You don't recall Bessie Carney, a seventy-year-old widow, living alone in a two-room flat?"

"I'm not certain."

"Isn't it a fact, Mr. McGrath, that Mrs. Carney agreed to pay you twenty pounds to do certain work in her flat?"

"I did work for many people."

"While you were also on the dole?"

"Yes."

"Didn't Bessie Carney refuse to pay you because she said your work had been inadequate?"

"She may have." McGrath's eyes darted around the courtroom. Still shifting in his chair, he was now rubbing his hair and tugging on his shirt collar.

Westgate sat motionless, his left hand pressed tightly against his chin.

Stafford looked back and forth between McGrath and Westgate, writing furiously all the while.

"Didn't you brutally beat Mrs. Carney when she wouldn't pay you?"

"I can't recall exactly what happened."

"Didn't the RUC arrest you when you ran from her flat?"

"I don't remember."

"Didn't the RUC take you back into her flat, where Bessie Carney was lying in a pool of blood?"

"Aye."

"Didn't the RUC take you to Castlereagh and say that if you did not become an informer, they would tell the IRA what had happened and turn you over to them?"

"I don't recall."

"So it is your testimony that even though you have total recall of events that you say occurred years ago involving the defendants in this trial, you have no recollection at all of what the RUC said to you at Castlereagh two years ago when they arrested you for beating Bessie Carney?"

"Aye." His voice was down to a whisper; nonetheless, it resonated through the silence of the courtroom.

Judge Stafford recessed the trial for the day and left the bench. McGrath sat motionless in his chair until his minders led him from the courtroom while the defendants shouted and whistled derisively.

Paddy arrived at Bernadette's home that evening just after dinner. Liz let Paddy in as Bernadette came down the stairs.

"Paddy," said Bernadette, "I knew nothing at all about McGrath and that poor old woman. That was brilliant, so it was."

"McGrath looked destroyed," added Liz.

"He did indeed," said Paddy. "And McEntegart was great. He led McGrath along and then sprang the trap on him. And once he had him, he was unmerciful."

"I thought the British would have expected those questions," said Jack, "and had him prepared."

"They didn't prepare him," answered Paddy, "because they never had a clue we knew about the arrest."

"Isn't there an official record?" asked Jack.

"Ah, there should be," said Paddy, "but the peelers made no record of the arrest."

"And still you found out about it," said Bernadette. "You're magic, so you are."

"No, it's just that we have several very good friends inside the RUC, and thank God the RUC doesn't know who they are," said Paddy.

"How come they kept it secret in the first place?" asked Jack.

"The peelers had heard McGrath was acting erratically and that the Ballymurphy IRA unit was threatening to throw him out," said Paddy. "So the peelers were following him, trying to get something on him. They were tipped that he was doing the double, collecting the dole and working besides. They never expected him to attack Bessie Carney. When they lifted him, they kept it very quiet. Bessie was living by herself and had no relatives. She was taken to Musgraves—that's the military hospital—and was there for about six months. She's been in a home ever since. The poor woman has never recovered."

"Did Frank put up much of a fight?" asked Bernadette.

"Indeed he didn't. They tell me he wasn't in Castlereagh for even a hour before he broke and agreed to tout. They let him go the next day."

"No one knew what had happened to Mrs. Carney?" asked Jack.

"The RUC were Special Branch, so they were in plain clothes. Frank went easily without any fight or carry-on. And the neighbors were told that Mrs. Carney fell in her flat and cracked open her head."

"Jesus," said Bernadette, "this shows the Brits to be bloody liars."

"It does more than that," said Paddy. "The Brits and McGrath have said he was in the IRA until last year, and that he didn't become an informer until he left the IRA. Today Ger showed he became a tout two years ago. If you remember, during his testimony McGrath described three shootings which occurred during the year we now know he was an informer. Two peelers were wounded, and George Barkley, the unionist politician, was killed. McGrath also said he knew about these shootings before they were carried out."

"I see what you mean," said Bernadette. "The Brits are trapped. Either McGrath knew the operations were being planned and never told the Brits—which would mean he deceived them—

or he did tell the Brits and they did nothing about it—which would mean they allowed the two peelers and Barkley to get shot—or McGrath never knew about any of these operations and has no idea who carried them out."

"Stafford must be raging," said Liz.

"The Brits have put him in a terrible position," said Paddy. "McGrath is as discredited as a witness could be, yet they still want Stafford to come in with a guilty verdict. And Stafford fucking well knows the world is watching this time. Not just Terry and Jack but, Christ, you see all the reporters."

"Are the judges that sensitive to public opinion?" asked Jack.

"Indeed they are," said Paddy. "That's the only reason Ralston is meeting with you tomorrow. He wouldn't see Terry when he was here, but now Ralston feels battered by negative publicity: newspaper stories, speeches by congressmen, letters from American judges. This is all new to him, something he's never had to deal with before."

"Will anyone else be at the meeting besides me?" asked Jack.

"He insisted on meeting with you alone," Liz said. "But sure, we never expected for a moment that he would meet with us."

"The meeting is tomorrow morning in the courthouse at half eight," Bernadette added. "We'll just leave a bit earlier for court. When the meeting is over, you can go right to the courtroom for the trial."

"Maybe I was just fortunate to get here on the right day," said Jack, "but I thought today's session was fascinating."

"Well, there's no doubt today was more dramatic than most," said Paddy. "But put in perspective, it was a capsule of what the trial has been all about. The Brits' entire case is based upon McGrath, and McGrath is a desperate liar. There's not a jury in the world that would convict anyone on his testimony. And no judge with any independence would convict anyone, either."

"How do you expect it to go tomorrow?" asked Jack.

"It should be another interesting day. As you saw for yourself today, McEntegart is an absolutely brilliant barrister. Just about everyone agrees that the case against Dermot is the weakest one of all. It's ridiculous on the face of it. An IRA man from Andytown executes a UDR man in Downpatrick using a pistol from Ballymurphy, and Frank McGrath knows all about it even though he had nothing to do with it! I think you can safely say that McEntegart will tear him apart."

"What I find devastating," said Jack, "is the implication in McGrath's testimony today that the RUC knew about the three shootings. That would make them accessories. How can they get out of that without discrediting McGrath and undermining their whole case?"

"It'll be a tough one, that's for sure," answered Paddy. "I'm sure what really happened is that McGrath did agree to become an informer two years ago. But I'm also sure he didn't have access to any information that would be helpful to the Brits."

"How can you be so sure?" asked Jack.

"Because McGrath hadn't been active in the Ra for years. They thought he'd become erratic—drinking and talking too much. Slobbering about in public. They'd never've let him know anything about their operations."

"So when he came up with nothing, the Brits put the heat on him?"

"Exactly. After about a year, the Brits told McGrath he would have to testify in court the way they wanted him to or they'd let the Ra know he was a tout. At that stage, Frank had no choice. He agreed to testify and the Brits wrote his script. They took unsolved incidents—mostly in the Ballymurphy area—and connected those incidents with the men they wanted off the street."

"And there's no independent evidence or corroboration to back up McGrath's testimony?"

"They claim there's corroboration, but there's none. For instance, in Dermot's case, the peelers say that when McGrath came to Dermot's cell in Castlereagh to identify him, Dermot had a hostile look on his face and told McGrath to fuck off. The prosecutor says Dermot's 'hostile reaction' was an admission of guilt. Also, McGrath said Dermot shot the UDR man with a .45-caliber pistol and the forensic testimony confirmed that. Of course, it was the peelers that told McGrath about the .45."

"There were a lot of reporters in the courtroom today," said Jack. "How've they been reacting to the trial?"

"From what we understand," said Liz, "the foreign reporters, especially the ones from Sweden and France, are amazed by what they're seeing, and that's having an effect on our local reporters. I suppose you'd call it peer pressure."

"The best coverage we got was for Terry's news conference," said Bernadette. "But the day-to-day stories in the Irish papers have none of the sense of outrage I saw in the American papers when I was over."

"Don't get too carried away with the American papers," said Jack, laughing. "Before I got into politics, I was a reporter, and the American media is far from perfect. But I suppose it has to be better than what you have here."

"Have you been involved in the Irish issue for long?" asked Bernadette.

"Even though I'm Irish-American, it's only in the last few years that I've learned much about the issue at all. Until then, it was just something I vaguely recalled my grandparents talking about when I was a kid."

"There wasn't much talk in Washington about it?" asked Liz.

"Not until the hunger strikes. Then it emerged as an issue not just in Washington but back in the district as well. It was during the hunger strikes that the Committee for Irish Justice was formed on Long Island. The committee picked up a lot of members— many of them from Congressman Ashe's district—and began meeting with us on a regular basis."

"Did that continue even after the hunger strikes were over?" asked Paddy.

"Yeah. The meetings between the congressmen and the committee have continued. He's not Irish or Catholic, but he thinks the Irish Justice Committee makes a good case and he supports their agenda."

"And the Congress itself?" asked Bernadette.

"Once the hunger strikes ended, the interest in Congress began to recede. With all the other trouble spots in the world, why get involved with Northern Ireland unless you have a particular interest in it?"

"You said Terry's report had an impact?"

"It certainly generated some interest. Probably the main reason is that it dealt with legal issues that people can understand. We're talking about juries, about informers, about intimidation, about fair trials. And that gets across to people, especially since they've always identified the American court system and the British court system as having so much in common."

"Serious as it is, there are times when we can hardly keep from laughing, it gets so ridiculous," said Bernadette. "The best was when Stafford had to stop the trial and talk to himself about McGrath. You tell him, Paddy."

"It's customary in British courts," said Paddy, "for the judge to warn the jury whenever the only evidence is the testimony of an informer. The assumption being that the word of a former criminal is not always trustworthy. Well, Jesus, in the middle of McGrath's testimony, Stafford realized he hadn't given the warning. But, of course, since there's no jury, he had no one to give it to except himself. So sitting there in his robes and wig, he stops the trial and reminds himself, in front of everyone, that it's dangerous to accept the uncorroborated testimony of an informer! And then, proud of himself indeed for carrying out his legal obligations, he tells McGrath to continue on with his testimony."

"That must've been some sight," said Jack, shaking his head.

"It was, all right," said Bernadette. "He made a real bollix of himself, so he did."

"But how about the informer?" asked Jack. "What will happen to McGrath when the case is over?"

"McGrath has already been in custody of one form or another for the past year," said Paddy. "Once the trial is over, he'll be sentenced for IRA membership. I'm sure the sentence will be whatever time he has served to that date. Then he'll be given a new identity and resettled in another country—perhaps England or South Africa—along with a substantial amount of money. Maybe as much as a hundred thousand pounds."

"Will the Brits be able to protect him?" asked Jack.

"I think they have to, at least for the next few years. Otherwise, they won't be able to get anyone to cooperate with them. But Jesus, even if they guarantee him lifetime protection, I wouldn't want to be Frank McGrath. Wherever he goes for the rest of his life, he'll be looking over his shoulder. Before he takes his final breath, Frank McGrath will have already died a thousand deaths."

"Well, he's already caused a thousand heartaches," said Bernadette, "so he won't be getting a bit of sympathy from me. Not a bit."

The morning session had just begun when Bernadette saw Jack enter the courtroom and walk toward them. Jesus, she thought, that was a long meeting indeed. Jack had been with Ralston for more than ninety minutes.

Jack sat down next to Bernadette and smiled. Before he could whisper anything to her about the meeting, Ger McEntegart's voice boomed through the courtroom and the cross-examination resumed.

"Mr. McGrath, you testified the IRA unit in Downpatrick requested the Belfast IRA to send a man to execute a UDR man in Downpatrick."

"Yes, my lord."

"And the reason they wanted someone from Belfast is because they feared a Downpatrick man might be recognized."

"Yes, my lord."

"You testified that Private Gordon, the UDR man, lived in Killyleagh—a 'loyalist enclave' you called it—just outside of Downpatrick."

"But the local man, the Downpatrick IRA man, who drove the getaway car—couldn't he have been recognized?"

"I, I suppose so, my lord."

"Then why ask for a Belfast man in the first place if a Downpatrick man had to drive the getaway car?"

"I can't answer that, my lord."

"The reason you can't answer, Mr. McGrath, is because this entire story is based upon nothing but lies. Isn't it?"

"No, my lord."

"Mr. McGrath, you testified that you just happened to be with Malachy Donnelly when Dermot Hanlon returned the .45-caliber pistol."

"Yes, my lord."

"And that Mr. Hanlon discussed the operation with Mr. Donnelly in your presence."

"Yes, my lord."

"Mr. McGrath, isn't it unusual for top-ranking IRA members to discuss any operation—let alone such a high-risk operation as this—in the presence of a third party, unless they fully trust that party?"

"Yes, my lord."

"So, Mr. Hanlon and Mr. Donnelly must have trusted you?"

"Yes, my lord."

"Because they considered you to be an active IRA man, isn't that so?"

"No, my lord."

"You mean they did not consider you to be an active IRA man?"

"No, uh, I mean that they may've considered me to be active in the IRA, but I really wasn't. As I said, I was always able to give reasons why I couldn't carry out missions."

"In other words you lied, and deceived them?"

"I don't know what you'd call it, my Lord. I just did what I thought was the right thing."

"In other words, you thought it was the right thing to lie and deceive Malachy Donnelly and Dermot Hanlon, just as you think it is the right thing to lie and deceive this court?"

"No, my lord."

"Isn't it a fact, Mr. McGrath, that your entire life has been a lie? That you are lying now and that you are a chronic and habitual liar?"

"No, my lord."

"That the RUC came to you and presented you with this entire story?"

"No, my lord."

"That you are willing to destroy a man you barely know to protect yourself?"

"No, my lord."

With McGrath reeling from the relentless interrogation, McEntegart suddenly paused for a moment. He glanced at his papers and then looked toward the defendants for a long moment before fixing his eyes once again on McGrath.

McEntegart's first words were barely above a whisper, but then his voice rose in a crescendo of outrage and scorn. "Mr. McGrath, I have just one final question. In all the times that Jesus has visited your cell, has He ever spoken to you about Judas?"

McGrath's mumbled answer was lost amidst the cheers from the gallery, the objection of the prosecutor and the judge's gavel.

McEntegart said nothing more. Secure that he had done all that could be done, he sat down and sipped water from his glass.

CHAPTER FOURTEEN

Bernadette was saddened whenever she went into Ballymurphy. Sure, there was poverty in Andytown, and she herself barely eked out a day-to-day existence. But the poverty in Ballymurphy was stifling. Unremitting and merciless, it pervaded every aspect of life.

Unemployment was more than 80 percent. Two and three generations of Ballymurphy families had never known work. Housing was overcrowded and decrepit. Most kids left school by the time they were sixteen and spent their days roaming Ballymurphy's grim and desolate streets. Many married before they were eighteen or nineteen, usually to someone else from Ballymurphy. Once married, they lost little time propagating the next generation of Ballymurphy children.

Somehow, through it all, the people maintained their defiant spirit. When Bernadette canvassed for Sinn Fein, she found no area more republican. And despite having heavily fortified Brit army bases located right in their community, no IRA unit was more effective. Even with all the arrests in the McGrath case, there had been no letup in successful IRA operations.

As Liz drove from the courthouse to Ballymurphy, Bernadette leaned toward Jack, who was loosening his tie in the backseat.

"Father Slattery will have lunch waiting for us," she said. "I'm delighted you'll be able to meet him. He's a wonderful man, so he is."

"If there's such a thing as 'doing God's work,' that's what Tom Slattery does in Ballymurphy," said Liz.

"We've heard a lot about Tom Slattery in America," said Jack. "I'm looking forward to meeting him. How long will we be able to stay?"

"We can stay for the entire afternoon," answered Bernadette. "Paddy told me he doesn't expect very much to be going on in court this afternoon."

"God almighty," said Jack, "after yesterday's performance, whatever happens this afternoon would be anticlimactic anyway. I thought I was watching an old *Perry Mason* show. McEntegart just cut him to ribbons. McGrath was helpless."

"And so were Westgate and Stafford," said Bernadette. "Their man was torn apart in front of them and they couldn't do a thing about it."

"Stafford can still come in with his guilty verdict," said Liz.

"Aye, so he can," said Bernadette, "but he knows he will sound like a whore when he does it."

"You're right," said Jack. "I was with Ralston for about an hour and a half this morning, and I never heard anyone sound so defensive."

"Jesus, Jack, I've been dying all morning to find out what went on with Ralston," said Bernadette.

"The first thing that struck me was how unimpressive he looked. In the pictures Paddy had shown me beforehand, Ralston was always wearing a white wig and robes, looking regal. But when I walked into his office, I saw this shrunken little guy with thinning gray hair, wearing a tweed suit, standing behind an oversized desk. From the moment we shook hands, he seemed ill at ease."

"Ralston did most of the talking?" asked Bernadette.

"He was almost nonstop."

"How did he defend the supergrasses?" asked Liz.

"He didn't. He spent the entire ninety minutes putting as much distance as he could between himself and the supergrasses. It's obvious Terry's report got to him. I don't know how many times he told me that the courts are not influenced by the Army or the RUC. He said he could understand why an outside observer might conclude that the RUC has developed a 'supergrass strategy.' But the judges, he said, can only look at each case individually, so that it's difficult to conclude that the RUC has concocted the entire case."

"Did he say why it was so difficult?" asked Bernadette.

"I asked him that, and he said that if a judge reached the conclusion that the RUC had created a fictitious case, he'd actually be concluding that the law enforcement system had broken down."

"Another thing which I'm sure Ralston didn't tell you," said Liz, "is that his life depends on the RUC. They protect him twenty-four hours a day. His house is bullet-proofed. His car is bullet-proofed. When he goes back and forth to court, his car is surrounded by an armed escort. Under those conditions, you can be sure he doesn't want to do anything to antagonize the peelers. Remember, Ralston knows full well what vicious bastards the RUC can be, so he does."

"You're right," said Jack. "He didn't mention that at all. But he did tell me something else that surprised me. And he said it pretty much out of the blue. He said that almost none of the Catholics who've been convicted in so-called terrorist cases would ever have been in trouble with the law if it weren't for the political situation. Then he went on to say—and this is what really hit me—that many of the Protestant paramilitaries were common criminals."

"Jesus, if that ever got out, Ralston would have serious problems indeed with the orangies." Bernadette laughed.

"I'm sure he would," said Jack, "but it can't come from me."

"No, you're right about that," said Bernadette. "It would be bad faith on our part. After all, he did agree to the meeting."

"Did he say anything that you found encouraging?" asked Liz.

"It's hard to figure what's real and what's not real. But he did say one thing that was promising. After telling me so many times that the judges can only look at each case individually, he did say near the end that perhaps the time was coming when that policy would have to be reviewed. If he meant anything by that, he was giving me a message that if the RUC keeps coming in with these obviously phony cases, the judges would have to do something—that even they would only go so far."

"Jesus, that would be wonderful if only it were true," said Bernadette.

"I don't think Ralston has decided what he intends to do," said Jack. "But the fact that he even mentioned it shows me he's uncomfortable with the supergrasses and that the time could come when he'll tell the Brits he can't go along with this charade any longer. And that's why it's so important that the pressure be kept on. You just can't let up at all."

"You can help us there," said Bernadette with a directness that surprised herself.

"You're absolutely right. I wouldn't have thought so before I came over, but now I can see how much these guys react to what we do."

Wearing an open-collar white shirt, an aging blue cardigan and old gray trousers, Father Slattery warmly welcomed his guests to his battered two-story building. Bernadette rubbed her hands together. Jesus, she thought, this place is always cold and damp, so it is.

Bernadette and Liz sat down on the small couch. Jack and Father Slattery sat in the two overstuffed and worn chairs opposite the couch.

"We should be ready to eat in about twenty minutes or so," said Father Slattery as an older woman served them all tea. "But tell me Bernadette, how is Dermot keeping?"

"Just fine, Father," she answered. "And the trial's gone very well this past few days."

"Jack, this must be some experience for you," said Father Slattery. "Do you think we're all mad?"

"No, Father, I think it's a terrible tragedy. I've been a reporter and I've been in politics a long time. So I consider myself to be a pretty cynical guy. But what I've seen just the two days I've been here has really gotten to me."

"How so?" asked Father Slattery, rubbing a hand through his wavy white hair.

"Well, the trial is a cruel farce. I would have more respect for the British if they were honest about what they were doing and just interned the ones they were after rather than making a mockery of the courts," said Jack.

"The Brits are seldom honest about anything involving Ireland," said Father Slattery with an ironic smile. "But I'm sorry I interrupted you. Go on."

"The conditions the people have to live under are far worse than I expected. Just now, driving into Ballymurphy, I couldn't believe the poverty I was seeing."

terrible
Beauty

"Yes, this economic poverty is disgraceful, and it's gone on for generations," said Father Slattery. "But there is no poverty of spirit."

"That's dead on," said Bernadette. "But a lot of that spirit is because of you."

"That's generous of you, Bernadette, but it's not true. The most I do—the very most—is help to keep the flame burning. But with or without me, that flame would still burn."

"That may be," said Jack, "but coming in here, I saw the people lined up outside this building. It certainly seemed to me they're coming to you for help."

"Listen," said Father Slattery, "I'm not into false modesty. What we've been able to do here at the community house has been helpful to the people. But without me or without this community house, the people of Ballymurphy would still carry their heads high. It's because these people are so good it's important we do all we can to help them."

"What exactly do you do in the community?" asked Jack.

"Well, I'm sure if you asked the Brits or the RUC, they would at least suggest to you that I'm an IRA priest, whatever that means."

"What would they mean by it?"

"They'd be suggesting either of two things. The first is that I'm actually involved with the IRA—perhaps even a member. That certainly isn't true, not so much because of any moral decision on my part but because, despite what other mistakes the IRA might make, they're smart enough to know I wouldn't be any help. I'd probably end up shooting myself in the foot—if not worse." He straightened his eyeglasses and went on.

"On the other hand, if they're suggesting that I'd give the sacraments to an IRA member, that I'd visit IRA men and women in prison and that I'd try to help prisoners' families, then I plead guilty. The republican movement honors me whenever it allows me to work with them to make their lives any easier."

"I suppose my real question, then, is what do you do day-to-day to help the people in this community?" asked Jack.

"First of all, our programs are available to all the people of West Belfast," said Father Slattery, "though most of the people who come to us are from Ballymurphy. We have what you'd call a soup kitchen to help the people who don't have enough food to live from one day to the next. They were the people you saw outside in the queue. Then, the wee office you saw just inside the front door is where we keep records of particular needs people have. Some need clothing, others furniture, others shelter. Some are having serious family problems. If we can get help from the government—which isn't often—we help the people prepare the paperwork. If, as is usually the case, there's no government assistance available, we give them the items they need from the donations we've accumulated. If it's a personal problem, we try to counsel them as best we can."

"I'm not doubting anything you've said about the spirit the people have," said Jack. "But this poverty is so oppressive. And you have so many fathers in jail. There has to be some breakdown in the social structure."

"Oh, God, aye," said Father Slattery. "We have our problems—especially the glue-sniffing and joyriding among the teenagers—but so far they haven't got out of control."

"Do you have any drug problem?"

Father Slattery shook his head. "No hard drugs at all."

"I understand, though, that Dublin is filled with heroin."

"That's true enough, but that's Dublin, not Ballymurphy. All the suffering our people have had has brought us closer together. You won't see families anywhere closer than they are in Ballymurphy. Also—and this is something the Free State government and the Church would never admit—but drug dealers wouldn't dare come to Ballymurphy for fear of the IRA."

"Father, you should also tell Jack about the education programs which have been set up," said Liz.

Father Slattery beamed. "First we should go into the dining room and start eating the delicious meal Maggie has prepared for us."

The dining room was a smaller area just off the living room. The rectangular metal table seated six. Father Slattery and Liz sat on one side, Jack and Bernadette on the other. Maggie served hamburgers, chips, onions and toast and refilled their cups with steaming tea.

"God love you, Maggie," said Father Slattery. "The food is delicious. I'm sure Jack would take you to America and get you a job in the White House, except that we need you too much over here."

"Keep up that kind of smart talk," said Maggie, "and I'll do my cooking on the Shankill. I'm sure their manners couldn't be any worse than what I've to put up with here."

"Jesus," said Bernadette, "if you went to the Shankill, the orangies would have you for dinner."

"You're probably right. I suppose I've no choice but to stay here with the likes of you," said Maggie, feigning disgust as she shook her head and marched back to the kitchen.

"As you can tell," Father Slattery said, "I'm very proud of the Ballymurphy people. Besides their spirit, they have a good bit of talent and ability. Upstairs we've converted two bedrooms into classrooms for 'O' levels and 'A' levels. We also have Irish language classes and a theater workshop which puts on two shows a year."

"And they are quite good indeed," interjected Bernadette with a smile.

"We also publish a literary journal—once a year—primarily of poems and short stories."

"As for artwork," laughed Liz, "that's on display on the walls of buildings, every day, year-round."

"God, I saw those IRA wall murals on the way in," said Jack. "There must have been at least one or two on every street. They were beautiful."

"Oh, they're well done, sure enough," said Father Slattery. "And they drive the Brits absolutely mad."

"And the slogans were very clever," said Jack. "I particularly like the one 'God made all men but the armalite made them all equal!' It must be damned annoying for the Brits to have to look at them everywhere they turn."

"It's more than just annoyance," said Father Slattery. "It comes back again to the total inability of the Brits to understand the Irish will to resist. It's been said so many times but it's so true: 'The Brits will never understand the Irish.' Never."

"Father, you keep saying 'we' do this and 'we' have this program. Who is the 'we'?" asked Jack.

"The 'we' is an enormous number of dedicated volunteers—and I don't mean IRA volunteers," said Father Slattery with a slight smile. "Everyone you see in this house is a volunteer. And that includes Maggie, the men and women in the soup kitchen and in the offices, the teachers upstairs."

"That's amazing," said Jack. "How long have you had the community house?"

"We started about ten years ago. It started with one adult Irish language class and grew from there. And last year, about three streets over, we took over an abandoned factory and are using it for craftwork and job training."

"Do you get any government assistance for the factory?"

"We get no help from the government at all. And to make it worse, we also get nothing from the Church."

"Why doesn't the Church help you out?"

"Because the Catholic Church in Ireland won't give money to anything unless it can exercise control over it," said Father Slattery, "and the people in Ballymurphy made it clear they want the factory to be a community-run project."

"There's also the fact that you're not particularly popular with the hierarchy." Bernadette smiled.

"No, I'm not, but they're not popular with me, either." Father Slattery laughed.

"So long as you brought it up, what is your status in the Church?" asked Jack. "We get different stories in America."

"I can tell you that I'm not a heretic," answered Father Slattery, "but other than that, I don't know just how you'd define my status. I'm not assigned to any parish. I say Mass in the room upstairs. Several years ago, Bishop McIntyre, who is the Bishop of Down and Connor, sent me a message through several of his aides saying that if I continued to speak and write about the political situation, I might well be silenced. I ignored the threat and continued to do what I had been doing, perhaps even more so. Since then I've had no communication at all with McIntyre or any of the hierarchy."

"Have you always been so strongly republican?"

"Certainly not. I was the traditional churchman who did what I was supposed to do: pass the collection basket and condemn violence. To be honest with you, I'm quite ashamed that it took me so long to realize what was happening in my own country."

"Ah, Father, don't worry about it. You've done wonders since you saw the light. You've atoned for all your sins, so you have," Bernadette laughed.

"Father, if I could use Bernadette's expression, when did you 'see the light'?" asked Jack.

"I have to say mid-1972. It was an accumulation of events, but primarily internment and Bloody Sunday. Internment convinced me the Brits had no regard for the law. And Bloody Sunday convinced me the Irish people had the moral right to use force of arms to resist British rule."

"Do you see any conflict between your position and Church teaching?"

"None at all. This is a just war. Our people are the victims of aggression and they have the right to resist. I never tell anyone they have the duty to use arms, only the right to do so. And once they assert that right, I have the duty to defend the morality of their decision."

"How do you justify civilian deaths caused by the IRA?"

"If the deaths are intentional or the result of recklessness, I make no effort to defend them. The IRA has the same obligation any army has to avoid civilian casualties. And I'm satisfied that it's IRA policy to go only after military or political targets. Certainly there have been errors, tragic errors. It's the Brits, though, that target civilians, murdering wee children like Mairead Brady with plastic bullets. That's what McIntyre and the rest of them should shout about, but they don't."

"That's the question," said Jack. "Why don't they?"

"God knows I've wrestled with that one for years, and I'm still not certain I have the complete answer. But one thing you have to keep in mind is that, at least in this century, the Church hierarchy has always sided with the Brits. They condemned the 1916 uprising, and they excommunicated the IRA during the Black-and-Tan war. But once the Brits pulled out of the twenty-six counties, the Bishops lost no time going up on the platform with the same men they'd excommunicated just a few years before. And, of course, ever since these troubles started in 1969, the hierarchy has continually denounced the republican movement."

"Except when they needed our help," Bernadette said.

"Ah, yes, there were times especially around 1970 and '71 when Catholic churches were under siege from loyalist mobs, and heavily armed paramilitaries were trying to burn the churches down," agreed Father Slattery. "The priests had no reluctance then about asking the boys to use their guns to defend Holy Mother Church—the 'church militant' as they used to call it."

"Jesus, they're bloody hypocrites," muttered Liz.

"It goes beyond hypocrisy," said Father Slattery. "The worst of the problem is that the Irish hierarchy are so authoritarian and committed to preserving the Church as an institution that they wed themselves to the state. Always remember that the Brits treat the organized Church very well. The government gives millions of pounds to the Church each year just to subsidize our schools."

"I'm not arguing with you, but do you really think it's that cynical?" asked Jack.

"It's even more cynical than that," said Bernadette. "The Church wants to be the dominant voice in the Catholic community. They see the IRA and Sinn Fein as threats to their power, so they're of one mind with the Brits in keeping the republican movement down."

"I agree with what Bernadette says, but I'd make one addition," said Father Slattery. "Difficult as it may be for us to accept it, I think the Bishops truly believe that what they're doing will be best for the Irish people in the long run."

"You're right," said Liz. "That is difficult to accept."

"Just hear me out for a moment, though, Liz," said Father Slattery with a friendly smile. "The Irish Bishops have such faith in the institutional Church, they're willing to pay almost any price to preserve that institution. Of course, in their zeal to preserve the institution, they've lost sight of Christ's teaching. And that's the tragedy—for us, but even more so for them."

On that note, they stood up and moved back into the living room, where Father Slattery poured each of them a glass of brandy. Bernadette sipped hers and smiled. She was pleased with the meeting.

"I hope this isn't too personal a question, Father, but have you ever given any thought to leaving the priesthood?" asked Jack hesitantly.

"I've never for a moment of my adult life thought of being anything but a priest. In my mind, the Catholic Church is the teachings of Christ and the people. And I've no doubt that if Christ were in Ireland today, He would be here working with the people of Ballymurphy. It's just unfortunate for the people of Ballymurphy they've got me instead," he said, laughing.

"Don't be slagging yourself, Father," said Bernadette. "You're one of the only blessings these people have ever received. They know that and you should never forget it. God love you."

Wednesday had been a grueling day for Bernadette, and she was looking forward to dinner with Seamus in Dunmurry that evening.

She leaned her head against the backseat and reviewed the day, which had begun when Liz and she had taken Jack to the press centre for an early morning meeting with Adams and Morrison. From there it was to the courthouse to watch an hour of cross-examination; to the American Consulate on Queen Street for a briefing from the Consul General; to the *Irish News* for an extensive interview; to Ardoyne to talk to some relatives of supergrass defendants; to Queen's University to meet Ian Grant, a unionist law professor who supported the supergrasses; and to Twinbrook to meet Mairead Brady's family.

Now Liz and Paddy were going to the Forum to make the final arrangements for Jack's news conference the next day. After that, they had a meeting with the loyalist relatives. Bernadette was glad her appointment with Seamus gave her an excuse to beg off. She was exhausted.

Paddy stopped the car and Bernadette got out. "Thanks for the ride," she said. "I'll see you again in the morning." They drove off, leaving her in front of the Greenan Lodge, a hotel and restaurant just outside of Andersonstown.

Although owned by Catholics, it had been bombed by the IRA a number of times. Sufficient warnings were always given, however, and there were never any casualties. It wasn't often that Bernadette would get to eat in a place as fashionable as the Greenan, but Seamus had suggested it and she was delighted. Besides, this would be the first time she'd seen Seamus since he began meeting with Cartwright.

He was waiting for her as she walked in, and a waiter led them to their table. As always, it was a white wine for her, Guinness for him. They ordered their meal. Lamb chops for Bernadette, steak for Seamus.

"How's the Yank doing?" he asked.

"Great. He's just like Terry, cooperative and friendly." She laughed. "And also like Terry, Jack will be in a state of total exhaustion by the time he finally gets on the plane."

"From what I hear about McEntegart's cross-examination, Jack picked the right week to be here. It must have been some show."

"Jesus, Seamus, McEntegart was brilliant, and it certainly made an impression on Jack, but he saw it as much more than that. He was raging that the Brits would make such a mockery of the courts."

"That should certainly be a help to us back in America, but what does Paddy think about the trial?"

"You know Paddy—always the realist. Stafford knows it's his job to find most of the men guilty, particularly Dermot. So long as McGrath doesn't break down on the stand and actually admit that it's all a lie, Stafford will do what he's expected to do. McGrath's performance will make it a bit more difficult for him, but Stafford will still give the Brits the convictions they want."

"And you'll keep fighting?"

"Jesus, you know I will. And so will Dermot."

"Of course, I know you will. But I love to see that fire in your eyes."

"Ach, the cheek of you!" she said, laughing. The waiter brought their meals and they began eating.

After a few moments, Seamus asked, "How is your Brendan? Is he doing any better?"

"I don't know how long it will last, but for the past few days, thank God, he's been like a new person. Once McEntegart started the cross-examination, Brendan just came alive, so he did. He wanted to know every last detail. And he enjoyed it so much

terrible
Beauty

when we told him what a fool McGrath has been. It's as if Brendan was waiting for our side to fight back." She took a drink of wine. "How've you been doing with Cartwright?"

"It's early, but so far I've been pleased indeed. For a man who shouted about electrocuting Catholics, he seems to have a genuine decency about him. He's also much smarter than I expected, very clever, very quick."

"I felt the same way when I met with him. I believe he can be reasoned with."

"What has impressed me is that he's not interested in reliving past battles. He's concerned about his people now and what's going to happen to them. He totally distrusts the Brits."

"Has he proposed anything you can tell me about?

"Christ, there are no secrets between you and me, not after what we've been through together. Both sides realize that right now we need symbols to shake the Brits and get world attention. At the same time we can't go too fast, or we risk a reaction from the people on the ground, particularly the loyalists who are still skeptical about sitting down with Catholics for any reason." He picked up his Guinness and took a long swallow before continuing.

"What we're considering is assembling prominent people from both communities to come together and issue a report not merely about supergrasses but the entire Diplock Court system. The participants would be readily identified as strong republicans and loyalists. For example, there'd be people such as Paddy Ferguson and Father Slattery from our side and George Hopkins for the loyalists. Cartwright tells me there's even a retired judge who may agree to take part."

"It would certainly get attention."

"Indeed it would, and I believe it would be a positive step

for us. The one problem I have—and I know I must put it aside—is that I'm still reluctant to be equating our side with theirs. We've never been sectarian. We've never had anything like the Shankill Butchers. But, despite all that, I know it's in our interest to move ahead with the loyalists whenever we can find common ground."

"And the leadership?"

"It's them I'm representing in these meetings. And whatever I propose to Cartwright has been coordinated with them. We're of one mind on this. We've been presented with the opportunity for a diplomatic breakthrough and we've no alternative but to take advantage of it."

"How many meetings have you had with Cartwright?"

"We've had three, and there's another one planned for tomorrow evening. The meetings alternate between their place and ours."

"Do the loyalists give him any flexibility in the meetings?"

"Far less than I have. As I said, I get my instructions from the leadership, but I'm given a certain leeway. Cartwright is kept on a tight rope."

"How about you, though? Is the school aware of what you're doing?"

"They're aware I'm meeting with loyalists, but they don't know it's Cartwright and they don't suspect anything. They think it's something to do with the work I do for the prisoners."

"Ah, yes, the Irish language books," laughed Bernadette. "How could I ever forget them?"

"How could either of us forget?"

The waiter came back and cleared the tables. They ordered dessert and coffee, which Bernadette enjoyed. Finally, she leaned back and said, "Seamus, this has been a wonderful evening for me.

The meal was great and conversation with you is always brilliant, and maybe I'm being unrealistic, but I have great hope for the talks with Cartwright. I truly think this might be the right moment, and I know you're the right man."

"Ah, Bernadette, luv, that one glass of wine must have gone straight to your head. But thank you very much indeed for the kind words. I'm sure we'll find out soon enough whether any of us is right!"

It was half seven on Friday morning. Bernadette had just returned from the airport, where she had seen Jack off. He had taken the early morning shuttle flight to London, where he was to attend a business meeting for Congressman Ashe before boarding a TWA jet to New York.

Bernadette already missed him. He'd been so easy to get on with. Like Terry, she already considered him a longtime friend, even though she'd known him for only a few days.

She was especially pleased with how well the news conference had gone yesterday. Jack had covered the same points as Terry, but the reporters seemed intrigued that an aide to a Republican congressman would not be following the Reagan line on Ireland. Jack not only defended himself and Congressmen Ashe but pointed out the number of other Republican congressmen—including Gilman, Fish, Lent—who were opposed to the Brits' policies.

In talking to reporters after the news conference, Bernadette could see that the consensus was that Jack had come across as sincere and knowledgeable, and, as Jack himself admitted to her later on, perhaps a bit more influential in the Republican Party than he actually was.

After a long, relaxing lunch at the Forum, Bernadette and

Liz had taken Jack to the stores and shops in town, where he did some shopping for his wife and children. In the evening, they'd gone off to the Felons, where they had a festive and friendly evening. Joe Austin was there, and during the break he got up and thanked Jack and all the Americans who supported justice and freedom in Ireland. As the evening wore on, Jack told Bernadette that now he knew why Terry had told him, "if you don't go to the Felons, you haven't been to Belfast."

But that was last night. Bernadette looked at the clock on the kitchen wall and shouted up the stairs to Brendan and Siobhan that they would be late for school if they didn't hurry.

Within minutes they'd finished dressing and were downstairs eating the cereal and boiled eggs she'd prepared for them. Most important to Bernadette, she could see straightaway that Brendan was still cheerful this morning.

With smiles and kisses and a minimum of confusion, Brendan and Siobhan were soon out the door and off to school. A few minutes later, Maura finished eating her final piece of toast and walked into the living room, where she sat down on the floor with her coloring book and crayons.

Outside, the day was bright and clear and the morning sun beamed through the living room window.

Bernadette would have some time this morning to tidy the house a bit and look through the newspapers. Eilish had to take her Veronica to the clinic and wouldn't be by the house to mind Maura until half ten. Bernadette would be late for court, but Paddy had told her not to worry. Most of the morning would be taken up with routine motions and procedures and more mumbling between Stafford and the barristers.

As she lit a cigarette, inhaled deeply and looked at Maura

busying herself on the sunlit floor, Bernadette realized that a calm and serenity had come over her.

The trial was in its last days. And all that could be done had been done. The trip to America, the news conferences, the meetings with the loyalist relatives, the observer visits by Terry and Jack, the daily visits to the court. And in the courtroom, McEntegart and Paddy had been a brilliant team. My God, she thought, it hasn't even been a year since Dermot was lifted. I'd never have thought we'd be able to do so much. And through it all, Dermot had been the pillar of strength he'd always been.

As for the next phase, she was hoping for the best and prepared for the worst. She was confident that she would have the strength to fight on and never falter. Like Cuchulainn, her knee would never touch the ground.

She put out her cigarette. It was time to go upstairs and straighten up the bedrooms. But first she paused for a moment by the bookshelf at the foot of the stairs. She removed the book of Irish poetry and opened it again to Dessie's note. She read it and smiled. After closing the book, she rubbed it softly with her hands and gently placed it back on the shelf.

CHAPTER FIFTEEN

Bernadette was awake and out of bed by half five. The moment
was upon her: Stafford was to read his verdict at half ten. She show-
ered, put on a neatly pressed dark blue skirt and white blouse and
carefully applied her makeup.

She awakened Brendan and Siobhan a half hour earlier
than usual. After they finished breakfast, Bernadette sat with them
in the living room and told them that no matter what happened
today, their daddy had already won. This trial had proved how
unjust the Brits were, and that no matter how much strength was
arrayed against him, their daddy had never weakened. Not even for
a moment. Both children smiled and told her they would try their
hardest to be as strong as their daddy. And as strong as their
mommy, said Brendan.

And then the taxi drove to the courthouse. The security
frisk at the entrance. The dark stares from the peelers in the rotunda. It was all the same as the preceding days—yet so different.
Bernadette sat anxiously in the courtroom with Eilish and Liz on
either side of her. She looked down toward Dermot and then
toward McEntegart and Paddy. More than fifty RUC were positioned throughout the courtroom. Judge Stafford entered and sat

behind the bench. She folded her hands tightly, placed them on her knees and leaned forward to hear every word of the verdict.

"There are thirty-five accused persons in this trial," said Stafford, as he began reading his lengthy opinion, "and one hundred thirty-one counts in the indictment. The counts include membership in the Irish Republican Army and relate to forty-two alleged incidents of a terrorist nature, ranging from murder to possession of firearms in suspicious circumstances. The principal Crown witness is a man called Frank McGrath, who states that he was a member of the Provisional IRA. He has pleaded guilty to membership in an illegal organization and is awaiting sentence." Stafford looked up and adjusted his glasses.

"In view of the great interest in the kind of trial in which this Court is now engaged, it will in my opinion be salutary if, in rendering this verdict, I openly set forth certain main legal principles.

"It is in the public interest to bring criminals to justice, even should this be done through informers. In such cases it is the duty of the trial judge to warn the jury . . ."

What jury? Bernadette wondered.

". . . that it is dangerous to convict on the uncorroborated evidence of an accomplice and to give himself the same warning when he is the tribunal of fact. This rule is not satisfied by a mere incantation of magic words. Nor can it be watered down. A person can be convicted on the uncorroborated evidence of an accomplice only if the tribunal of fact is satisfied that evidence is reliable. The reason for this caution is clear. An accomplice-turned-informer, or a mere paid informer, has an obvious ax to grind. He is an interested party and for that reason his evidence must be treated with suspicion."

Bernadette squeezed her hands more tightly. Stafford was acknowledging the seriousness of the defendants' main argument.

"On the other hand, it is recognized that the presence of a strong motive to misrepresent the facts is not a bar to hearing a person's evidence and accepting it in a proper case. The rule of law is paramount, but the old rule of thumb gives way to reason."

Bernadette closed her eyes for a moment and took a quick breath. Stafford, that bastard, was going to convict them after all.

"I would just like to make one general point before going further. The resort to 'supergrasses,' to use the popular name, has been described by some people as a method of *convicting* suspected terrorists. But the expression 'method of conviction' is a complete misnomer, since it is likely to give the impression that the executive and the judges are together implementing a trial process with the joint object of convicting and imprisoning suspects. It is for the executive, no doubt, to prosecute a case, if on the available evidence, that seems to be the right course. But the function of the judges, *acting quite independently*, has not altered. It is simply to decide whether the allegations of the prosecutor have been proved.

"Today, peace, order and society itself are under fierce and constant attack. This war is being waged by organizations that style themselves as armies and observe military procedures, but it has not invaded, and will not be allowed to invade, the courts. The rule of law has prevailed and will continue to prevail here.

"I shall introduce my consideration of the case by making an assessment of McGrath, who, as I have said, is the main Crown witness. He is thirty, divorced and was almost continually unemployed. His chief recreation was frequenting social clubs. While he joined the Ballymurphy unit of the Provisional IRA in the early 1970s, he stated that he never committed any terrorist offenses.

He testified that he voluntarily agreed to cooperate with the Crown after he became disillusioned with the IRA and underwent a religious experience.

"I must state at this juncture that I find McGrath's insistence that he never participated in IRA terrorist actions to be devious—a clear and brazen attempt to avoid responsibility for his deeds.

"There is, however, another side to this man and the evidence he has given. First, he was a member of the Provisional IRA when his unit was undertaking a good many local operations. Therefore, he must have been thoroughly familiar with his fellow terrorists, and his knowledge of them was by no means casual or transient. Secondly, he did voluntarily agree to cooperate with the Crown at a time when, from a worldly point of view, he had absolutely no need to do so, since he was neither in custody nor the subject of investigation. At this point I comment that defense counsel has attempted to make much of the fact that almost one year before McGrath agreed to cooperate with the Crown, he was involved in a minor civil disturbance. That incident was so minor it did not even warrant any arrest being made, and I find counsel's argument to be without merit."

Bernadette stared blankly for the next forty-five minutes as Stafford pronounced defendant after defendant guilty. At last he came to the count against Dermot.

"Hanlon is charged with the murder of Private Gordon. McGrath described this incident in his direct examination. Independent evidence, including the murder weapon, confirms McGrath's account in the most important respects and, despite counsel's misgivings, I have regarded certain supposed inconsistencies as insignificant if indeed they are inconsistencies. For instance, the fact that it would be so unlikely for a member of the Belfast IRA to carry out a murder in Downpatrick is precisely why the IRA would have ordered such an operation.

"I must also address the confrontation between McGrath and Hanlon when Hanlon was being interviewed in Castlereagh on Holy Thursday evening by Constable Nicholson and Constable Grant. A contemporaneous note was taken by Constable Grant indicating the look of shock on Hanlon's face when he saw McGrath and the profanity he uttered against McGrath. This note bore the stamp of genuineness, and I accept its accuracy. I also accept the oral evidence the police gave about the confrontation.

"My confident inference from the confrontation is that Hanlon's demeanor confirmed McGrath's evidence that he knew him to be an experienced member of the IRA. While Hanlon did not corroborate McGrath's allegations, it would be unrealistic to fail to notice that McGrath's communications to the police were causing Hanlon great anxiety. Hanlon's attitude makes me very ready to accept that McGrath was telling the truth when he described Hanlon's reputation in the IRA." Stafford paused and looked around the court.

Bernadette held her breath.

"I am satisfied beyond reasonable doubt that Hanlon murdered Private Gordon and I find him guilty on count 91. I also find him guilty of membership in the IRA under count 117."

Bernadette looked at Dermot, who turned and looked up at her with a reassuring smile. She returned the smile, but as Dermot turned back toward Stafford, her eyes filled with tears and for a moment she feared she would pass out.

Eilish reached for Bernadette's hands and grasped them tightly. Liz placed a hand on her shoulder.

Bernadette forced herself to take a deep breath and wiped her eyes with the tissue Liz gave her. Folding her hands again in front of her, she set her jaw and fixed her gaze on Stafford.

Stafford continued reading his decision for another twenty minutes. Though Bernadette appeared composed, she heard almost nothing he said, except when he declared Tommy Malone not guilty of membership. Tommy was the only one of the thirty-five to be acquitted.

As soon as Stafford finished reading, he got up from the bench and left the courtroom. More than twenty RUC and prison officers formed a cordon around the defendants and rushed them from the courtroom, except for Tommy Malone, who was being embraced by his wife and brother. Bernadette looked toward Tommy and smiled. She was happy for him.

Eilish placed her hand on Bernadette's arm as they inched their way out of the courtroom into the lobby. Paddy was waiting for her.

"Jesus, Bernadette, I'm sorry," he said. "But at least we weren't surprised."

"No, we weren't. Except I must admit that a few things Stafford said at the beginning got my hopes raised a bit. But not for long."

"He wanted the media to think he agonized over the bloody decision," said Paddy. "He didn't mean a word of it."

"We still have the appeal, Paddy," said Bernadette.

"We do indeed. And there's reason to have some hope. The fact that Stafford had to explain himself so much today shows how concerned they really are. Stafford never would have done all that justifying if it weren't for the pressure you've brought. I've seen Stafford read many a ruling, and I've never seen him as concerned as he was today."

Still wearing his powdered wig and black robe, Ger McEntegart came toward them.

"God love you, Ger," said Bernadette. "Dermot and I can never thank you enough. You were brilliant."

"Thank you, Bernadette," answered McEntegart. "I was proud to represent Dermot. He was always like a rock. All he said to me today when it was over was 'Tell Bernadette I'm fine'."

"When will the sentencing be?" she asked.

"In two days."

"Do you expect he'll get life?" she asked in a firm, clear tone.

"You've already received so much bad news," said McEntegart with a bit of hesitation. "But yes, he'll almost certainly get a life sentence."

"Dermot told me from the start he expected to get life," said Bernadette. "I'd better be going home now so I'll be ready for Brendan and Siobhan when they get home from school. They'll want to know everything that went on, so they will."

"Be sure to tell them there's still the appeal," said Paddy.

"Aye, Paddy, I will indeed," she answered. "Don't worry yourself. We'll all have hope and we'll always keep our heads high."

Bernadette was encouraged by the way things had gone during the three weeks since Dermot was convicted.

She had not expected the ferocity of the reaction to the verdict. Editorials not just in the *Irish News* and Free State papers, but in some British papers as well, denounced Stafford's decision as a terrible miscarriage of justice. The Protestant *Belfast Telegraph* suggested the time might have come to reevaluate the use of supergrasses. Free State politicians in Dublin criticized the Diplock courts. Human rights organizations in France and Sweden demanded a

United Nations investigation of the British legal system in the six counties. In the United States, labor leaders and politicians, led by Congressman Ashe, issued statements and held news conferences to assail the verdict. Even the Irish Bishops felt compelled to decry the verdict, saying "it raises the most serious questions about the British commitment to justice." The Bishops went on to warn that "the continued use of supergrasses will only play into the hands of the men of violence."

Bernadette was also gratified by the personal support she had received. Eilish and Liz and Father Slattery came by the house often and did so much to maintain her spirits. Brendan and Siobhan did all they could to help her, and even wee Maura seemed to be on her best behavior. Within hours of the verdict, Bernadette had received telephone calls from the Tierneys, Terry and Jack.

And a week after the verdict, she received another type-written note from Dessie: "Wounded but never vanquished. You shall prevail. All the best." Again, a large "D" was scrawled across the bottom of the note. She placed it alongside the other in the Irish poetry book in the bookcase at the foot of the stairs.

One problem she did have to adjust to was the restricted visiting at the Long Kesh, which was outside Belfast. She had been accustomed to visiting Dermot three times a week at the Crum, and for the past several months, seeing him in court almost every day.

Still, she was fortunate that Liz was able to drive her to the Kesh for her visits. Security procedures there were more stringent and time-consuming than at the Crum, so that by the time she came home from a visit, the day was almost gone.

From her three visits with him and from his letters, Bernadette felt that Dermot was adjusting well to the Kesh. Certainly there was no break in his spirit. Today, she had brought Brendan and

Siobhan with her the first time. Dermot was delighted to see them.

Now it was late afternoon and Bernadette was back at the house. Brendan and Siobhan were upstairs doing their homework and Maura was taking a nap after being with Eilish all day.

After smoking a cigarette and reading the *Irish News*, Bernadette walked to the kitchen to start getting dinner ready. The phone rang and she picked it up.

"Bernadette?"

"Aye."

"It's Paddy."

"How's things?"

"Not so good. It's very bad."

"Mother of God. What's happened?"

"Bobby Cartwright. He's been shot dead."

"Jesus, Paddy. Who did it?"

"The fucking IPFF. They shot him from a car as he was coming out of a shop on the Shankill."

"When did it happen?"

"No more than an hour ago. It should be coming across the radio soon."

"God," cried Bernadette, her voice quivering, "Where's Seamus? Has anyone seen him?"

"No, not yet. He'd already left school before we could contact him. We're looking everywhere for him."

"Paddy, you know the loyalists will have to retaliate. And Seamus is the first one they'll go after."

"That's why we must find him before they do."

"Can I do anything at all?"

"Just stay by the phone. I'll ring you as soon as I hear anything."

CHAPTER SIXTEEN

The next three hours were agony for Bernadette. She fixed hamburgers and chips for the children, then sat on the couch, smoking cigarette after cigarette, listening to the rain and waiting for the phone to ring.

At half seven there was a knock at the front door. She got up from the couch and opened the door. It was Paddy. Bernadette looked at his face and began to sob. "My God. No! No!" she screamed again and again as Paddy held her in his arms.

After a few moments, they walked toward the couch. He sat her down and poured her a glass of brandy. Then he took off his raincoat, sat down beside her and helped her light a cigarette.

Brendan and Siobhan came downstairs warily. "Is it our daddy?" asked Siobhan.

"No, it's Seamus," answered Paddy.

"Is he dead?" asked Brendan.

"I'm afraid he is," answered Paddy. "Now, it would be a great help to me if you'd go back upstairs for a while and take care of Maura while I talk to your Mommy." They did as he said.

Bernadette continued to cry bitterly, tears streaming down her face. Paddy poured himself a brandy. He sipped it slowly and, as Bernadette struggled to regain her composure, began to speak.

"Apparently they were waiting for Seamus outside St. Columba's. As soon as he came out of the school, three men threw him into a car and drove toward the Shankill."

"Who was it?" asked Bernadette through her sobs.

"UVF. They've issued a statement claiming responsibility."

"My God, the UVF. How bad was it?"

"Very bad. The body was dumped in an alley off the Shankill. His throat was slashed from ear to ear."

"Was there anything else?"

"Nothing you have to hear now."

"Why, why did the IPFF kill Cartwright?"

"Because they're a bunch of fucking madmen. They said Cartwright was a 'war criminal.'"

"How did they know where Cartwright was to be found?"

"We think some of the orangies who were against the talks may have tipped them. But we'll never know for sure. And it's really no matter. What matters is that Bobby Cartwright was murdered by Catholics, and because of that, Seamus had to die. It's a fucking nightmare, Bernadette. A fucking nightmare."

Although Seamus Fitzpatrick had successfully evaded controversy in life, it swirled about him in death. The morning after he was murdered, the IRA announced that he had died as a member of the Belfast Brigade and would receive a republican funeral.

The reaction was immediate. Bishop McIntyre denounced Seamus as a "diabolical man who dishonored the trust which so many good people placed in him, a treacherous man who brought scandal upon his Church."

Ian Paisley assailed Seamus's IRA membership as "contemptible Papist treachery."

Father Slattery extolled Seamus as "a noble warrior who sacrificed his life for freedom and justice."

Among the rank-and-file Belfast Catholics who read the glaring headlines and watched and listened to the dramatic revelation, the reaction was one of astonishment. Thousands of Catholics had encountered Seamus, either as students themselves or as relatives of students. To all these people he had seemed scholarly, bookish, remote. Never at all political, let alone republican. His appearance had been so tweedy and rumpled. There was no way, even now, they could envision him as a paramilitary.

As Bernadette smoked a cigarette and listened to the radio, she remembered how startled she'd been that night in the P.D. when she found out that Seamus was in the Ra. And how much she'd come to depend upon him since then. For his intellect, of course, but also for his strength and genuineness. Now he was dead. And for no fucking reason.

Bernadette could not help thinking of Bobby Cartwright as well. She'd only met him the two times, and sure, he was probably a bit of a header, but he had the courage to open talks with the republican movement. And he ended up murdered by fucking Catholics.

Paddy and Liz were to come by the house around noon to discuss the arrangements for Seamus's funeral. Bernadette poured herself a cup of tea while she waited. She was composed only to the extent that she felt all emotion had been drained from her. After going to bed last night, she had cried for hours before falling asleep sometime after half three, the last time she had looked at the clock. When she awoke this morning, Bernadette felt no sorrow or anger.

Just a gnawing void. Once again, someone close to her had been torn from her life, never to be replaced.

When Paddy and Liz arrived, Paddy told Bernadette what he had refrained from telling her last night. Not only had Seamus's throat been slashed but his eyes cut out as well and rosary beads strewn between the sockets. "UVF" had been carved into his chest.

"Jesus," said Bernadette, "those orange bastards."

"The only fortunate aspect is that it appears they slashed his throat first and that Seamus died instantly," said Paddy.

"Do you expect this to go on much longer?" she asked.

"No, the republican leadership has decided there's to be no retaliation, and I don't believe the loyalists want to pursue this any further."

"I suppose this has put an end to the talks," said Bernadette. "Have the IPFF said anything more?"

"Not a word," answered Paddy, "and I don't know if they will. There's not ten men in Belfast in the IPFF, and there's not a brain among the ten of them. They're fucking headers that the republican movement would never have a thing to do with. But we're going to get the blame for them."

"We are already," said Liz. "I understand the news reports in America are saying it was the Ra who shot Cartwright."

"Jesus," sighed Bernadette, "and what do you think the reaction here will be to Seamus being in the Ra?"

"You've already heard the shouting from McIntyre and Paisley," answered Paddy. "But I honestly don't have a clue how the people will finally react. Right now, I believe they're still trying to sort it all out."

"I'm sure they are," said Bernadette with a sigh. "I'm sure they are."

That evening, Paddy and Bernadette drove to the Markets area for Seamus's wake. As they neared his home, they knew straightaway there would be an enormous turnout. Already the line of mourners stretched for several streets.

Paddy parked the car and he and Bernadette went to the rear entrance of the home. John McCadden, a Sinn Fein worker, opened the door for them, and they walked through the kitchen to the living room. The closed casket was against the wall opposite the fireplace. Two uniformed, masked IRA men stood at attention next to the coffin. The front door had not yet been opened for the mourners to come through.

Liz had arrived earlier, and she introduced Bernadette to Tom and Maureen, Seamus's brother and sister.

"I'm so sorry for your trouble," said Bernadette, shaking hands with Maureen and then with Tom.

"Seamus was always so quiet, so reserved," said Maureen. "This is all such a shock to us."

"It had been two years since I saw Seamus last," said Tom. "My wife and I came over as soon as we heard."

Staring blankly, Tom and Maureen said nothing more. They seemed bewildered and dazed. Neither appeared at all angry, however, at the revelation of their brother's life as an IRA man. A life he had kept so secret from them.

Bernadette walked to the front window and pulled the curtain back slightly. In the rays of the streetlamps she could see throngs of mourners still gathering. Many were saying the rosary. This might be the largest wake since the hunger strikes, she thought. Thank God the people were not listening to Bishop McIntyre.

Bernadette heard the back door open. Gerry Adams had arrived. He was accompanied by Danny Morrison and Sean

McKnight, the Sinn Fein leader in the Markets. Paddy led the men into the living room and introduced them to Tom and Maureen. After Adams expressed his condolences, Tom took him to the rear of the room and introduced him to his wife. Maureen introduced him to her husband. Adams then went to the casket, where he blessed himself and stood with head bowed. My God, thought Bernadette, how many of these wakes must Gerry have been to?

Adams, Morrison and McKnight each said hello to Bernadette and asked her to give their best to Dermot. "I will indeed," she said.

Moments later, the front door was opened, and for the next six hours more than two thousand mourners filed past Seamus's coffin. It was clear to Bernadette that many of them had no involvement with the republican movement. She could see the looks of apprehension on their faces when they saw the masked IRA volunteers standing beside the coffin. There was no indication, however, of any discord among them. Whatever their political views, they were there as one in their respect for Seamus.

It was past two o'clock in the morning when the last of the mourners filed by. The neighbors who had tidied up the house after the wake had just gone home. Bernadette sat at the kitchen table sipping tea. She looked at Paddy and then at the coffin in the living room. She could think of nothing to say that had not already been said. She sipped her tea some more. The funeral would be at half ten in the morning.

A number of Sinn Fein stewards had remained in the house to be with the coffin. Two of them walked toward the rear door and opened it. A man entered and shut the door behind him. A brown cap was pulled down over his eyes and the collar of his jacket was turned up. It was Kieran McAloran. She had not seen him since that night in the farmhouse in Ballyshannon.

"Mother of God, Kieran!" exclaimed Bernadette. Hands outstretched, she rushed to greet him.

"Bernadette," he said softly and clasped her hands in his.

"It's so dangerous for you to be here," she said, thinking of the massive Brit patrols all over Belfast and of the helicopters beaming their floodlights up and down the streets of the Markets throughout the night.

"Don't worry, I'll be away soon. But I couldn't let Seamus be buried without being here for at least a few minutes. He was a good man."

Bernadette introduced Kieran to Liz and Paddy. Kieran told Paddy he had known his brothers. Liz and Paddy told Kieran how much they respected him. No one asked Bernadette how she had come to know Kieran McAloran.

She walked with him into the dimly lit living room. For a moment they stood at the coffin together, then she went back to the kitchen so that Kieran could be alone with his old comrade.

Several minutes later, as suddenly as he had arrived, Kieran was out the door and off into the dark of night, once more to elude the probes and snares of the Crown Forces.

When Bernadette arrived at Seamus's house the next morning, the air was filled with a tension unique even for a republican funeral. The Brits had issued a statement that morning that they would take "all necessary measures" to prevent the IRA from firing vollies of shots over Seamus's coffin.

The firing of shots was the traditional republican salute to a fallen soldier. The Brits claimed it was a "cynical and inflammatory paramilitary display." Bastards, thought Bernadette, they won't even let us bury our dead as we want to. Dirty bastards.

Bernadette knew the Ra would have to resist; they couldn't back down. On the way over with Paddy, she'd seen the Brits out in force. Rooftops were lined with troops. Streets were cordoned off. And there were more helicopters than she'd ever seen.

The question was where along the procession route the IRA would attempt to fire the salute, and whether the Brits would have enough forces at that location to prevent the shots from being fired.

Bernadette went back into the house and stood silently for a long moment in front of the coffin. Blessing herself, she kissed the coffin and whispered, "Thanks for the Irish books." Then she went back outside with Paddy. They would wait on the street and follow the hearse to St. Malachy's Church nearby.

It was a clear, cool day. There was bright sunlight and a slight wind. Above, the helicopters still hovered. On the ground, the crowd swelled further. Television crews from around the world jostled for position.

Bernadette and Paddy stood in the street behind the hearse. She could see black flags everywhere.

At five minutes past ten, the front door of Seamus's house opened, and six Sinn Fein pallbearers carried the coffin, draped in the Tri-Colour, out to the waiting hearse. Seamus's brother and sister and their families followed. Seamus's black beret and gloves were affixed to the Tri-Colour.

The helicopters began to move away toward the route of the funeral procession.

At the rear of the hearse, the pallbearers halted. They lowered the coffin onto a trestle. Then they stepped aside and three masked and armed IRA volunteers emerged from the crowd. The crowd cheered.

The three volunteers took their positions beside the coffin and were called to attention in Irish by a fourth. The crowd fell silent. For a moment, all that could be heard was the fading roar of the helicopters.

Suddenly, the volunteers aimed their rifles skyward and fired three sharp, piercing vollies over the coffin. After each volley, Bernadette grabbed Paddy's arm.

The final vollies delivered, the volunteers removed their berets and bowed their heads in silent tribute.

By now the Brits had realized what was happening. The helicopters were returning and their roar grew louder. Troops would be arriving in minutes. The volunteers turned and vanished into the crowd, which milled about them, closing the path they took.

The pallbearers lifted the coffin from the trestle and into the hearse, which then pulled away slowly. Seamus's brother and sister and their families were directly behind the hearse, followed by Adams and McKnight and a number of other Sinn Fein officials.

Bernadette and Paddy marched with the Sinn Fein delegation. When they had gone a short distance from the house, Bernadette could hear noise behind her. Brits were coming through the alleys from the surrounding streets and wading into the crowd, desperately seeking the volunteers who had so defiantly flouted their decree.

The mourners kept marching.

"That was a brilliant stroke," whispered Paddy. "The Brits never expected the volley to be fired outside the house. And tonight the world will see it on television."

"How will the volunteers be?" asked Bernadette.

"I'm sure they're safe already. Let men like that get into a crowd like they did and give them two or three minutes and they'll never be caught, so they won't."

The hearse arrived at St. Malachy's at twenty-five past ten. The Sinn Fein pallbearers lifted the coffin out of the hearse and carried it to the church door. Before bringing it inside, they removed the Tri-Colour, beret and gloves.

Bernadette and Paddy sat in the third row from the front on the left side of the church. Father Slattery sat next to them. He told them the Brits had beaten quite a few mourners and were raiding homes all through the Markets. But the four volunteers were indeed safely away.

The church soon filled to capacity. Thousands more stood outside.

The celebrant of the Requiem Mass was Father Michael Mullaney. During his twenty years as a priest, Father Mullaney had never taken any political position other than to instruct his flock to "pray for peace and understanding." Now that McIntyre had condemned Seamus as a virtual heretic, Bernadette feared what Father Mullaney might say in his sermon.

As he ascended the pulpit, Bernadette folded her arms in apprehension. Glancing to her side, she saw that Father Slattery had folded his arms as well. Father Mullaney began.

"Today we gather to honor a man who has taken his place in the proud ranks of the Fenian dead. A man of letters, a man of the arts and, yes, because he wanted his people to be free, a man of the sword."

Bernadette breathed a contented sigh and placed her hands in her lap. Father Slattery unfolded his arms as well.

A lone piper led the cortege as it entered the gates of Milltown

Cemetery and made its way to the republican plot.

Standing with Paddy at the gravesite and waiting for the burial ceremony to begin, Bernadette marveled at the thousands of people throughout the cemetery for as far as she could see.

The ceremony began with the playing of the Last Post. Then a masked volunteer appeared and presented the Tri-Colour, beret and gloves to Seamus's sister Maureen. The volunteer withdrew into the crowd and the Sinn Fein pallbearers lifted the coffin from the stand on which it had been resting and lowered it into the grave.

Helicopters hovered overhead.

As a light rain began to fall, Father Slattery led the mourners in prayer and Danny Morrison delivered a moving oration that extolled Seamus and called for *"Bura do Shaighduiri Arm Phoblacht na h Eireann!"* Victory to the Irish Republican Army!"

When the ceremony concluded, Bernadette walked to the grave, reached down, grabbed a handful of rain-damp soil and dropped it gently onto the coffin. She stood over the grave and smiled a last smile at her friend. Then she turned and walked with Paddy toward the front gates.

The Brit troops that had massed on the Falls were in a frenzy. Enraged by the volley of shots, by the appearance of the volunteer at the gravesite and by the mammoth crowds, they were throwing mourners to the ground and threatening to "kill every fucking one" of them.

That's what you'll have to do, thought Bernadette. Kill every fucking one of us. Because so long as even one of us is alive, we'll never be defeated. Never.

Bernadette stayed at home that evening. Sitting alone in her living room, she went from channel to channel watching the extensive television coverage not just of Seamus's funeral but of Bobby Cartwright's as well.

And she was moved—even more than she'd expected—by the scenes of Cartwright's burial. Yes, his coffin was covered with the flag of the hated North Belfast UVF, but as she watched it being lowered into the ground at Roselawn Cemetery, all she remembered was what Cartwright had tried to achieve when he reached across from the Shankill to the Falls.

It's failed for now, thought Bernadette. But only for now. It will happen someday. I know it will.

CHAPTER SEVENTEEN

It was five months since Dermot had been convicted. Now the day she had both anticipated and dreaded had come. Bernadette could hardly breathe as she waited for the Lord Chief Justice to begin reading his decision concerning Dermot's appeal.

It was not until a few moments had gone by that she allowed herself to absorb what Ralston had just said. By then the courtroom had erupted in wild cheers, and she was locked in Eilish's warm embrace.

"Therefore," Ralston had concluded, "because the accomplice testimony was so bizarre, so contradictory and essentially uncorroborated, the convictions must be reversed and the defendants released."

A wall of warders and peelers formed between the gallery and the defendants until Ralston and the other two judges rose from the bench and left the courtroom. Then the screws and cops stepped aside and the relatives and defendants rushed toward each other.

Bernadette and Dermot threw their arms around each other while tears streamed down her face.

The defendants congratulated one another, and Dermot

squeezed Ger McEntegart's hand. Then, as Eilish, Paddy and Liz led the way, Bernadette and Dermot hurried from the courtroom.

"Get out of here before they try to charge you with something else," said Paddy as they dashed through the lobby and out onto Crumlin Road.

Paddy's car was parked in the lot next to the courthouse. Bernadette and Dermot climbed into the backseat while Eilish sat down in the front with Paddy. Liz took her own car, after saying she'd be at Bernadette's house in about an hour. She was going to the press centre to telex a statement to the media around the world.

"Jesus, Paddy, I still can't believe I'm out," said Dermot, his right arm firmly around Bernadette. "I'm in a dream, so I am."

"You're out sure enough," said Paddy. "But Christ, it is hard to believe."

"And all the other lads as well," said Dermot.

"Paddy, you always said there was a chance on the appeal," said Bernadette. "But you'd never let me get my hopes too high. Tell me now, what did you really believe?"

"I was being as honest with you as I could be. I knew that at the end of the day, it was to be a political decision. How much the Brits were willing to pay in world opinion to keep Dermot and the others in jail."

"So, fortunately for you, Dermot," laughed Eilish, "it looks as if you're not as important as world opinion."

"Thank God for that," said Dermot.

"What encouraged me the most, Bernadette, and I must admit I didn't tell you this at the time," said Paddy, "was what Terry and Jack were telling you: that Ralston was sending long, personal letters to every American judge and congressman who wrote to

him, and that he was putting considerable distance between himself and the supergrasses. I thought that was a tip-off."

"Well, thank you very much indeed for not telling me,"
said Bernadette, feigning anger. "God forbid you'd ever give me
any encouragement."

"It was for your own good, my child." Paddy laughed.

It had been more than a year since Dermot was arrested. And now,
with Maura in his arms and Bernadette beside him, he walked from
room to room and touched the walls. Speaking softly so that Eilish
and Paddy couldn't hear him, Dermot said, "Bernadette, you've no
idea how many times I've dreamed of this moment. And, to be
honest with you now, there were times when I doubted it would
ever happen."

"Ah, Dermot, that's all behind us now, so it is. You're home
and that's all I want to think about."

"Maybe so. But there's one thing I'll always think about and
that's what you did for me. Going to America. The news conferences. The television shows. The pickets. That's why I'm out, and
I know that. What Paddy said was right. The case was a bollix. But
that wouldn't've been enough to get us out. It was all the pressure
you caused that did it."

"You'd better watch yourself," she laughed. "You might be
saying something you'll be sorry for later."

"I'm not joking, and it isn't just today's decision I'm talking
about. It's also how quickly the appeal was heard. That was because
of you as well. You never stopped. You drove the fucking Brits mad,
so you did."

The phone rang all afternoon. Terry, Jack, the Tierneys,
Michael Garvey, news reporters, Jerry O'Donnell, Martha Mc-

Entee, and Brenda Johnson and Sarah Williams from the loyalist women. And people came by the house. Bernadette's mother, Mrs. Brady, Liz, Alex and Father Slattery.

Eilish told Bernadette to stay out of the kitchen. She would fix the sandwiches and the tea, and she'd cook the dinner.

The homecoming was complete when Brendan and Siobhan came racing through the door and into their daddy's arms. They had heard in school that Dermot was free and had run home as fast as they could.

Dermot hugged them and kissed them. And for the first time ever, Bernadette saw his eyes fill with tears.

Later, at quarter past ten that evening, after their friends had gone home and the kids were in bed, they were alone.

Tomorrow night there was to be a party at the Felons for all the defendants. But tonight Bernadette and Dermot were to be by themselves, alone.

After so long, they were together in bed again. And they reveled in each other's bodies. The touch. The caress. The kiss. And the ecstasy of the lovers' embrace. An embrace where she held him more tightly than she had ever thought possible.

And then she lay quiet. And he kissed her gently.

There was hardly room to breathe in the Felons that night. The defendants, their families, their mates, and republican supporters were all there to celebrate victory over the Brits. The band played. The pints flowed. Congratulations were offered and embraces exchanged.

Bernadette and Dermot were seated at a table with Eilish, Liz and Paddy. So many people were coming over to shake

Dermot's hand that his pints were backing up.

Kathy, the waitress, was working on the other side of the room. But at the first chance, she rushed over to congratulate Bernadette and Dermot.

"I'm so delighted for the both of you, so I am," she said, squeezing Bernadette's hand and shouting to be heard over the almost deafening din.

"Thank you so much," said Bernadette. "And how's your Gerard?"

"He's great. It's just wonderful to have him out. I don't know how I was able to get on without him all that time he was inside."

"Ah, but that's behind you now," said Bernadette.

It's behind you as well," said Kathy. "Thanks be to God."

When the program began, Gerry Adams spoke briefly. But the most resounding roars were for each of the defendants as they were introduced and asked to come onto the stage.

Watching Dermot accept the cheers of the crowd and salute back with his fist, Bernadette's only regret was that Seamus was not there to share the moment with them.

It was almost midnight. Bernadette was finishing a white wine and Dermot still another pint of Harp as the band played the final song of the evening.

> *Glory, glory to old Ireland*
> *Glory, glory to this island*
> *Glory to the memory of the men who fought and died*
> *"No Surrender" is the war cry of the Belfast Brigade*
> *Come all you gallant Irishmen and join the IRA*
> *We'll strike a blow for freedom when it comes our*

certain day.
You know your country's history and sacrifice it's made
Come join the 1st Battalion of the Belfast Brigade.

Afterward, as Bernadette and Dermot inched their way down the crowded stairway to the front door, Bernadette saw a man speaking with excitement. A crowd was gathering around him. Straining her ears, she heard him say, "It was an hour ago. Just outside Lisburn. The Ra ambushed the Brits, so they did. Three Brits are dead. But two of ours as well. There's no names released yet."

Before she could say anything, she felt a hand grasp her arm. It was Eilish, her face ashen. As they walked out into the street amidst the confusion and talk, Eilish whispered to Bernadette, "Alex went out early tonight. He said nothing, but I know he was on a job."

"Try to calm yourself, luv," said Bernadette in hushed tones. "Don't say a word to anyone."

Bernadette took Dermot aside.

"I've no way now of knowing if he was on that operation," he said.

"I can't leave her alone tonight," said Bernadette. "She's petrified."

"You take a taxi with her to Twinbrook. I'll have Paddy drop me at home. Stay with her as long as you have to."

When Eilish and Bernadette arrived at Eilish's, they were greeted by Nora, a girl from down the street who had minded Veronica for the evening.

"Did anyone ring or stop by?" asked Eilish, attempting to appear calm.

"No, there was nothing at all," answered Nora.

After Eilish left to take Nora home, Bernadette went into the kitchen and put on the tea. Jesus, she thought, it can't be. Not now. Not after all we've been through. Not after all Eilish has done for me.

When Eilish returned, Bernadette poured her a cup of tea and fixed her a cheese sandwich. They went into the darkened living room, where Eilish sat in a chair beside the fireplace. Bernadette put some more wood into the fire and sat down next to her.

Sipping her tea and looking into the fitful glow of the flaming hearth, she knew that it would do no good to give her sister false hope. Eilish was too smart for that. She had seen too much. No, Bernadette would just sit with her for as long as she had to.

After several hours they both fell off to sleep, only to be awakened by Veronica's crying. The final embers of the fire had gone out. As Eilish went upstairs to calm Veronica, Bernadette turned on the lamp so that she could see the clock on the wall. It was half four.

After a few minutes, Veronica was back to sleep and Eilish came down the stairs. She handed Bernadette a jumper. "Put this on. You'll be catching the death of cold."

Someone knocked at the back door. Eilish darted over and opened it. It was Alex. He closed the door quickly behind him and came into the kitchen.

"I heard about Lisburn," he said. "I knew you'd be worried, but there was no way I could contact you."

"You weren't at Lisburn?" asked Eilish.

"No. I knew nothing about Lisburn. That must've been a special operation."

"You'd better get up to bed in case the peelers come looking," said Eilish.

"Aye," he said. "And thank you, Bernadette."

Bernadette smiled and went to the phone to ring Dermot.

"The child is fine," she told him. "The fever's gone down and she's sleeping soundly. I'll sleep here for a while, but I'll be home by half six."

"That's good news indeed," he said, putting down the receiver.

Bernadette pulled a blanket over herself and lay down on the living room couch. She fell into a deep sleep and slept soundly until Eilish gently awoke her about an hour later.

"Bernadette, it's six o'clock. The taxi's here for you."

Bernadette put on her shoes. As she got up from the couch to put on her coat, Eilish said, "My God, your skirt is a mass of wrinkles from you sleeping in it."

"Ah, it's nothing to worry about. I do have an iron at home, you know." She laughed, then grew serious. "I'm glad Alex is safe. Thank God for that."

"Thank God indeed," said Eilish.

As Bernadette entered her house, she could feel exhaustion coming over her.

The children were still sleeping, but Dermot had a cup of tea waiting for her. She placed her coat over a chair and sat down with him at the kitchen table.

"Alex knows nothing about Lisburn," she said. "He thinks it must've been a special operation."

Dermot nodded. Bernadette lit a cigarette and sipped her tea.

At half six, Dermot got up from the table and turned on the radio. They heard the voice of the newsreader. "The Northern Ireland Office has released the names of the two IRA terrorists who were killed in last night's ambush attack near Lisburn, which left three British soldiers dead."

Dermot stepped back from the radio and folded his arms. Bernadette put down her tea and listened for the names.

"Daniel McCloy from the Short Strand area of Belfast. . ."

"Jesus, Danny McCloy," said Dermot, shaking his head.

Bernadette inhaled the smoke from her cigarette.

"The second man has been identified as Desmond Maguire, formerly of Belfast."

Bernadette's heart stopped.

"Intelligence sources report that Maguire recently returned from New York, where he had been in hiding for more than five years."

She could see nothing in front of her but shattered light. She felt as if she were hurtling through space.

"Dessie Maguire," said Dermot. "He was from Ballymurphy. He's been away for years. Do you remember him at all?"

Bernadette couldn't speak. She tried to clear her throat.

"You must remember him," he said.

"I think my brother knew him," she answered in a whisper. "I think he was one of Rory's mates."

She crushed her cigarette into the ashtray and got up from the table. She walked slowly toward the living room and stopped at the foot of the stairs. There, she looked at the book of Irish poetry resting peacefully in the bookshelf. She reached up and gently touched it.

Then she heard Maura roaring from the bedroom upstairs.

terrible
Beauty

Bernadette breathed deeply and squared her shoulders. She walked up the stairs.

She had to be ready. Ready for the day that had already begun. And ready to endure Dessie's funeral in solitary anguish.